MAGGIE'S
FAT
ASSETS

LYNN CARROLL

Maggie's Fat Assets

Blaze Press
Imprint of Orison Publishers, Inc.
PO Box 188
Grantham, PA 17027
717-731-1405
www.OrisonPublishers.com
Publish your book now, marsha@orisonpublishers.com

Printed in the United States of America

Acknowledgements

A very special thanks to my beloved *G* who always supports me in whatever crazy ideas I might have. Equally, I'm indebted to the Wilkes University professors whose imparted wisdom is truly invaluable. To my first outside readers, Barb Taylor and Sheri Abel, thank you for your honesty and valuable suggestions. To Mollie Pryzblick, thanks for your unfeigned interest and for loving the novel. As well, much gratitude goes to Lisa Frese who has read all versions of *Maggie's Fat Assets* and never once wavered. You were my biggest cheerleader in all this, and it means the world to me. And lastly, thanks to ALL my girlfriends who have shared silly stories about ridiculous relationships—there's a piece of all of us in this novel.

Counting Down to Paris

CHAPTER

1

Halloween Candy and Corny Clichés

Maggie lifted the back of her flared red-and white-striped miniskirt to snap a picture of her freshly inked backside—a sweet little heart that showcased her husband's initials, *AMSIII*. Surely, Andrew Michael Spencer III would be turned on by a sext message featuring a snapshot of his wife's monogrammed butt cheek.

A little corny and cliché? Perhaps. But Maggie didn't care. It was her birthday. Her *fortieth* birthday. Her college gal pals had told her several years ago that their own husbands loved little outside-of-the-box surprises like a personalized tattoo or a couple's massage or the occasional lap dance. Of course, *they* had all gotten married in their midtwenties when their energy and imaginations ran hot and wild. Forty-year-old Maggie was just getting started.

She practiced several seductive poses in her sexy candy-striper costume. She wasn't sure what it was about the Spencer family lake house in Laurelton, but she always felt so carefree and uninhibited when she and Andrew spent a weekend there. Even when she indulged in some alone time *without* Andrew, the lake house was her solace, where she'd wind down from her career as a therapist at her father's practice and other stressors that life tended to inject.

Maybe it was the color of the fall leaves. Maybe it was the crisp, clean air. Or maybe it was the way the artsy community of Laurelton celebrated everything, but fall was Maggie's favorite time of year, especially at the lake house. And Halloween was extra special—not because of her late-October birthday but because dressing up and being someone or something else was an escape from the everyday humdrum.

I hope Andrew enjoys this little getup, she thought, wincing as she adjusted the bustier that plumped her breasts up and nearly out of her costume. And why wouldn't he? He loved Maggie's imagination. Surely, he'd appreciate her candy-striper humor, since she'd played nurse to him a few weekends ago when he was a little under the weather. His being a very busy, well-established business lawyer kept him on a tight schedule. Ever since their June wedding, Andrew's already successful career had escalated, which necessitated his working longer hours and taking frequent business trips. But Maggie didn't mind one bit. She didn't necessarily understand his business dealings, but she was pleased that his incessant determination to thrive would soon allow her to resign from what she considered her rather unglamorous position as a therapist.

Nonetheless, she'd been missing Andrew's spontaneity—and his energy! When they'd first met a little more than a year ago, he was doing business with her father, who was heading for retirement and merging his practice with that of a colleague, Ted Worthington. That Andrew Spencer's a mover and a shaker, her father would say after their meetings. Yep, he sure is, Maggie would agree, thinking of the crazy sex sessions she and Andrew conducted in her office down the hall. She'd begun to block out "paperwork" time, so they could conduct their *own* business practically under her father's nose.

She knew her husband quite well. No matter how exhausted he might be after one of his business trips, she could get him to do anything as long as there were no clothes involved. Naked cooking…naked changing-the-lightbulb…naked Scrabble! So even though he'd get a kick out of her Halloween garb, Maggie would be just as pleased to peel it off, layer by layer, while performing her best lap dance…or taking a few turns on the cedar column in the center of the cottage. Or, she could simply forget the costume and greet Andrew in her finest birthday suit, then lead him into the kitchen for naked-baking. After all, what's a birthday without a little cake batter?

***

Andrew burst into the lake house at ten o'clock that evening. Maggie was still a little buzzed from her Friday evening relationship with gin and tonic.

She wasn't quite as energetic as she'd been four hours earlier, but she could still work up some birthday-girl adrenaline.

"Hi, babe!" said Andrew. "You look exhausted. Let's get you to bed. Had no idea I was going to be so late. These damn trips are getting to me."

"Oh…uh, hi, honey," said Maggie, pulling herself forward on the couch and rubbing her eyes. "Uh…well, I'm not exactly ready to go to bed…"

"Oh, sweets, you certainly are. You can barely keep your eyes open. Besides, I need to get some rest. We'll just celebrate your big four-o tomorrow…when we're both rejuvenated from a good night's sleep. We'll be here till Sunday evening. We have the next two days to party."

"Well, um…okay," she said, pouting down at her seemingly wasted costume and leaning sideways to rub her swollen heart tattoo.

"I'm gonna grab a shower, then snuggle up to my little piece of candy," said Andrew, suddenly eyeing Maggie's sexy costume. "But I'll be out like a light in no time."

Maggie was quite used to Andrew's long, steamy showers. In fact, she knew exactly how long she had to whip up some cake batter she'd found in the pantry and position herself in her best "sexy baker" pose on the master bed, naked…and ready to *bake*.

Damn it! she thought. This is *my* big birthday, and we're gonna celebrate tonight!

She quickly threw some ingredients into a bowl with the cake mix—water…oil…milk? Didn't matter. She had no intention of heating the oven to 350 degrees.

Six more minutes. She scooched around on the mattress, trying to assume her most flattering pose. She watched herself in the bedroom mirror, judging every little angle. Every. Little. Forty-year-old. Angle. Ugh! This tattoo makes my ass look fat, she thought, noticing the swelling in her right cheek getting bigger. Oh, to hell with it…Andrew's getting his cake in the shower!

***

It was now three o'clock in the morning, and the birthday girl had awakened to the log-sawing sound of a snoring husband. She reached over and gently removed a piece of cake batter clinging to a wavy lock of Andrew's dark-brown hair. She smiled as she rolled the batter between her index finger and thumb, recalling the X-rated events of the night. True to form, Andrew had been easily seduced by Maggie's naked role playing. Who knew that forty was the new twenty-five? Andrew might've lost a little bit of his zing, but her energy and imagination was sure to keep this marriage alive, she thought, as her very played-out husband continued to rock the house with his thunderous snore.

Unable to fall asleep again, Maggie decided to go for a little stroll on the cottage deck. *So serene,* she thought, ogling the rippling water and zoning out to a few faint squawks of geese. Who would ever get tired of this view? She snuggled into a lounge chair and wrapped a plush blanket around her slightly shivering body, still mesmerized by the tranquility of her surroundings.

"Hey, Betty Crocker." The voice came from the open french door.

Maggie chuckled. "Oh, hi, honey. Couldn't sleep?"

"I just wanted to get some water. Speaking of water…" He hesitated. "That was *some* shower visit."

"Sure was. I knew you'd get your second wind. You still got it, babe," Maggie said with a flirtatious giggle.

"Well, why wouldn't I?"

"Oh, I just meant…"

"We're in our forties, Maggie. Not quite over the hill," said Andrew.

Stand down! It was just a stupid expression, she wanted to say…but it was her birthday night. No sense in spoiling it. "It's lovely out here, isn't it?"

"Uh-huh," said Andrew as he slugged back his water. "The only thing lovelier would be seeing your phat ass swing around a steel pole."

Maggie's face jerked a little. "I'm sorry, what? What did you say?"

"The steel pole, Mags…remember? I thought it would be fun for us if you took pole-dancing lessons." Andrew turned away.

"No…before that. Something about my ass?"

He turned back around. "Mags! Now come on. Phat! With a *PH*. So, it's a little corny. But I thought you'd catch on after the way I *loved* your tattoo."

Her face returned to its blissful state. Yes, you sure did love it, she recalled. "Coming right behind you."

Maggie stopped in the kitchen for a glass of water before returning to bed. She leaned over the mini-island, resting her frame on her elbows. *Pole-dancing…hmmm.* Andrew had been suggesting it for quite some time. *Forty years old…pole-dancing.* She chuckled, then smiled with delight at the trick-or-treat candy bowl. She wasn't exactly sure why she'd bought a heap of candy for the weekend. She was quite certain there weren't any children in the lakeside community. Perhaps it was the spirit of the season…or that the beautifully displayed bowl added some life to the rather nondescript cottage décor, which she'd be more than happy to upgrade with a dose of her superior decorating skills. The cottage would become her new project. Her labor of love.

As Maggie contemplated all the changes and improvements she'd make in the cottage, she mindlessly munched on the perfectly displayed Halloween candy. Hmmm…open floor plan works well, but this wood needs to be refurbished…the kitchen area could use modern floor tiles…and it's in desperate need of updated appliances…these casement windows are fairly new…they still look good…

"Mags, you okay?" came from the master bedroom.

"Yep! Coming." Maggie looked down at the five Snickers minibar wrappers that lay on the kitchen island. Surprised at the body count, she scrunched her face, threw them away, and then glided toward the bedroom, ready to sleep off her sugar buzz.

CHAPTER
2

Mediocre Gifts
and Naked Kayaking

The following afternoon, Maggie decided to give herself a facial as she waited for Andrew to return from a liquor run. "Soooo, this is forty?" she said as if expecting the bathroom mirror to answer her. She examined various spots on her face that needed a little more coverup. A few errant hairs had sprung up overnight too. They stood straight out of her chin—the very focal point of her well defined, heart-shaped face Oh, dear God! One more place I need to groom, she thought while rummaging for her tweezers.

She finalized her facial by applying a dime-size squirt of red-raspberry serum, which would serve as a little sunscreen while she enjoyed the late-afternoon sun. She then strolled onto the cottage deck, satisfied with her DIY spa treatment, and sank into a cushy lounge chair. Even though the sun seemed to be at full blaze, Maggie had gotten a slight chill. I need to grab a sweater, she thought, and Andrew needs to return with the wine!

"Yuck…hideous…too nappy…hell, no!" Maggie said, flipping through the sweaters and jackets that Andrew's mother had left in the spare closet. "Too wooly…too musty…too old lady." As she shut the closet door, Maggie caught sight of something that didn't quite fit with the unsightly jackets and sweaters. She nudged the door open as if peeking at something forbidden. There it was: a foot bath massager—never used, its box unopened. What an odd thing for Andrew's old-school parents to stow in the closet, she thought. Nonetheless, she was up for some foot pampering! She ripped through the packaging and set it up on the deck.

Now swathed in a throw blanket, Maggie sank her feet into the tepid, effervescent bubbles. Pure stimulation! She slid into a wonderfully euphoric state of mind. No work…all play…

Her mind drifted, once again, to their naughty dating period—the prewedding days. The crazy things she and Andrew would do…the sexy clothes he'd lay out for her at his suite…the martini marathons…the wine marathons… the spontaneity of it all…

"Hi, darling!" said Andrew, interrupting Maggie's meditative state.

She quickly removed her pruned feet from the massage basin and sprang forward to meet him at the french doors. "Hi, babe. You caught me in the middle of a wonderful foot massage."

"I see that. Hope you enjoyed it." Andrew came closer, backing Maggie onto the lounge chair, straddling her swaddled figure, and taking her freshly exfoliated face into his hands. "Happy belated birthday, pretty girl," he said, while gently butterfly-kissing her chin, heading for her lips. "Hold on a sec! I'll be right back."

Startled and confused, Maggie sat up, looking around in case a hidden pack of partiers was waiting to jump out and yell, *Surprise!*

He wouldn't, she thought, panicking as she looked down at her somewhat exposed, naked body. She swiftly repositioned the blanket that had slid to the side when Andrew got up. *He knows I wouldn't want to be surprised looking like this.* The thought of a surprise party at that moment was debilitating.

So, when Andrew returned to the deck with his hand wrapped around something small, she was instantly relieved. Phew!

Maggie couldn't determine what sort of bling was about to be presented. Andrew clasped it tightly and straddled her again, reaching out with the other hand to tilt her face up toward him. She closed her eyes, breathlessly waiting for an uninterrupted kiss.

"*Ouch!* What the hell did you do?" she said, rubbing her chin.

"There was a hair! It jabbed my lip, Mags. That sucker could have taken out an eye," Andrew said, chuckling as he blew on the tweezers.

Maggie wasn't sure if she was in pain from the deep plucking or simply mortified that she'd overlooked an obvious hair. Maybe it was both. Not wanting to ruin her belated birthday celebration, she excused herself to go pout somewhere. Had she become more sensitive at forty? She guessed so.

"Babe! It's no big deal. You're gorgeous. Wouldn't you let me know if I had an unsightly something or other hanging off my face?" he shouted into the cottage.

***

Andrew and Maggie strolled down Dane Street hand-in-hand, like a giddy couple of lovebirds. The hair-plucking humiliation had subsided after a few martinis and some naked kayaking inside the boathouse. Maggie walked with great confidence in a short, sequined cocktail dress with a sheer, silky shoulder wrap for later in the evening. The gentle autumn breeze lightly tousled her loose, wavy hair. And she ogled her husband, who swaggered down the street, greeting others who passed by as if he owned the town.

"Reservation for two—Spencer," said Andrew as they stepped inside Connor's Place.

"Oh, good evening, Mr. Spencer," said the hostess. "Your table is right this way."

Andrew and Maggie slipped into a back-corner nook that was barely lit except for the streetlights bouncing off Lake Keasley.

"This view is stunning," said Maggie.

"*You're* stunning," said Andrew. "Happy birthday, babe."

Maggie smiled at him.

"Good evening. Is this your first time at Connor's Place?" the server asked.

"No, but this is our first time under the new ownership. How are the martinis? I didn't recognize the bartender when I walked through," Andrew said. "Teri knew exactly how to make my martinis. Does she still work here?"

"No, sir, I'm afraid not. But we have an awesome staff here. Can I get you started with a martini, then?"

"Well, I wouldn't expect anything less from Joan and Connor...I'm sure they hired only the best staff," said Andrew.

"Oh, so you know the new owners."

"I do. They're our lake-house neighbors. And, yes. We'll get started with martinis. Mags, what would you like?"

"I'll have an apple martini, chilled," she said.

"Mags, are you sure that's what you want? You got a little sticky from those earlier," Andrew said. "She had a few apple martinis while kayaking," he added, looking up at the server.

Maggie cringed. Why is he telling some millennial stranger about our kinky afternoon? She fired daggers from her eyes to his.

"Wow, I'd think martinis would be hard to balance," said the naïve server.

"Oh, my wife is *very* talented," Andrew replied.

Okay, what has gotten into you, Andrew?

"I see." The young man shifted uncomfortably. "And for you, sir?"

"Dry Grey Goose martini, up with olives."

"Very well. By the way, my name is Jeremy, and here's a list of our specials. I'll be right back with your drinks."

"Andrew," Maggie whispered. "What *was* that?"

"What, babe? I was just having a little fun with Jeremy. He doesn't need to know that the kayaks never left the boathouse. And how are you feeling? I'm a little bruised up from your boathouse birthday party."

Maggie rolled her eyes and smiled. "You're a piece of work."

"I know."

"But it would be nice to actually take the kayaks out on the lake, Andrew. I miss that. Don't you?"

"I know you miss that, babe. There just hasn't been a lot of time, lately," he said. Then he brightened. "Tell ya what; why don't we celebrate your birthday with *real* kayaking tomorrow?"

"Oh, that would be great!" Maggie said. But when his eyes immediately dropped to the menu, a pall settled over her party mood. She couldn't help but wonder when Andrew would present her with a gift. She didn't want to be greedy or selfish, but it was her fortieth birthday weekend. Shouldn't there be *something*? A piece of jewelry? A blender? Even a scratch-off ticket!

Maggie sighed and tried to distract herself by looking around the busy room, scrutinizing the décor. It now seemed more lackluster than romantic. Connor's Place had been much more charming from the outside.

***

By 10:30, Maggie and Andrew were back at the cottage, stuffed with crab-filled filet mignon and sloshy from a variety of martinis. Although Maggie hadn't intended to be so sluggish on her big birthday weekend, she and Andrew *were* somewhat played out. But where was the gift?

"I think I'll wind down the night with the last of the cab sauv. Care to join me on the deck?" said Andrew.

"Of course, babe."

Maggie excused herself in order to change into her comfy silk lounge pants and matching tank top. She also pulled on an old tatty, oversized sweatshirt, as the air had returned to a crisp autumn chill. She couldn't help but snoop around the bedroom, looking for a receipt or any other clue that would assure there was a gift coming her way. She came up with zilch.

"Really, Mags?" Andrew said when she finally joined him.

"Really what?"

"Silk lounge pants with an old sweatshirt. Might as well eat caviar on a hotdog roll."

"Oh, silly. You know I get cold easily. I thought you would've started a fire," she said.

"Nah, I'm just gonna finish this and head off to bed. I'm beat," said Andrew, yawning as he spoke.

Soooo, where's my dynamo husband from this afternoon? Where's a steel pole when you need to rev things up? And where the hell's my birthday gift? Maggie quickly squirmed out of the tattered sweatshirt, exposing the silky, low-cut pajama tank, and curled up with Andrew.

"Ya know, Mags," he continued, "I didn't want to say anything earlier…but you sort of spoiled my surprise for you."

"What? What do you mean?"

"Well, you found your birthday gift," said Andrew.

"I did?" Maggie said, sitting up and pulling away from him.

"Yeah, you did."

Maggie's head was spinning. Not from the martinis…not from the cab sauv. But she was at a loss. She stared into space, speechless.

"The foot-massager," said Andrew, nodding toward the basin that was still sitting by the deck chair full of water. "You seemed to be enjoying it earlier today, but I had planned to have it all set up for you when we came back from dinner. I wanted you to have a nice foot soak while I drew a bath for you. A perfect wind down to a wonderful day for my hot-for-forty wife."

That's my gift? A foot massager? Please tell me this is a joke. Maggie remained calm. In fact, she was quite certain she'd turned to stone.

"I can see you're quite taken," said Andrew as he reached beneath his chair. "Here's your birthday card, babe. Maybe you'll appreciate what's inside."

Hmmmm…this could be interesting, Maggie thought as she tore through the bright-yellow envelope.

"Let me go work on that bath while you read it," said Andrew.

As she opened the card, a gift certificate popped out. Carrington Heights Day Spa. Oh, he's doing a theme here, an underwhelmed Maggie thought as she looked over at the foot massager. She tried not to be ungrateful, but really? A day at the spa? She could do that any old time for any old birthday.

Maggie was bewildered. What was up with Andrew's odd behavior this weekend? The phat-ass comment. The chin-hair plucking. His lack of birth-day creativity…it's my fortieth, for heaven's sake! They'd been married for only five months. Was Andrew suffering from marital Alzheimer's? Was he finished with the honeymoon phase?

After sulking, Maggie began to reason with herself. Andrew could never do better than last year's birthday gift—a trip to Paris. A lovely walk and a picnic in Luxembourg Gardens…the fountains…the flowers. Alfresco dining and people-watching in Saint-Germain-des-Prés. Strolling down the tree-lined Champs-Élysées…the Seine River at sunset. And best of all, the most awesome view of the city from atop the Eiffel Tower, where they'd sipped champagne…and Andrew proposed! He'd even suggested that Paris be a do-over for their first wedding anniversary.

Sooooo, it's a day at the spa…Forty is just a number, Maggie thought.

"Betcha can't wait for your trip to the day spa," said Andrew, stirring her from the trip down Paris lane.

"Uh-huh…can't wait."

"Take as long as you'd like in the tub, Mags. I'm sure I'll be crashed when you get to bed. Your bath is hot, steamy, and bubbly…just the way you like it."

"Yep…just the way I like it."

"Okay, good night then," he said.

"Oh, hey Andrew!"

"Yeah, babe?"

"Ya know what I was just thinking about?"

"What's that?"

"Do you remember the night you proposed?"

"Well, yeah, Mags. It was a year ago."

"Right, but we also discussed going back…for our first anniversary."

"Oh, uh…yeah. I vaguely remember tossing around the idea."

"It was the most wonderful time of my life, and I think it's worth a do-over!" she said.

"Mags, can we talk about this later? I'm off to bed."

"Yes, of course. By the way…you meant what you said about *real* kayaking tomorrow, right?"

"On one condition, Mags."

"Oh? What's that?"

"That we go naked."

Maggie was speechless…again. Andrew's moods had been running hot and cold over the past few months, but naked kayaking…on the lake? Was that a little *too much* zest to keep the marriage fiery? I'd better be careful what I wish for, she thought.

"Well, Andrew…I'm not sure. I mean, what would the lakeside residents think?" she said in a hushed voice.

"Mags! Don't be ridiculous!" Andrew began to roar with laughter. "I'm joking. You should see your face!"

"Oh, good night, you rascal!" Maggie said, relieved.

As Andrew left the deck, Maggie tried to pull herself back in time. Back to a time when she was on top of the world. Sure, things were still good*ish*. But her overworked husband was starting to fizzle out. Then she rallied herself. June was eight months away. Andrew had plenty of time to rejuvenate and dump some of his workload. She'd see to it that they'd thoroughly enjoy round two of Paris for their first wedding anniversary. The countdown was on!

CHAPTER

3

Rhetorical Questions and a Sixteen-Pound Turkey

November rain had always disappointed Maggie by washing away the last of the colorful foliage that she so loved. Nonetheless, the lake-house scenery created a calmness all year round, which is why she invited her college girlfriends for a "friendsgiving" weekend. They'd gotten away from their tradition of getting together for beach weekends once kids and growing families took over. But this year, everyone had turned forty. Surely, their husbands could handle a couple preteens for the weekend.

Maggie set off for the lake house early Saturday morning, as Andrew had left for a business meeting in New York. His trips had begun to blur together, and she could no longer keep up with his schedule. He promised that work would slow down in the new year, but for now, he'd remain working and traveling as duty called. At least Maggie saw a positive side to all this coming and going. She'd soon be a stay-at-home wife, dabbling in various projects, which thrilled her to no end. His current absenteeism was a small price to pay for the chance to leave her unfulfilling career. Besides, she'd developed quite a passion for interior design and decorating. She had hinted to Andrew several times that the lake house would be her first project, but his mother would have to give her approval. After all, the house belonged to his parents.

Since they would do anything for Andrew, however, she knew that a little sweet talking about an overhaul would clinch the deal. Andrew could charm the pants off anyone, Maggie thought.

***

Immersing herself in the serenity of the lakeside cottage, Maggie became concerned that none of her girlfriends had called or texted to say she was on her way…to ask if Maggie needed anything…to double-check on the address…nothing. They had all been so excited to see each other at Maggie's wedding that promises were made to rekindle their lost tradition of getting together. They'd been planning this girlfriend weekend for a couple of months. Where were they?

"Ah, Katie!" said Maggie as she answered her phone. "Where are you guys? I was thinking that everyone was gonna bail on the weekend."

"Yeah, Mags…well, I'm afraid you're right about that. Jules and I aren't going to make it."

"What? Are you serious?"

"We're so sorry, but, well, you know that Jess got divorced last year, right?"

"Didn't find out till my bridal shower, but, yes, she told me. She also told me *weeks ago* that it would be too hard to arrange things with the kids for this weekend. But what's going on with you and Jules?" said Maggie.

"Well, we just don't feel right going without her. I mean, it wouldn't be the same. I know it's been forever since we've gotten together for a girly weekend, but it was always about the four of us."

"True, but, I…I guess I'm just a little disappointed. I came up here really early to prepare the turkey for tonight's dinner. I stocked the house with everything we'd need for a pampered weekend. What the hell am I going to do with a sixteen-pound turkey?"

"You got a sixteen-pound turkey? Wow!"

"Yes…I figured everyone could take leftovers."

"I'm so sorry, Mags. I don't know what to say."

"Well, it's just so last minute, and I'm a little hurt," said Maggie.

"Again, I'm so sorry. But here's the thing, Mags…we all have kids. I know you don't understand this, but it's hard sometimes to just drop everything on a whim for a weekend get-together."

"Wasn't exactly a whim, but whatever. So, yeah…have a great Thanksgiving," Maggie said while biting a hole through her tongue.

"You do the same," Katie said in a low voice. "Tell Andrew we said hello."

"Will do."

"Talk soon, I hope," said Katie.

"Yep. Buh-bye."

Maggie rolled her eyes and sighed heavily as she stared out at the lake. What was up with these so-called friends? Sure, they hadn't really been in touch for the last several years, aside from an occasional text or Christmas card photo that showcased their lovely kids and pets. But they all came together for Maggie's wedding…as if they were fresh, young college grads… carefree…spontaneous…celebratory. The friends-giving was supposed to be a new tradition…a new beginning.

Maggie balled herself up on the couch and drifted off to pouty land. What would she do with a sixteen-pound turkey? She chuckled for a second, and then her thoughts turned away from disappointment as she compared her own life with her friends' lives, specifically Jess's life.

Poor thing…strapped with three kids. She recalled Jess telling her that her ex-husband was now living with his much-younger someone. She also recalled Jess telling the whole gang that the best way to keep a man is to do whatever he wants in bed. Hmmm…she's probably too damn tired to take her own advice, Maggie thought, envisioning Jess with all the kids and dogs and whatever else was plastered on the Christmas card photos every year.

Maggie's thoughts were interrupted by a call from Andrew. "I didn't expect to hear from you, babe. What's going on?"

"Well, you haven't answered my texts," said Andrew.

"Oh, sorry. I guess I was preoccupied."

"Just wanted to check on your weekend and see if Dean fixed that tiny leak in the roof. Remember? The one in the spare room?"

"Oh, yeah, I checked…it looks good."

"Okay, great. He's a hell of good handyman. Soooo…how are the girls?"

"Phf! Couldn't tell ya! They bailed!" said Maggie.

"Are you really surprised?"

"Well, yeah. I am," said Maggie, slightly jarred by Andrew's reply. "All of a sudden, Jules and Katie feel it wouldn't be the same without Jess. I'm just disappointed…I miss them."

"How so?" said Andrew.

"Uh, well, whatta you mean?" Maggie said.

"Seriously, Mags. You saw them at the wedding, but before that…what was it? You said it was like ten years or something?"

"Well, yeah. But we kept in touch…enough."

"Babe, listen to yourself. Kept in touch *enough*? Face it, Mags. They've moved on. Weddings bring out the best in people. So, of course they were all caught up in a nostalgic moment when this friends-giving plan came up," said Andrew.

Okay, you're being a little douchey, she thought. And you sound like a therapist.

"So, here's an idea, why don't you and I have our own friends-giving party. Business wrapped up early here, and I can be on the road within the next hour. To hell with those bitches!"

"Andrew, I know you're trying to make me feel better, but they're not exactly bitches."

"Okay, you're right. That was a bit harsh," said Andrew. "So, I'll see you in a couple hours."

"See you then," said Maggie, thrilled by the spontaneity of Andrew stepping in to save the weekend.

Oh, well…friends-giving could've been a wonderful new tradition, Maggie thought. But maybe Andrew was right. How well did she really know these people anymore? People who methodically send a holiday photo with no real message and no real sentiment.

Her thoughts turned toward Jess again. Maggie wondered if she'd send a photo of her and the kids this year. Or would the holiday photo be a thing of the past now that Jess was divorced? *Do whatever he wants in bed*…Maggie chuckled. She couldn't get Jess's famous words out of her head. She began to perk up. Andrew was on his way to the lake house, and Maggie's disappointment over a flop of a weekend had begun to fade.

***

By six o'clock, Andrew had arrived with takeout from Chef Wong's.

"Thanks for picking that up, babe. Had no idea the oven was in such poor condition," said Maggie.

"I gotta say, I was both surprised and disappointed by your call. I was only about thirty minutes away and so looking forward to a home-cooked meal," said Andrew. "And what the hell will we do with a raw, sixteen-pound turkey?"

"I know, babe. It was my first time preparing a turkey. I was looking forward to it as well," said Maggie. "We always go out to dinner when we're here, so how would we have known about the oven, really?"

"One more thing that needs to be fixed. I'm surprised Pops hasn't sold this place by now. I mean, he and Mother never come here."

"Ya know, Andrew…I was thinking. Maybe it's time he just handed the cottage over to you."

"I don't know, Mags, it's becoming too much maintenance."

"Oh, but we love it here," said Maggie.

"Well, *you* love it here," Andrew replied. "This is more your thing."

She sat in silence and confusion. Andrew had always seemed to enjoy their getaways at the lake. Was his disappointment pulling him into a negative vortex? Maggie knew one thing for sure—she'd do whatever it took to keep the lakeside cottage in their possession.

"So, I guess we'll just plow into Chef Wong's," said Andrew, who had already begun eating his kung pao chicken over the sink.

Maggie's appetite had died right along with the idea of devouring any part of big bird. She continued to play with her chopsticks, swirling the pork lo mein around its cardboard container, having no real intention of eating more than a few bites.

***

By eight o'clock, Andrew had turned on the TV in the master bedroom and propped himself up with a stack of pillows. Maggie had gotten over the disappointment that consumed the better part of the day, and she had suppressed any thoughts of her in-laws selling the cottage. But it was hard to watch Andrew's moodiness get the best of him. She heard Jess's voice once again…Do whatever he wants in bed!

"Honey? Are you tired?" said Maggie as she slithered her way inside Andrew's hunky arms.

"I am, actually."

"Really?" She reached for the remote and tuned into a sensual music channel.

"Maggie? What the hell?"

"Well, it's time for a little pole dancing," she said, tossing her robe aside and taking a spin around the cedar column in the bedroom.

"Mags, come on. Stop it. You'll get splinters from that old pole. Besides, you need a dancer's pole…and stilettos if you're gonna do it right. You look ridiculous."

"Seriously, Andrew," said Maggie as she lunged forward for the remote to mute the TV. "For several months, you've hounded me about some…some pole-dancing fantasy. Could you at least indulge me for a hot second and not make me feel like an ass?" Maggie stormed off to the bathroom for a cool-down shower.

Andrew sprang out of bed to follow her. "Mags. Hold on a sec," he said, watching her from the bathroom door.

Just about to step into the shower, she heaved a sigh, shut the water off, and wrapped herself in a towel. "What?"

"I'm just a little overwhelmed right now. It's not you," he said, walking toward her with arms wide open. "You didn't look ridiculous. I shouldn't have said that."

"Well, I appreciate your apology," said Maggie, giving in to Andrew's manly hug.

"Why don't you take a shower and then come curl up with me. Let's talk more about that anniversary trip…to *Paris*?" he said, playfully.

"Oh, Andrew! I would love that."

As Andrew returned to bed, Maggie proceeded with her shower. Her make-shift pole-dancing attempt was a flop, but perhaps a little romantic pillow talk would add some spark to an otherwise dissatisfying night. Ahhhhhh, Paris… all over again! Could she be any happier?

CHAPTER

4

Holiday Getups... and Get Downs

Christmas came and went with all the traditional hoopla. Family dinners, mother-daughter shopping spree, Maggie's father's office party. All that was a bit of a snooze-fest for Maggie. But aside from those social obligations, Maggie loved how everything seemed so magical throughout December. Mesmeric holiday displays adorned with twinkling lights. The glistening, ice-laden trees. The smell of pine.

The jewel of the holiday season, however, was the big Spencer, Decklyn, and Mackenzie New Year's Eve party. Andrew's firm traditionally threw an extravagant party for all the employees, special clients, and a few of Andrew's friends. Last year, she'd attended as Andrew's fiancée, and he had proudly shown her off, asking guests, "Isn't my fiancée an absolute rock star?" He couldn't take his eyes off Maggie, who'd donned a long-sleeved, fitted crop top and a pair of subtly sequined black palazzo-style pants with a sheer overlay. This look put Andrew completely over the top in lust. He loved Maggie's sense of style and the way her beach-wavy hair had just enough messiness.

Caught up in the elation of that most exquisite night, the two of them had retreated to Andrew's office suite, which was well-equipped to serve as a private romantic nook, so she could play one of their favorite games—naked runway. Unfortunately, a tipsy guest had barged into the office suite with his own date, looking for some privacy just as Maggie was parading around in her lacy lingerie and plush suede "Loubi-red" booties—a Christmas gift from Andrew. Oh, God…so embarrassing, she remembered. Andrew had been so excited to sneak away with her that he forgot to lock his office door.

But this year, she was Andrew's Mrs. Perhaps they could excuse themselves once again from all the carousing and go for a naked runway do-over. They'd already scheduled a secret 11:30 p.m. meeting on Andrew's office terrace. Maggie was more than happy to dodge the countdown crowd by sneaking off to their own private world, overlooking the river, where they could take in the city's spectacular display of fireworks.

Unexpectedly, Maggie's phone buzzed, interrupting her blissful thoughts of what the night had in store for her. "Darling, hello," her mother screeched as Maggie answered her cell phone.

"Oh, hi, Mother. Happy New Year!"

"Maggie, that's really more of a January greeting."

Oh, it is not! she wanted to reply, but nothing could spoil her festive spirit. "It's, good to hear from you. Are you and Dad still joining Rita and Ted at the country club?"

"Oh, of course. And please tell Andrew that we certainly do appreciate the invite to his firm's holiday party. But we traditionally go to the country club for New Year's Eve."

"I will certainly tell him," said Maggie. "He's been out running around all day…dealing with the caterers and so forth. In fact, I'm surprised he's not home by now, getting ready."

"I'm sure he's done a remarkable job. Everyone who's ever gone to a Spencer gala has simply raved over how spectacular they are. Now, will you and Andrew be coming to dinner next weekend? Or will he be out of town?"

"Uh, actually, I think he *is* out of town, Mother, but *I* can make it."

"Well, that's fine, darling. It's a shame, though. We miss seeing the two of you together. But I realize he's awfully busy…inheriting his father's firm and all that goes with it."

"Yes, very true. Always busy."

"Well, I simply called to tell you and Andrew to have a wonderful time tonight."

"Oh, we certainly will," said Maggie as she began to lay out her sexy outfit.

"I can just picture the two of you," her mother said, "corralling everyone at midnight toward the fireworks as they shoot from the river barge."

Yes, you just keep that picture in your mind, Maggie thought, imagining Andrew and herself far from the party crowd, having their *own* celebration on the office terrace. "Well, happy New Year's...Eve," said Maggie.

"By the way, dear, the Worthingtons will be throwing their annual Winter Blues party at the end of January. Do you think it's something Andrew would like to attend?"

Ugh! Gag! Not a chance of us getting together with those pretentious snobs. "Oh, how nice. I'll write myself a note on that." *Not!*

"Well, be sure to tell him how wonderful it is. Ted and Rita hire the most wonderful blues band...everyone seems to have a ball!"

"Oh, geez, Mother. That probably falls on Andrew's birthday weekend. Bummer."

"Yes, well, whatever the two of you decide, then. I'm sure you're getting ready for your fabulous evening," her mother said. "What are you wearing, by the way?"

Maggie looked down at her bed, where she'd laid her holiday-red, fitted cropped top and black flared cropped pants with subtle red piping along the sides. "Oh, I'm wearing a fitted black cocktail dress," she said, while brushing her hand across the red sequins on the crop top.

"With understated accessories, I assume. Remember, less is more, dear. But you always put yourself together so nicely. I'm sure Andrew will be very proud to have you by his side."

"Well, Mother, I really do have to run. Have a wonderful time!"

"Same to you, dear."

Click.

***

"Andrew! Honey? Where are you?" said Maggie as she stepped into his office at precisely 7:30 p.m.

"Babe, hi," he said, as he came from his adjoining overnight suite, wrapped in a towel. "Just got out of the shower. Thanks so much for bringing fresh clothes."

"So, what happened? What did you say about the caterers? I wasn't following your message, " said Maggie.

"Oh, babe, there's no time to go into all that. The party starts in half an hour, and I'm sure people will be starting to roll in soon. I need to go greet them," said Andrew as he pulled on his pants. "Howie and Tom are probably already down in the lobby. Did you see them on your way in?"

"No, I didn't, actually," said Maggie.

"Oh, okay. Well then, we definitely need to get going," said Andrew, while buttoning up his shirt. "Is that what you're wearing, Mags?"

"What? Yes, this is what I'm wearing…you love this look on me," she said.

"Of course I do…you look hot, babe. Just looks so similar to last year's getup."

Getup? Maggie was thrown off by his disinterest. She wanted him to love the way she looked.

"I'm sorry, babe. That came off wrong. Let's get you, *Mrs. Spencer*, down to the party, so I can show you off."

Much better, Moody Dude! "I'd like that," said Maggie, who was more than thrilled to be introduced as his Mrs. She took hold of his collar and fixed his tie but recoiled, nearly bowled over by the strong hint of several Grey Goose martinis.

"You're amazing, Mags. Thank you," said Andrew as Maggie finished up with his tie. He leaned in for a kiss.

Maggie stopped him. "Babe, don't take this the wrong way, but I think you need a breath mint."

"Grey Goose a bit much, is it? " Andrew said with a slight chuckle as he headed toward his overnight suite.

Maggie plopped herself down onto the office couch, taking in the layout of the place, thinking that she'd only been there a few times in the past year. She'd been quite the regular when she and Andrew were dating. In fact, he lived there, for the most part, which was something he could do, since his father owned the building. Andrew had designed his office to include personal amenities such as a small but luxurious bathroom off to the side of his cozy overnight quarters. And the shower was the best! A large walk-in with dual shower heads…very spa-like…very exhilarating…very much a part of their premarital romantic life.

What's taking him so long? she wondered. "Andrew!" she called as she walked into the overnight suite.

"I'm just looking for my phone."

"Why is the futon such a mess?" Maggie asked, looking around.

"Babe, I'm not gonna lie to you. After the catering mishap, I had a few drinks to calm my nerves…I mean, this is a big night with a big reputation. I came in here to take a nap but overslept. That's why I called you to bring my clothes. The phone has to be here somewhere…help me shake out this blanket."

"There it is," said Maggie, pointing to the lower corner of the bed.

Andrew grabbed the phone from the folds of the blanket and stuck it in his pocket. "Ya know, this just isn't the way I wanted to start the evening." He sighed. "I wanted to have a pre-party with you, babe, but time—"

"So, let's have one! Let your partners greet the guests till we get there." Maggie started toward Andrew's office bar.

"As much as I'd like to, we just can't." He tapped his watch, then pointed toward the office door.

"Let me just freshen up a bit," said Maggie, having caught a murky glimpse of herself in the reflective martini shaker.

"Mags, come on! You look great!"

"I promise I won't be more than five minutes."

"Okay. But please hurry, Chubba Bubba," said Andrew as he tapped Maggie's butt. "Amy and Susan will be wondering where you are."

"Chubba Bubba? What's that about?" said Maggie. It was true she'd put on a few pounds since the wedding, but it was happy weight. She was happy to be married and let down her guard around carbs from time to time.

"Oh, Mags. You just look a little Kardashian in these pants," said Andrew, while rubbing the curvature of Maggie's butt. "It's not a bad thing!"

Uh, okay, but let's ditch the Chubba Bubba tag, she thought.

"So, I'll see you in five?" he said.

"Yep! See you in five."

As Andrew rushed from his office, Maggie decided to take a moment for herself. She stepped out onto the terrace and sucked in a deep, refreshing breath of frosty air. She gazed out over the river, mesmerized by the city lights and the festive sounds of noisemakers and horn blowing on the street below. Maggie was so caught up in the jubilation, she barely minded the frigid air. But her appreciation for the majestic night came to a screeching halt when she detected a little drizzle that could quickly ruin a head full of dramatic beach waves.

She rushed back inside and took a quick look at herself in the bathroom mirror. She brushed a subtle glittery powder over her face—a special indulgence just for the night. And she tousled the waves in her hair until she achieved the perfect amount of disarray.

"All set," said Maggie, taking a final look at herself.

As she stepped out of the bathroom, something familiar caught her eye. The corner of a beige box with a Paris logo jutted out from beneath the futon. Maggie's face lit up. As if she'd found a chest full of gold, she snatched the box and brushed her hand across the opulence of the ornate Louboutin signature sprawled across the lid.

That little rascal, she thought. Naked runway in new stilettos! Hmmm…a little higher than I'm used to. Not sure how I'll ever walk in these bad boys, but I'll give it a whirl.

Maggie kicked off her Loubi-red booties and slipped her size seven-and-a-half narrow feet into the European size thirty-eight shoes. She wobbled around for a bit until her feet became numb, then she threw back a shot of Jack Daniels from Andrew's office bar, deciding to surprise Andrew by wearing her new shoes to the party. Surely, he'd appreciate her doing a little *teasing* for what he apparently had planned for later. Besides, if she were going to take his pole-dancing fantasy seriously, she'd better get used to the feel of these extravagant, most exquisite shoes.

***

Maggie stepped off the elevator into what appeared to be the party of all parties. The mammoth corridor was circular and lined with string lights. There were cocktail servers and massive marble tables holding appetizers…canapés…carving stations with the works! And a jazz-funk band set up in the far corner of the lobby was covering some fun dance tunes. Maggie was awe-struck. Beautiful people. All dressed gorgeously…many with high-class labels.

She strolled through the crowd, searching for Andrew, making eye contact with people she didn't know, nodding her head, and mouthing hello. As she passed by a small group of men, she heard them commenting on someone who they considered "quite MILFy"—as in, a mother I'd like to f***. She tried to think of hot moms who might be present, but no one came to mind.

"Maggie! Hello!" said Howie Decklyn. "Happy New Year!"

"Yes, Happy New Year to you and Susan. Is she here?"

"She's off to the ladies' room, I believe. Ahhhh, here comes the man!" said Howie, turning his attention toward Andrew as he approached. "Your wife's a stunner!"

"Yes, she certainly is," said Andrew as he took a look at his watch and then spotted Maggie's feet. "Howie, will you excuse us for a minute?"

"Of course, of course. Great seeing you, Maggie. I'll see you a little later for the toast."

Doubtful…I'll be "modeling" by that time, she mused. "Okay, Howie. See you later."

"Mags…it's 8:30," said Andrew as he gently pulled her aside. "What've you been doing?"

"Well, I spent a few peaceful moments on the terrace and—"

"People have been asking about you," he interrupted.

"Time just got away from me, Andrew. So…*you've* never been late for any-thing?"

"Maggie, let's not get into that. Besides, that's always been about business."

"Okay, whatever."

"And I see you've been snooping around," said Andrew.

"What? Whatta you mean, *snooping around*?"

"The shoes, Maggie," he said, staring down at the new Louboutins. "I was going to surprise you with those *later*."

"Oh, Andrew. Is that really an issue? I thought I might surprise *you* by wear-ing them! Don't they look great?" said Maggie, raising her left foot behind her knee and craning her neck to get a good look.

"Quite frankly, Mags, I think they look a little sleazy with your outfit. Those shoes aren't meant to be worn in public."

"Geez, okay! I'll go change back into the booties!"

"The booties are classier…and not so…so hooker high! How can you even walk around in these?" he said, pointing to her shoes as if they were defective rejects. "But don't bother changing, now. People will notice."

"Andrew, you sound ridiculous. If I can't walk in these shoes now, how will I strut around in them later?" she said in a hushed voice, noticing that Tom and Amy Mackenzie were coming their way.

"Hey, guys!" said Andrew. "The party's great, isn't it?"

"Yes, it sure is. A lot more people this year," said Tom. "No wonder you were in a tizz over the new caterers."

"Yeah, they really came through for us," said Andrew.

Maggie could not stop looking at Amy. Her curvaceous figure was smoothly poured into a fitted, red, sequined dress…slightly low-cut… with a front slit starting just above the knees that bared miles and miles of legs as she walked. How on earth could she look like that after cranking out three kids!

Aaaaaaand, she's the trending MILF! Maggie thought.

"Oh, there's Jake Youst. I need to see him for a second. I promise I won't talk too much business," said Tom, walking away and blowing a kiss to his wife.

"Maggie, I love your shoes!" said Amy.

"Oh, thank you. A belated Christmas gift from this one," she said, playfully nodding her head in Andrew's direction.

"Nice, Andrew!"

"Thanks, Ames," he said, leaning in to kiss her on the lips.

Aaaaaaand, apparently Andrew thinks she's the MILF as well, Maggie thought of her too-soon-to-be-tipsy husband.

"I think I'll go over and say *hi* to Jake and Tracey. Great seeing you, Maggie. See you later on, Andrew," said a slightly flustered Amy.

"Doesn't Amy look fantastic, Mags? Can't believe she had a baby a few months ago…at her age!"

"Yeah, she looks great. I ran into her a few weeks ago at the spa. Said Tom hired a nanny."

"Yep. Best idea Tom ever had was to hire that nanny. Clearly, Amy's gym and spa time is paying off."

Maggie smiled, feeling a tad deflated for a reason she couldn't put her finger on.

"Hey, bud! Can you bring me another scotch on the rocks?" Andrew said to a passing server.

"Sure thing, Mr. Spencer."

"Andrew…really? *Another* scotch?" said Maggie.

"Mags…stop! Don't be a buzzkill. It's New Year's Eve!" said Andrew as he began to walk slightly in front of her.

Maggie plastered a gotta-get-through-the-night smile on her face, thinking that her lofty expectations for the most entrancing night of the year might have to be reined in. She lagged further and further behind Andrew as she tried to mask her hobbling gait.

"Andrew, hi! Great party!" said an oncoming client.

"Thanks, Gil. And I see you brought your daughter," he replied.

"You sneaky devil," said Gil as everyone fake-chuckled. "This is my wife, Kathleen."

"Kathleen, hi! This is my Maggie," he said to them, motioning to his side… to no one.

"Hi!" said Maggie as she made painful strides to catch up.

"Hello," Kathleen said as she gave Maggie the once-over, stopping at her feet, fixating on the shoes.

"So, you're Dr. Maggie," said Gil as Kathleen gazed around the party, lacking interest in the conversation.

"Oh, ha ha, *Dr. Maggie*…too funny! Not an MD but a clinical therapist. Not for much longer, though," Maggie replied, seeking a look of approval from Andrew, who'd joined in with Kathleen's boredom.

"Oh? Changing careers?" said Gil.

"No, just ready to pursue some personal interests," said Maggie, now getting Andrew's attention as he shot her a look.

"Well, Maggie and I have a lot more to discuss on that matter," said Andrew.

We do? Maggie thought, remembering that during premarital discussions, he was completely on board with her transitioning out of an unfulfilling career.

"Hey, party animals!" said Howie, who'd walked up to the foursome, unknowingly quelling the awkwardness.

"Havin' a good time?" said Andrew.

"This party rocks!" said Howie, spilling a bit of his cocktail as he raised it in a toast. "Maggie," he said, "Susan's not much of a dancer. Wanna get down with this old dog?" He nodded his head toward the dance floor as the band played its version of "Get Down Tonight."

"Andrew, you mind?"

Hello! I mind! Maggie wanted to say. How will I dance in hooker shoes? she wondered, recalling Andrew's "hooker-high" comment earlier.

"Not at all," said Andrew. "Mags, go for it."

A panic-stricken Maggie began to tremble inside. And then she caught a glimpse of a few ladies on the dance floor who'd tossed their shoes aside. Give a girl a few drinks, and etiquette goes straight out the window, she thought, watching the shoeless women flail around to the KC and the Sunshine Band tune. She quickly stepped out of her shoes and rushed to the dance floor, content to dance the night away if it meant not having to walk another step in those feet grinders.

***

Maggie had done most of her mingling for the night sitting with others at a cocktail table, hiding her shoe-free feet under a long linen tablecloth. The night hadn't turned out as she'd hoped, but it was now 10:30...only one hour to go until she'd sneak to Andrew's office suite. She could peel herself out of her holiday getup and toss those damn shoes back into the box.

A woman who smelled like old-lady perfume and appeared to be quite bloated in her ill-fitted holiday dress staggered to the table then. "You must be Dr. Maggie!" she said.

Ugh! Enough with the Dr. Maggie stuff. "Yep. That's me," Maggie replied, disappointed she'd been trapped in another shoptalk conversation.

"I have a question," the woman said.

Seriously? Is there an invisible booth around me, inviting tipsy partiers to start personal conversations? As hard as she tried, Maggie couldn't figure out who would bring his or her advice-seeking, boozy mother to the firm's New Year's Eve party.

"Maggie! I see you met Ms. Deirdre," said Tom Mackenzie.

Tom! You wonderful savior! "Um, yeah," she replied. "Who is she?" Maggie mouthed to Tom as Deirdre's head hit the table.

Tom pulled a barefooted Maggie aside. "She's Harold Thompson's, um, lady friend."

"Oh, so she's not someone's mother, then?" said Maggie."

"Ha ha. No. Maybe you don't know Harry. He retired about five years ago. Good friend of Andrew's father. He's a first-timer here at the big New Year's blowout."

"Yeah, he's before my time. But Deirdre called me *Dr. Maggie*. How does she know me?"

"Who knows? Maybe Andrew said something to Harry?"

"Apparently, many people have been misinformed about my therapist status."

"Ha ha. All in good fun, Maggie. Good talkin' to ya. I'd better go find Harry...let him know his date's ready to call it a night." Tom chuckled as he walked off.

By now, Andrew's private suite was calling out to Maggie. She'd had enough of the party and would now set her sights on a fresh start to a new year with a rejuvenated Andrew. But where had he gotten to? Maggie hadn't seen him in quite some time, and her feet hurt too much to go looking for him. She certainly couldn't walk around barefoot, could she?

But thoughts of leaving the party a little early, persuaded Maggie to take a lap around the room to find him. She slowly began to slip her feet back into the Louboutin's, but they simply would not fit. Her size seven-and-a-half feet had swollen to the size of watermelons, and she'd never wanted so badly for sexy shoes to morph into a pair of canyon-sized clodhoppers.

To hell with it, she thought, as she stood up with shoes dangling from her fingers. She was on a mission to find Andrew and coax him into leaving the party. She'd walked only a short way, when he popped out of crowd, gaping at his shoe-toting wife.

"Mags," he said, approaching her. "What's going on?"

"What's going on? Well, quite frankly, I've had my ears talked off by too many people who wanna speak to Dr. Maggie, and I'm not here to give therapy, Andrew."

"I know, Mags. I guess I've bragged about you a little too much. These people are just making conversation. Plus, I could tell you were in pain…thought it'd be best for you to sit for a while."

"Yeah, I guess so," she said. "And yes, my feet are killing me. So, I was wondering…why don't we go ahead and get our own little party started. I can't listen to one more person's problems."

"Mags! That's a little harsh."

"Maybe it is. But I just wanna go back to the suite now. Are you coming?"

"Um, no. I will meet you at 11:30 as planned. Why don't you take a hot shower? Have a drink or two? The view from the terrace should be quite interesting by now," said Andrew. "The festivities are ramping up."

"Okay," said Maggie, disappointed but too exhausted to put up a fight. As she hobbled toward the elevator, Maggie couldn't help thinking the whole evening had been some kind of bizarre dream…a nightmare, perhaps. Had she not yet entered the massive lobby that housed the most spectacular party of the year? Was the real party about to jump out and surprise her? She sure hoped so.

***

Maggie heard the faint sound of premature fireworks that some hard-core partiers had been setting off. It was now 11:45. She had dozed off, waiting for Andrew, the slightly scuffed Louboutin stilettos kicked into a corner of the overnight suite. Her feet were throbbing as she attempted to rise from the futon.

"Ouch!" she said, sitting down again. Where's that stupid foot massager when I need it? she thought, recalling her lame birthday gift.

"Mags?"

"Andrew?" she said, surprised to see her husband standing inside the doorway. "Got here just in time."

Still wearing her now very wrinkled holiday getup and taking another look at the tossed-aside Louboutins, Maggie said, "So, I wasn't dreaming? This very disappointing night really happened?"

"Mags, can we try to salvage the last few minutes of the year and not focus on the negative?"

"I guess so," she said, looking up at her husband who was struggling to loosen his tie.

He leaned over to give her a hand getting up from the futon. "Let's get this champagne off the ice and enjoy!"

Maggie began to loosen up. "Yes. Let's."

"By the way, Mags, you weren't feeling well."

"Well, it's just that my feet were on fire. I admit, it was stupid of me to wear my new shoes to the party," said Maggie as she looked down at her swollen feet, now forming blisters and looking the worst kind of nasty.

"No, what I'm saying is *that's* what we'll tell people if they ask where you disappeared to," said Andrew as he filled their champagne flutes.

"Oh. Okay. Can't imagine that anyone paid that much attention to my whereabouts," said Maggie.

"Just a precaution...no need to fuel the gossip tanks."

"True."

Maggie slipped on the soft, cozy Uggs she'd stuffed into her overnight duffel, and she and Andrew proceeded to the terrace. She shivered in his arms as they watched the city folks run amuck with their streamers and horns, shouting, Happy New Year! as the most magnificent fireworks display lit up the sky. They clinked their champagne glasses as Andrew leaned over and kissed Maggie on the forehead.

***

After all the festive hoopla, Maggie and Andrew returned to the suite, exhausted and chilled to the bone. They quickly stripped down and hunkered under the futon blankets.

"Up for a little chat, babe?" said Maggie.

"Um, sure," Andrew mumbled as he turned over to face her.

"Well, I've been thinking...I know we're talking about a Paris trip in June, but would it be too much to do something tropical for your birthday?"

"Mags, that's only a few weekends away."

"Oh, I know. There's not much time for planning. But we can pull it off... don't ya think?"

"Hmmm, I dunno, Mags. January is a very busy month at the firm."

"January weather is just so depressing. Wouldn't you like to go to the Caribbean for a few days?" said Maggie.

"Of course I would. But like I said, it's a very busy month. Come to think of it, I have to be in New York over my birthday weekend."

"Seriously?" Maggie said, sitting up.

"Settle down, Mags. I'll be back on Sunday…my actual birthday."

"I just think you've been working way too hard, Andrew. You need a break. And you said things would slow down in the new year."

"And they will…after January. It sounds like someone else needs a break. You sure you're not pushing this trip to get *yourself* out of *your* office?"

"Okay, so we both need to get away," said Maggie. "Here's what our New Year's resolution should be: we'll make the effort to get back to our honeymoon phase…even if that means spending quality downtime with each other."

Andrew looked at her with very tired, bloodshot eyes and said, "Mags, this honeymoon phase stuff? I don't really know what you're talking about. And I definitely don't wanna talk anymore. Stop worrying so much. Can we *please* get some sleep now?"

Maggie didn't respond. She simply forced a smile and nodded. Andrew leaned over and kissed the top of her head. He muttered, "Happy New Year," and rolled away.

As Maggie started to drift, she suddenly realized that Andrew hadn't even asked her to play naked runway. Then she caught another glimpse of the glamorous red underbellies of the sleek, shiny feet grinders that lay abandoned in the corner as if they were on a time-out. Maybe it was just as well that they'd skipped the role playing. Those shoes were little demons, as far as Maggie was concerned.

CHAPTER

5

New Year's Resolution Interrupted

Maggie stared playfully at Andrew's one-of-a-kind birthday gift—the tall, sleek, steel pole newly mounted in the center of the master bedroom. The fantasy dancer's pole that Andrew had envisioned for his wife's live performance. She was well pleased that she'd pulled off a sneaky installation while he was out of town for the weekend on business. He'd most likely arrive home at his usual post-business trip time, between 6:00 and 7:00 p.m., expecting the typical light Sunday dinner and even lighter conversation. But on *his* special day, he'd be blown away by Maggie's promise to resurrect the honeymoon phase. Their sense of adventure had taken a little hiatus, but Andrew promised his schedule would be lighter soon, and this surprise gift would surely reignite his passion. It was the new year—time for new ideas and creativity. And it was perfect timing for a perfect gift.

Maggie had planned a wonderful evening, for which she'd rehearsed tossing herself around the steel pole, trying to mimic the moves of a twenty-something dancer on YouTube. And there was still plenty of time to practice before Andrew's return that evening.

She swung herself around in a pirouette a few times, repeating the instructor's words with the flow of her movements; hips out, turn into pole, let go, grab it again. She was fairly confident of her beginner moves, so she went on to something called the back spin. As much fun as it was, her knees suffered scrapes on the hardwood floor. So, she decided to stick with what she knew, which was really just a glorified spin around the pole with a few impromptu hand gestures. These seductive moves would be good enough for Andrew on his birthday night. Besides, she'd eventually work her way into the fan kick and the pole climb—he'd always have something to look forward to.

As Maggie stopped to take a breath, her phone buzzed. "Hello, Mother."

"Maggie, dear, you sound out of breath."

"Oh, yeah, I was just doing a little housework before Andrew gets home."

"I'm not sure why you won't hire Janice to come over and do that. She does a fantastic job on *our* house."

"Well, that's something Andrew and I need to talk about, I suppose."

"But she doesn't work on Sundays," her mother said.

Yeah, well, neither do I, Maggie thought, grinning at the dancer's pole. "So, how's everything?"

"Everything is quite well. Now, Maggie, since you and Andrew didn't make it to Ted and Rita's Winter Blues party, I wanted to remind you to wish him happy birthday from your father and me."

"That's so nice of you, Mother. I will do that. He should be home around sixish.

"Oh, you kids with your *ishes*…everything's an *ish*."

"Ha ha. Okay, then, Mother. I'll see you soon," said Maggie, wanting to move on with more important things—like sliding down the dancer's pole into as much of a split as she could possibly muster.

"Now, hold on, dear. We haven't seen you and Andrew together for a family dinner in quite some time."

"Well, you're right about that. Not since Christmas dinner."

"Let's get something on the calendar, Maggie. We all seem to be running in circles these days—especially that Andrew. He's certainly not afraid to work."

"Yep, he's the quintessential workaholic," said Maggie. "I'll get with him on this, and we'll nail something down, I promise."

"Okay, dear. The two of you have a wonderful evening."

Oh, we sure will! Maggie's eyes were drawn to the pole once again. "Thank you. Talk soon."

Mother's passive-aggressiveness had always irritated Maggie, but she'd learned to deal with it over the years. Her parents had consistently provided her with a healthy dose of vexation, often pushing Maggie into yoga or meditation or a nice long run in the park. She couldn't think of a better way to release today's pent-up frustration than by polishing her moves on the pole. She swung around the thing time and time again, adding her own kicks and provocative facial expressions, building up her mojo. Finally, she had enough vigor to go for it, and she slid down the pole into her best gymnastic split.

"Ouch! Damn it!" Maggie's hamstrings hadn't stretched that way in decades. She hobbled to her bed and began rubbing her inner thighs. *Maybe I should've gone with the naked selfies,* she thought. But the pole had already been installed.

She lay there thinking about Jess's famous marital advice: do whatever he wants in bed. Then her cell phone rang.

"Hello."

"Maggie, it's Jess."

"Whoa! That's weird. I was just thinking about you. Must've somehow channeled your call. What's up?" said Maggie.

"I just wanted to see how the new year was treating you. How were the holidays as a new Mrs.?"

"Oh, how nice of you to ask. Well, the holidays weren't exactly what I expected—"

"Yeah, marriage is hard work, isn't it?" Jess interrupted.

"I suppose it can be...I was just a little disappointed in the—"

"Yep! I get it. It's nothing but disappointment all the time!" Jess interrupted again.

"So, what I was saying was—"

"Hey, listen, Maggie. I only have a couple minutes before Chris drops the kids off. Do you think I need therapy?"

An awkward silence followed. *You need meds,* is what Maggie wanted to tell her friend. "Uh, I don't know. What do you think?"

"Maggie you're no help," Jess said, laughing nervously.

"I can refer you to someone in your area if you'd like," said Maggie.

"So, you think I need to see someone, then?"

"Just give it a try, Jess. You'll feel better. I assume things aren't going well with the divorce and the kids and all."

"I just can't get passed the betrayal, Maggie. On top of that...managing the household with three kids and their schedules...I'm exhausted all the time."

And this conversation is exhausting, Maggie thought. "Oh, I can only imagine, Jess."

"I'm tellin' ya, Maggie. Keep Andrew happy...that's all I'm sayin'! Do what you have to."

"Well, I hope Andrew likes his birthday gift. I had a pole—"

"Oh, shit! Chris just pulled in. Gotta go, Maggie."

Click.

What the hell? Maggie thought. I'd better make that referral…fast.

***

After a long day of rehearsing and primping and making sure the house oozed with romance, Maggie's spirit was defeated. It's not like Andrew had never been late before, but where was he at eight o'clock? On his birthday?

He hadn't been answering his phone, and she was one text away from stalker-ville. She sighed heavily, threw herself flat onto the bed, and drifted off to the land of what ifs. She thought about the time she'd met Andrew. He'd been passing by her office on his way to a business meeting…

What if I hadn't bent over into downward-facing dog, she thought. What if Andrew hadn't lingered outside my office, peeking in on my secret yoga time, ogling my ass? What if he hadn't barged into my office and introduced himself? What if I'd simply gotten the damn latch fixed on that office door!

Maggie could play the what-if game indefinitely, but fact was that she despised her career as a clinical therapist—that was the stressor that compelled her to practice yoga during work hours. And she was rather pleased that someone like Andrew had found her hard-earned backside appealing. She was actually quite impressed by the brazen manner in which he'd approached her—he was resolute yet whimsical and full of gusto. She'd quickly become smitten.

In need of some fresh air, Maggie decided to give her feet-grinding Louboutins another try before Andrew got home. She wobbled onto the new cedar deck they'd added outside the bedroom. To her dismay, she caught one of the tall red heels in what appeared to be a newly formed crack in the wood. How could the new deck be rickety already? As she breathed in the January frigidity, prickly needles of cold pierced her face. Trying to shake the frostiness of a cold, lonely night reminded Maggie that Jess was right: marriage was *indeed* work.

She swiveled her foot and with great effort, dislodged the shoe from the cracked board. She then scampered into the bedroom, wincing at the throbbing in her toes. Was it New Year's Eve all over again?

What's so great about these shoes, anyway? she thought, glaring at the bedroom clock, which now displayed 8:30. She rolled her tear-filled, emerald eyes and reached for a box of tissues beside the king-size bed. "Ouch!" she cried knocking her head into the headboard.

Downhearted, Maggie resigned herself to spending Andrew's birthday night alone…with his cake—chocolate ganache, topped with a praline buttercream. She'd been saving this scrumptious little surprise for a bit of playful frolicking that night, but her sweet tooth and disappointment overtook any sort of plan for anticipated adventure. So, she padded barefoot into the kitchen and stabbed a slightly tarnished silver fork into the irresistible hunk of decadence, then shoved it into her mouth. Mmmm, delish! She went for bite number two.

***

By 9:30 p.m., Maggie was sluggish from a worn-off sugar buzz. She drifted in and out of aggravated sleep, while a marathon of *Sex and the City* episodes ran on the E! channel. Impossible, she thought, watching Sarah Jessica Parker run around Manhattan in designer spike heels. Maggie's wrath toward her beloved cast of girly girls was interrupted by vigorous knocking on the front door.

Who'd be at the door at this time of night? she wondered, and then panic set in. Was it the police? Had Andrew been involved in an accident? She tightened her sexy robe with nervous hands and rushed to the door, opening it a crack and craning her head around to see who stood on the front steps.

"Oh, hi," Maggie said, flustered to see her obliterated husband, propped up by a couple of guys who smelled of booze and smoke. "I didn't realize you were having a guys' night tonight."

"Sorry, Maggie. We just sort of bumped into each other," said Andrew's heavyset friend, Pete. "Neil and I met up with Andy, here, on our…uh, business thing over the weekend, and, well, we sort of got carried away over at Moby's once we got back from the trip. We were only gonna have one drink, but you know how that goes sometimes!"

No, I *don't* know how that goes, she thought, anger replacing her concern. "He was at a bar?" Maggie asked in bewilderment. "Did he even *mention* that I had a big night planned for his birthday?"

"Um, no. He didn't. Again, we're so sorry we kept him out," said Pete.

"Well, if you could just lug him into the master bedroom, I'd appreciate it." That was all Maggie could muster. She no longer cared if they saw her in a short, sexy robe.

After Andrew's frat-boyish attorney friends got him into bed, Maggie led them gruffly to the front door, relieved they didn't mention the dancer's pole. "So, thanks for driving him home," she said in an insincere voice.

"No problem, Maggie," said the other boozed-up fool, Neil. "You two have loads of fun tonight!" he said, howling with laughter as he swung around the outdoor lamp post, demonstrating his best drunken pole-dancer moves. She firmly closed the door behind them. Jerks!

Maggie, now fully awake, plunged onto the couch, trying to focus on anything that would keep her from losing her temper. She began twirling strands of the disheveled upsweep she'd so carefully crafted—and had planned to shake loose seductively during her performance. But now, her nearly ten o'clock bedhead served as a reminder that married life had become a little messy.

This is getting old, she told herself. What would she tell clients when they'd go on about their spouses' poor behavior and spew out rationalizations and excuses for them? They were fooling themselves, she always thought while listening to them. They were not going to change their spouses' behavior. Their only hope was to take off the blinders and make their own lives better.

While mulling this over, Maggie somehow managed to switch gears. She wanted to refocus on something positive—anything positive. She sauntered into to the bedroom and dropped into the beige- and black-striped reading chair. She couldn't help but wonder why she'd picked out that prison-look pattern. The mouthwatering appetizers, catered by Bella's, that she'd beautifully arranged on platters and placed in the bedroom earlier that evening had developed a rather unsavory film. The perfectly puffed-up *arancini di riso* now looked like mashed-down tater tots, and she realized her thoughts had drifted, once again, into all that was ugly.

Focus! Focus on the positive, she reminded herself. She decided to go with the reasons she and Andrew had married in the first place. She recalled their strong attraction to one another and how she adored the fun side of him. His unpredictable sense of adventure was also appealing. But mostly, she'd been swept away by the fact that Andrew Spencer III, Esq., who could've chosen *anyone*, wanted to marry *her*—Margaret Elizabeth Walters. She'd certainly had her share of dating accidents, which had soured her toward the concept of spending her life with another person. What a blessing when someone like Andrew popped into her life!

He loved her naughty side…and her backside, which he'd go on about. And he loved the fact that she had no baggage. Sure…he, himself, had had a right-out-of-college marriage that lasted for about a hot two seconds, but Maggie was free and clear of any such attachments. He loved that she was independent and wise enough to wait for the right man—her very best asset, according to him. She was his clean slate.

She curled herself into the mud-colored satin sheets of the bed, thinking about what had drawn them together and continuing to twirl her hair. Then her finger became tangled in what now felt like hairspray-sticky dreadlocks. She reached out to smooth Andrew's disheveled hair—chocolate-brown, swirled with a few grays here and there. Andrew would make up for this little mishap, she told herself; he often did. She envisioned a little blue box sitting on their dinner table the next evening. He'd most likely gift one of the items she'd circled in the dog-eared Tiffany catalog. What if he no longer cares about this pole-dancing nonsense? she agonized, taking one last look at the ridiculous nonrefundable dancer's pole.

Maggie's head now pounded from too many what ifs, which hindered her new year's resolutions. She massaged her face, which often relieved her headaches. To her delight, she discovered a tiny speck of praline buttercream on the outer edge of her fingernail. She licked it then frowned at its oddly brackish flavor.

Things will slow down…after January, she recalled Andrew's promising on New Year's Eve. "I'm not giving up on us," she whispered, sheepishly snuggling up to the sweaty, beefy mass that consumed what now seemed more like a single bed.

***

Beep beep beep beep beep beep. Maggie's alarm clock drilled right through Andrew's two-ton head at six o'clock the next morning.

"Good morning!" said Maggie as she bulldozed around the bedroom, opening drapes and picking up the barroom-smelly clothes that were strewn about.

"Mags, shut that damn thing off," said Andrew from beneath his pillow.

She couldn't keep her tormenting behavior at bay—he deserved a little Monday-morning abuse after last night's shenanigans.

"What the hell are you doing up so early?" Andrew said, edging out from under his pillow with squinty eyes. "And what's with the alarm clock. You always use your phone alarm."

"First of all, I'm going to work. And you know I use the alarm clock for backup," said Maggie. "Are *you* going to work?"

"Definitely not," he said as he buried his face again.

"Well, if *you're* not going, then neither am I."

"Mags," he said, "I know you're pissed about last night. And I can't say I blame you. But I wanna be left alone today."

"Actually, I think we need to talk. I'll call Margery and let her know that I won't be in till later on."

"Whatever…just let me sleep for another hour. That's all I ask."

Maggie clanged around the bedroom some more, gathering the nasty, spoiled appetizers and cheese board, which contributed to the stench of the room. He hasn't even mentioned the dancer's pole, she thought. Probably can't see the damn thing. She proceeded toward the kitchen with the wasted party platter and threw it into the sink.

Margery! She thought. Gotta call Margery and have her cancel my 8:30 a.m. appointment.

By 7:00 a.m., Maggie was still feeling a little devilish in wanting to torment her very hungover husband. She simply couldn't help herself! She decided there was no sense in wasting the hours of dance practice she'd put in the day before. Andrew could just sit back and enjoy the show.

"Alexa, play 'Closer' by Nine Inch Nails," she said. As the song hammered away, Maggie performed her best amateur routine, spinning around the sleek steel pole, whipping her hair and provocatively pursing her lips. Certainly, this was better than a wake-up call.

Andrew crawled out from beneath his sound-blocking pillow and soggy, rumpled blankets, staring in disbelief. He slowly approached Maggie with that look he'd get when she successfully enticed him into doing anything *naked*. He pulled her into his chest with a big manly hug. Maggie's New Year's resolution hadn't been stalled after all. They were on their way back to the honeymoon phase!

"Alexa, stop!" he said.

Dead silence.

Maggie stood naked in his arms, not understanding why he'd want the grinding music to stop. Weren't they on their way to some seriously kinky shit?

"Andrew?" she said, making sure he hadn't died in her arms.

"Mags, I love the pole…I truly do. And I feel like a real piece of shit ruining what must've been my birthday surprise. But I really don't wanna do this right now. In fact, if I don't get back in bed, you're gonna have to scoop me up off the floor." He kissed the top of her head and staggered back to bed. "But you'd better believe…later tonight, I'll be ready to go. That was hot."

CHAPTER
6

Valentine's Day Charm

Maggie sat alone in a cozy little corner of Bella's Bistro, anxiously spinning a single bead on the new charm bracelet she'd found on her nightstand that morning. She was waiting for Andrew to wrap up some important business with new clients at his downtown office, so the two of them could spend their first Valentine's Day as a married couple together. She'd thank him over dinner for such a sweet gift.

Late as usual, she thought, as she began flicking the bead as if it were an unsightly piece of lint. She couldn't really complain too much, since Andrew had remained *somewhat* true to his word about his workload. His pace had slowed down quite a bit, and he hadn't been out of town since his birthday. The frequency of their intimacy had picked up some, too, though it mostly took place very quickly in the morning.

Maggie carefully studied the atmosphere of the newly renovated restaurant, which seemed to be filled with love-struck couples sipping wine or gazing into each other's eyes and holding hands across the polished mosaic tabletops. She couldn't help recalling her commitment to keeping their honeymoon alive. But it was hard to delete last month's birthday debacle from her mind. Although Andrew had apologized profusely, and they'd enjoyed a couple of affectionate nights in which Maggie barely had time to swing herself around the pole, she wasn't *completely* over the humiliation and the disrespect. He'd also managed to dodge the we-really-need-to-talk conversation, merely insisting there was no need to belabor the birthday fiasco and reminding her that he'd already apologized. And while he thanked Maggie for the dancer's pole, it was with as much enthusiasm as if she'd gifted him a pair of socks. These thoughts rang out as if the mute button in her mind were malfunctioning. She continued to ping the single pink hibiscus bead that spun rather loosely on the sterling silver bangle. She dropped her head and frowned at the thing as if it were some cheap little bauble from a gumball machine.

Then, an epiphany perked her up. Maui! He's commemorating our honeymoon! Maggie cast her mind back to lolling on the shimmering white sand, listening only to the soothing hush of waves. No phone calls, no clients, no distractions whatsoever. Just island cocktails, sand, surf, and other activities in which honeymooners indulge. She'd worn a different Hawaiian flower in her hair every night—the pink hibiscus was his favorite. He really does wanna be in the honeymoon phase, she thought. Maggie had no idea Andrew was capable of such unspoken creativity.

But when she glanced at the time again, her face tightened. She took a deep breath. I'm *choosing* love, she decided. She pulled out her compact mirror to ensure her lipstick—Valentine Red—was flawless. She ran her fingers through her fresh, new, beach-waved bob, which Andrew hadn't seen yet. He loved her hair messy, and the new shorter cut would bring out the bounciness of the wavy curls.

Her cell phone vibrated on the table. It was Andrew calling.

"Hello, there," said Maggie in her sexy voice.

"Biscuit, is that you?"

Biscuit? she scowled, thinking nothing could be worse than the Chubba Bubba name he called her on New Year's Eve. "Uh, it's Maggie. Where are you?"

"On the road, so go ahead and order the pasta sampler for two and a bottle of red—your choice. Oh, and have a martini waiting for me when I get there. Bombay Sapphire, up, with two olives."

"Not Grey Goose?"

"Nah…I'm up for something different. Oh…and make it dirty."

"I know what you like, babe," she playfully purred.

"Huh?" Andrew replied.

"Oh, nothing…see ya in a bit." Maggie ended the call and chuckled at her silliness—though she wouldn't have minded if Andrew had played along with the sentiments of the sappy holiday.

Make it dirty, she said to herself, mimicking Andrew. The sound of his robust, commanding voice had always melted her. And even though he'd been a real jerk lately, she could forgive him if he was willing to make the effort to win her over again. Their Paris trip was only four months away. There was plenty of time for Andrew to decompress and get back in the game.

Nonetheless, she'd pulled herself out of the negative vortex of her earlier reflections and became revved up at the thought of their after-dinner date. She'd be getting down to some overdue nighttime bedroom business. Maggie was now determined to break in that pole. Time to really make up for the lack of affection, the misunderstandings, and anything else that created a wedge between Andrew and her. What better time than Valentine's Day to do just that?

I almost wish we could skip dinner—

"Ma'am, can I bring you another drink?" the server said, interrupting her thoughts.

"Uh, you know what? Could you just bring my check?"

"Certainly."

Maggie's love goggles had resurfaced. And though she'd been breathing in Bella's wonderful, enticing clam sauce aroma, she was quite confident that Andrew would be willing to skip the Valentine's Day hoopla and have dinner in bed.

She eagerly tapped the speed dial. "Hi there," she purred.

"What's up? A problem at Bella's?"

"No, no problem. Although service is a little slow," she said.

"Just go tell the management I have a VIP account there," said Andrew.

"Well, they are extremely busy tonight, so I was wondering, how does dinner at home sound? You know, appetizers in bed? I'll see if I can flag someone down to put in a takeout order of your favorite arancini di riso with a side of *formaggio*," said Maggie. "I'll open a bottle of cabernet and have a martini waiting, since I'm much closer to home than you are. How 'bout it?"

"Ya know, that's actually a great idea. Get home quickly…I'm quite hungry."

"I'll see you soon," she replied with a victorious spark in her tone.

Maggie frantically searched for her very busy server. She desperately wanted a redo on the beautiful presentation of Andrew's favorite appetizers that had been wasted on last month's birthday dud. But she hadn't even gotten the check for her vodka martini yet. She continued to strain her neck, looking in every direction for the server who'd apparently decided to devote his time to the big spenders over in the private nooks.

"Oh, to hell with it! I'll just throw together a meat and cheese platter from the fridge," she muttered, throwing a ten down on the table and practically tripping over her slightly worn boots as she tried to bust out of the place. As she made her way toward the exit, a tall, beautiful woman who could have been a model poked her head out from under some dangling-heart streamers.

"Maggie! Hi!" said Amy Mackenzie.

"Oh, geez, Amy. I didn't quite recognize you behind the streamers."

"Oh, I know. It's a bit much, I think. But this is what we get for taking a last-minute table. Tom's on his way."

"How funny. Andrew was going to meet me here, too, but I tempted him into staying home for a more private party for two."

"Oh, good for you! Yeah, we took advantage of having a nanny tonight… last minute, of course. Tom's always last minute with everything."

"Well, with Andrew, it's his travel schedule. It's really worn him down over the past several months."

"Yeah, Tom said he travels a lot."

"He does. But he's been home for the past couple of weekends. I think he's learning to balance things a little more. But hey, whaddo I know? I really know nothing about his business," said Maggie.

"I know. I'll hear Tom on the phone saying stuff like 'contract negotiations,' 'merger-this, acquisition-that…'"

"Same here. I just let Andrew do his thing." As long as I can resign soon, I couldn't care less if he's out dumping porta-potties, Maggie thought. "Oh, shoot, Amy, I'd better get going. I wanna get home and prep some things."

"Okay, good seeing you, Maggie. Have fun!"

***

"Damn!" Maggie cursed as she pounded the steering wheel. It had started to snow, and heavy traffic was delaying her potentially beautiful Valentine's night by nearly an hour. She called Andrew again. "I'm so sorry, but apparently there was an accident or something. I've heard several sirens. But I think traffic is starting to move now. I should've taken the back way home like you did."

"Yes, you should have," he replied in his I'll-stifle-the-lecture-for-now tone.

"Shouldn't be *too* much longer."

"See you when you get here," he said.

Click.

Tension tightened her temples as traffic continued to creep at a snail's pace. "Who taught these idiots how to drive? It's just a few flurries!" said Maggie.

***

Maggie *finally* arrived home and rushed into the house, tossing her bag and keys onto the foyer table. No Andrew in sight.

He's in the bedroom…waiting for me!

She slinked down the hallway, thinking she'd go straight for the pole.

She stopped for a second and playfully thought of giving herself a dancer's name. *Magnolia!* Yes! Tonight's the night for Magnolia to take center stage.

She chuckled with giddiness.

As she got closer to the bedroom door, however, she'd heard Andrew on the phone. Some sort of…business call?

"Uh huh, yep, that's it! Ride that pole, cowgirl! Ahhhhhh…now be a good girl and put your panties in my cowboy hat."

Oh, my God…is someone riding my dancer's pole! thought Maggie as she burst through the door.

"Oh, hi, Biscuit…you're home, finally," Andrew said in a nervous, quivering tone as he squirmed under the covers.

Maggie was not sure whether to be angry or embarrassed that she'd expected to see someone grinding on her pole. Her mouth gaped, and she was speechless, still baffled by what she'd just overheard. "Uh, hi," she replied in a chary voice. "Andrew, did you just tell someone to put her panties in your cowboy hat?" She faux chuckled.

His eyes widened. "What? Uh, no. Ha ha! I was messin' around with Bill. You know…Bill Mason. My client. He and his wife are Dallas Cowboy fans. I, uh…I just like to razz him now and then about the season they had. Failing to make it to the Super Bowl once again! He had a few legal questions…and, well…it turned into a friendly bout of harassing each other."

"Oh, well, I could've sworn you said something about riding a pole."

"Oh, we were just yakkin' about nonsense. And I was telling Bill how excited I was about my birthday gift," he said, nodding his head toward the dancer's pole. "I'm sure that's what you overheard."

"And what about the *panties*?" Maggie asked, blowing right by the pole nonsense.

"Huh?"

"You said something about putting panties in a hat," she repeated. "And why would Bill be making a business call on Valentine's Day? This is all very strange to me, Andrew!"

"Just as this conversation is to *me*," he snapped back. "Now, I didn't mean for you to hear me talking so foully, joking around with Bill like that. And who really gives a crap about some hyped-up gimmicky holiday? My clients know they can contact me any time."

Dead silence.

"Had you gotten home earlier," he said, "we'd have given the pole another whirl," He chuckled as if the pun were intended. "And I wouldn't have taken any calls. But these things happen. You got caught in traffic…I took a call." He was not making eye contact with Maggie. "As for tonight, it's nearly ten o'clock, and I am absolutely beat. Let's just make ourselves another pole date for later in the week. What are your thoughts on that?"

Only that I'd like you to stick the pole and the whole idea up your ass, she seethed.

"So, anyway," Andrew continued, not waiting for her to respond, "did you see your flowers and chocolates on the kitchen island?" A mist of sweat had broken out on his forehead.

"Uh, no, I didn't."

"Well, I've already eaten a few snacks since you said Bella's was a bust. So, I'm gonna take a big swig of Nyquil for this looming cold and call it a night. Why don't you go read your card and put your flowers in a vase?"

"Didn't know you had a cold brewing. Seems a bit sudden," she responded.

"Yeah…another reason I was glad to come straight home," Andrew replied, coughing into his fist.

Oh, shut your lying face! And bone up on faking a cough! "Okay, g'night," she said coldly. "I'll be in bed soon, I guess." To light your ass on fire, she so wanted to scream, recalling the old Farrah Fawcett movie she'd seen on TCM.

"By the way, your hair's cute!" he called after her as she walked to the kitchen to see flowers and candy that had about as much appeal to her as dog poo.

***

Maggie sat on a kitchen barstool, sniffing the multicolored carnations that were bunched in Superthrift Grocery cellophane. They had already begun to wilt. She picked out a couple of mysterious chocolates from the heart-shaped candy box. Dark malted, ugh! She ate them anyway.

Her ego deflated, Maggie couldn't avoid reflecting on the downward spiral of what she'd hoped would be night of reconnecting with Andrew. What was up with that business call? The hogwash about a looming cold? And where was this card he told her to read?

And Biscuit? What kind of ugly pet name is that? she wondered as she shoved another chocolate into her mouth.

Suddenly, her eyes detected the corner of an unopened Valentine's card that had somehow blended in with a pile of mail. Noticing that the Tiffany catalog was missing from the messy pile of mostly junk mail in the wire basket, Maggie couldn't resist hoping for another Valentine's Day present—perhaps Andrew would redeem himself with a Color Splash Heart Tag Charm.

She ripped the envelope, even though it hadn't been sealed. Aside from a white card with a raised, red-velvet heart and a sappy message about love, there was nothing. Nada. Zilch. Zipperoo. He hadn't even put so much as a paw print inside, let alone written his name.

I guess he forgot to sign it, being so encumbered by everything, she rationalized, cucking the card into the basket of junk mail.

Again, she sniffed the drooping carnations. Puzzled, she lifted her face to look at the flowers. They seemed to have lost their scent.

CHAPTER

7

March Madness

Maggie tapped her fingers impatiently as she waited for someone to take her drink order. She wasn't quite up for the Saint Patrick's Day crowd at McCrery's Pub, but her father loved the Irish stew there, and she and Andrew were *way* overdue for a family dinner—a tradition her parents had set in place when she started to date him. She couldn't help being hung up on her husband's refusal to see a marriage counselor—an idea she'd brought up after the Valentine's Day massacre of her ego...and her heart.

Mags, we don't need some bullshit counselor to tell us that marriage isn't perfect. There's nothing wrong with us, he'd said to her. *You're way too sensitive.*

"Excuse me, young man!" Maggie now said to a boy with a bus tub filled with dirty dishes. "I'd like to order a vodka tonic while I wait for the rest of my party. Could you send a server?"

"Uh, okay, Ma'am. I'll try to find her."

"Thank you."

"Maggie, dear. Must we sit in the smoking area?" a voice interrupted.

"Oh, hi, Mother. Hi, Dad. Well, this *is* a nonsmoking pub. That law's been in effect for quite some time now," Maggie replied as she stood up to welcome her parents with lukewarm hugs.

"No need to sass your mother," her father growled.

"That gentleman over there in the corner is smoking up a storm. I'm not sure how long I'll be able to take this," her mother announced. "Everett, perhaps you should say something to him."

Maggie's father rolled his eyes. "Liz, hush. He's far enough away, for God's sake. Let the management take care of it! Where's that son-in-law of mine?" her father snapped, shifting his attention away from his wife, who was flicking a small piece of lint from Maggie's sweater and waving her hand as if to fan smoke away.

"He's working late, Dad. Should be here soon, though."

"Oh, that Andrew. Such a hard worker," her mother said.

"Yep, that he is," Maggie replied dispassionately as she looked around the pub, watching the millennials across the way stumble up to the bar with their Guinness mugs.

"You've landed a great provider! And he has fabulous features," her mother added.

Oh, shutty…he's not that great, Maggie wanted to say.

"New blouse, Mother?"

"Yes, it is," her father butted in. "Your mother certainly knows how to dress like a classy, feminine lady."

"Of course, your father's favorite look on me is anything ruffled," her mother said.

"Why is that, Dad?"

"Oh, there's no need for fashion banter, Maggie. They'd better have my Irish stew this evening," her father said, while eyeing other patrons who appeared to be enjoying their fare. "I'd be very disappointed if they run out of it!"

"Oh, Everett, you say that every year."

Maggie's father scowled at his wife and changed the subject quickly. "I'm actually rather pleased that Andrew is running late, because I'd like to discuss a very important family matter."

"Oh, gosh, Dad. What is it?" Maggie fidgeted with her green kilt-patterned miniskirt.

"You skipped out of the office a little early today, or I would've discussed this then," said her father. "Your mother and I noticed that you were overly excited at baby Ashley's baptism last week."

I was? Maggie thought.

"Now, we're very thrilled for Cousin Meg and her growing family. But we just assumed any sort of maternal thoughts on your part had fled a few years ago when you realized you weren't going to be a young bride."

Uh, boundaries, please! And let's lay off the age crap, Maggie snarled inside.

"Lately," her father went on, "it seems you've taken quite an interest in motherhood. Your mother said you asked what she thought of Meg's late start at raising a family…questioning the medical risks and so forth. So, your mother and I would like to know if you and Andrew are thinking about starting a family of your own. Do you realize that a woman your age would have a very high-risk pregnancy? Plus, Andrew's well into his forties with a very heavy workload. He wouldn't be around much for childrearing."

I'm guessing you mean "parenting," and this conversation is downright maddening, Maggie thought with a muted growl.

"If you are seriously considering this tremendous responsibility, perhaps you should look into adoption," he continued. "Your mother and I were hoping you'd keep us up to date on such matters. We haven't seen much of you and Andrew, and I barely see you at the office anymore."

Maggie stared at him, unable to muster an instant reply. You've gotta be kiddin' me, she thought. Please, someone tell me this is one of those cruel jokes people play with hidden cameras. But the concern in his eyes told her that he was serious.

"Uh, well, first of all, Dad…no! We've never really discussed having children. I mean, we realize we're a smidge past the traditional age for starting a family. And as far as my conversations with Mother about Meg, I was merely curious." That doesn't mean I want children, you obnoxious meddler!

Her mother twitched a quick smile. "We just wanted to double check on your intentions, darling. I know it seems a bit invasive…all these personal questions and so forth."

Ya think? Maggie's eyes grew wide, but she muffled her sarcasm.

"We just really care, dear. We realize that you're a grown woman, and I feel a little silly having this conversation, but we want you to understand that for a woman in her forties, childbearing is extremely risky," said her mother.

Okay, we've established the age thing…can we just move on? "Well, I appreciate the concern, Mother, and I'm sorry there was some misunderstanding over my curiosity regarding Meg. But I do have to say, this sort of thing really isn't uncommon. In fact, my neighbor, Erin Bowers, just had a baby two months ago, and she's forty-one. Oh, and Amy Mackenzie had a baby not too long ago."

"And they were very lucky to have had healthy children. I can only imagine that both were riddled with anxiety during their terms," her mother interjected.

"Hi, may I get you something to drink?" asked a server with perfect timing, whose novelty shamrock nametag lit up and belted out a string of bagpipe notes. "So sorry! This thing goes off at the most inopportune times."

"Yes, it certainly does. You folks didn't wear those noisy things last year. And the crowd seems to be a bit rowdier than before," said Maggie's father. His squinting brown eyes peered over his readers, looking at the gang of Guinness drinkers, who were now dancing a little jig at the bar.

Wish I was part of *that* group, Maggie thought, noticing the party crowd. In fact, I'd rather be in a cage full of horny leprechauns than be sitting here listening to this…this over-the-hill-for-childbearing lecture.

The server looked in the direction of Dr. Walters's disapproving stare and quickly said, "Everyone seems to be having a good time, huh? So how 'bout those drinks?"

"Yes, my wife will have a glass of sauvignon blanc. I'll have a dry martini straight up, two olives. The young lady has a full enough drink there, and we're ready to order our dinner."

"Oh, okay, sir. Ma'am, I'll start with you. What will you have?" The server looked in the direction of Maggie's mother.

"We'll all have the Irish stew," her father interrupted. "And I trust it's a fresh batch, Miss? I wouldn't want to have to send it back."

"Always fresh, sir." Her bagpipe-playing nametag interrupted. "Your order shouldn't take long at all."

Maggie noticed that her sweaty palms were sticking to the booth's bench. She continued to stew over her parents' meddlesome interrogation. This is absolute madness, she told herself. And where is my husband? We need to get this fake "lovely dinner" show on the road.

"Your mother and I were simply hoping that you'd reconsider any sort of frivolous baby whim." Her father was relentless. "We do, however, think it's wonderful that you and Andrew got together at an advanced age."

Maggie sighed heavily. Oh, dear God! I'd rather chew off my right arm than be having this conversation. "So, again, this subject is completely unnecessary. There's no need for any further discussion on babies and age or whatever." Besides, there's not a shot in hell that I'll ever get pregnant from my dud of a husband, she thought, considering the dancer's pole was now a dust collector—along with the stuffed-away charm bracelet he'd given her to apologize for missing the birthday party she'd planned.

"Very well, then," her father said, having the last word, as usual.

Maggie's stomach rumbled as she glanced around the pub, looking for anything with steam rolling off it to come her way. But her appetite subsided when she spotted Andrew walking toward the table, stopping to shake hands with a few patrons as he approached.

"Mom. Dad. Lovely to see you!" Andrew said as he gave Mrs. Walters a sloppy hug and kiss. "Sorry I'm late."

"Oh, nonsense! You have a lot going on," Maggie's mother replied.

"No worries, son." Dr. Walters patted Andrew's shoulder. "Excuse me, young man," he called to a bus boy passing by with a tub of dirty plates.

"Oh, Dad, no. He simply clears the tables," said Maggie.

"Nonsense. I'm sure this lad can whip up a drink for Andrew," he snapped, humiliating Maggie, who now wanted to hide in the bottom of the youngster's bus tub.

Andrew shook his head and held up his hand. "No thanks, Dad. I just stopped in to say hi, really."

Shocking! Maggie thought. Let me guess...you have business to take care of...you're tired...you have a cold...blah blah blah. Maggie turned her head and rolled her eyes.

"Darling, sorry to disappoint you...Mom, Dad, I apologize. Got to entertain clients tonight. I hate when these things come up so suddenly. Dad, you know all that's involved with mergers, right?"

"I certainly do," said Maggie's father, looking across the room.

"I'll be late, sweetheart. But I wanted to give you a heads-up. I thought it would be nice to spend next weekend at the lake house. We haven't been there in quite some time. How does a nice, relaxing, client-free weekend sound?"

"Oh, Andrew, that sounds fabulous!" Maggie's mother inserted as her husband shot a look of contempt her way.

Darling? Sweetheart? You phony jackass! Take your own self to the lake...load your pockets with that soon-to-be-hacksawed dancer's pole and take a plunge! "Sounds great," she replied halfheartedly, giving Andrew a suspicious once-over.

"Okay, then. I'll be on my way, folks. Mom, Dad...great to see you as always. And I promise we will have a real sit-down dinner very soon. Again, my apologies," he said as he picked up Maggie's hand to kiss it, brushing his fingers over her bare wrist. "By the way, isn't Maggie's hair absolutely stunning?"

"It certainly is," her mother replied with twinkling doe eyes, boring in on her freshly coiffed daughter.

Maggie retracted her hand with a slight jerk, thinking, Oh, shut up! You've only ever called it "cute."

"We understand, Andrew. And please tell your parents we said hello," Maggie's mother responded.

"Will do."

***

After Andrew departed, Maggie excused herself for a visit to the ladies' room. As she turned down the shamrock-lined corridor, she tripped on a gnarled floorboard. Regaining her poise, she glance around to see if anyone had noticed her little stagger. From a distance, she observed Andrew standing at the back bar, chatting with a tall, slender woman who appeared to be in her late twenties or so and was sporting a tight, white, sweater dress and what appeared to be see-through stiletto platforms. She was twirling long strands of her bleached-blond hair and laughing at whatever he had said. He then moved along to a couple of gentlemen in suits, seated at a corner table, who got up to shake hands with him.

Who's the hooker? she wondered, still fixated on the blonde.

Maggie tried to envision herself in a dress like the mystery woman's, doing a little striptease on the dancer's pole—for anyone but Andrew. She wanted to gape at the vision that stood before her, but the mystery woman glanced in her direction, so Maggie quickly ducked into the ladies' room. To her recollection, she'd never hyperventilated before, but something funky was now going on with her breathing. All the *I'm exhausteds* and *not tonights* and *gotta entertain clients* nonsense flashed before her eyes. Likewise, many other weighty issues had been gnawing at her since their wedding—issues such as the career that was holding her back from life. Why was Andrew dragging his feet in giving her the go-ahead to resign? She splashed some water on her face and patted it dry with a sandpaper-textured towel.

Outside the ladies' room, she took one more peek at the back bar. No Andrew in sight. Hooker girl was now seated alone, with her six-foot-long legs crossed, sipping what appeared to be a pomegranate martini.

"Excuse me," Maggie said, flagging a server who was passing by with a tray of clanging beer mugs.

"Yes?" the young woman answered with forced sweetness, her arm trembling under the weight of the tray.

"Do you know that woman over there…the one in the white sweater dress?" she asked, pointing behind one hand.

"Yes, that's Gemma. Top dancer over at Lillian's Tigress Club. Just hangin' out for a coupla drinks before she goes on tonight."

"As in a *stripper*?" Maggie asked, recalling there was a popular gentlemen's club just outside of Carrington Heights.

"Yes, as in a stripper! Wouldn't mind havin' that bod! She's a real hottie, ain't she? Looks like a Barbie doll!"

"Yes. Yes, she does." Hooker Barbie, in fact. "Sorry to have bothered you. I thought she was someone else. Thank you, Miss."

Maggie returned to her parents, who'd been dutifully waiting for her to rejoin them, so they could eat their stew. "Mother, Dad…I'm suddenly not feeling so hot. I'm a little queasy. Please forgive me. And Dad, have my stew packed up for your lunch tomorrow."

Red spread across her father's face, which sported his standard irritated look. "Okay, Maggie. Run along and take care of yourself. Your mother and I would like to enjoy our stew. Although, I'm sure it's lost quite a bit of heat by now. And let Margery know if you're too ill to come into the office tomorrow. There's a lot of work to be done before Ted takes over, and I'm counting on you."

"Yes, yes, please eat," she replied, watching the steam roll off their overrated canned soup. In fact, burn your tongue to a crisp, so I don't have to listen to the same old babble about how much you depend on me, she thought devilishly.

"Oh, darling," her mother cooed. "So that's why you seemed rather underwhelmed by Andrew's lovely gesture?"

"Huh?"

"Your romantic getaway at the lake house! I hope you'll feel better by then."

"Oh, yeah. I'm sure I will." If he doesn't bail on me.

"And I bet you can't wait until June! I'm so excited for you to revisit Paris."

"Yep…can't wait," said Maggie. Oh, Mother, if you only knew!

"Also, dear," her mother added, while reaching out to touch beach-waved strands of Maggie's newly crafted do, "this haircut is much more becoming to you…for someone—"

Please do not utter another crack about age, or I will dump this lumpy Irish soup on top of that helmet-head hairdo of yours! Maggie had had about all she could take.

"Liz, will you let Maggie leave, for God's sake!" her father said, having to pause before he polished off his last spoonful of stew. "You've barely eaten."

"I was just going to say that her hair really flatters her face, nicely…for someone with such well-defined cheekbones."

"Well, thank you, Mother," she said, feeling a pang of sympathy for her mother, who'd spent decades with a man who squashed her every thought. "I'm glad you like it. So, I'll see you both later."

Maggie rushed out of the pub, fighting a crowd of partiers wearing leprechaun hats and toasting with overflowing, frothy mugs. She pushed the massive oak door open and stepped out into the brisk mid-March air, banging into none other than stripper girl.

"Sorry," Maggie said, but stripper girl barely acknowledged her as she continued to hand what appeared to be business cards to the drooling millennial guys Juuling on the sidewalk.

***

While driving home, Maggie couldn't shake her uneasiness. Suffering her parents' exceptional ability to push every single one of her buttons was all too familiar. She'd always been able to talk herself off an emotional ledge when it came to family matters. But thinking her mother was a bamboozled bonehead and hoping her father burned his tongue to a crisp were proof that she'd become jaded, and her own shoulder was no longer a soft place to fall.

Maggie drove around aimlessly as the pit in her stomach grew, which provoked a bit of hanger, so she decided to treat herself to an authentic Saint Patrick's Day treat.

"Hi, welcome to McDonald's. May I take your order, please?" rang out from the drive-through speaker.

"Yes, may I have a shamrock shake and a large order of fries?"

"What size shake, ma'am?"

"Large, please."

"Does that complete your order?"

"Well, do you have any special Saint Patty's Day desserts, or do you just have the usual hot apple pies?" she asked, hoping there was some sort of crème de menthe novelty.

"Uh, no," replied the irritated teenager. "Just the usual pies, ma'am."

"Oh, okay. Throw in one of those."

"Does that complete your order?"

"Yes, thank you."

"Your total is six sixty-five. Please pull around."

***

Maggie pulled aside in the nearly vacant McDonald's parking lot and plowed right into the pie, scorching the roof of her mouth with hot apple filler. She soothed herself by lapping up the mint-green shake like a puppy that had gotten into the coveted trash bin. She felt the lock fasten on her emotional box of pain as she sucked up the last bit of her tasty treat. The typical euphoric sugar buzz, a most satiating fix, had lifted her to a place of stern reflection. Is this what married life is really like? she wondered. Andrew couldn't possibly have fallen out of love so soon, could he have? She'd have to work harder to keep him interested.

I'll give the lake-house getaway a chance, she decided. I do love it there! Plus, Andrew and I really *do* need to discuss marriage counseling.

A faint smile painted its way across Maggie's face. She began to make a mental list of fun activities they could do while on their little excursion. Then she caught sight of the empty grease-speckled fast-food bag. The french fries were gone, but she couldn't remember eating a single one. Suddenly, she recalled Andrew's new nicknames for her: *Chubba Bubba* and *Biscuit*. She needed to get herself under control.

CHAPTER 8

April Showers

Maggie sat in her easy chair with a steaming cup of coffee, listening to the pitter-patter of rain. She could've easily returned to bed on this damp, chilly morning, but she was eager to get on with her trip. Soon she'd be packing her bag for the lake-house excursion, which had been postponed two weekends ago. Andrew's all-too-frequent business trips had been replaced with the all-too-frequent necessity to "entertain clients." Often times, he'd Uber to his office and crash in the overnight suite when "business got out of hand," he'd say. Just the same, a much-needed breather and some alone time with Andrew was in order to hash out a plan to work on their marriage. After all, he had not said no to marital counseling.

She'd be missing the Saturday afternoon bridal shower for Ted and Rita Worthington's oldest daughter, Paulina. She wasn't particularly close to any of the Worthington sisters. She'd interacted with them at social functions, but she recalled they were naturally beautiful, immaculately groomed, and the most uptight women in Carrington Heights. Normally, Maggie's mother would have guilted her into attending the shower, but *a lovely weekend away with Mr. Perfect takes top priority*, she thought, mocking her mother's uppity voice.

***

Though the rain began to pour down in buckets, Maggie remained determined to make use of the secluded weekend away. Maybe they'd do some good, concrete planning for their trip to Paris, which was just two months away. They hadn't even booked their flights yet. And would it be too much to ask for the weekend to serve as restitution for the miserable Valentine's Day, for openly flirting with mysterious blondes, or for any other offenses on Andrew's marital rap sheet? She had already decided not to pry about how he knew Gemma, the dancer. Andrew had said Gemma was just a former client who'd once sought legal advice. *Yeah, okay…whatever!* she thought.

Maggie was pleasantly surprised that by one o'clock in the afternoon, Andrew hadn't called to cancel the weekend. Her oversized Louis Vuitton duffel bag was packed and ready to go. Being fair-minded in how things might pan out, she'd packed her most comfortable sweat pants and hoodies; likewise, she hadn't neglected her more playful outfits, which been stored away in their original package—a cheetah-print box embellished with red-velvet lip prints in the corners. Although she had intended to wear these outfits on Andrew's birthday, maybe they'd make their debut this weekend. Maggie also thought there was no need to waste a perfectly erect pole in the center of one's bedroom, so she'd been secretly practicing her moves. She was more than thrilled about her inner thigh strength and how her whole body seemed to be toning up quite nicely.

She'd become caught up in reinventing her sense of adventure. There was something exhilarating about visiting one of those novelty-toy stores way across town, where she'd carefully selected her risqué garb. What would the country-club set think of her shopping in such a tawdry store?

Ha ha…how funny if I'd gotten Paulina's shower gift there, she thought, picturing snooty Paulina opening the cheetah-print box and pulling out crotchless panties and edible thongs!

"No!" she screamed at her cell phone when Andrew's name flashed up. "You'd better not be blowing off this trip!"

"Hi, Andrew. What's up?"

"Hi, lovely. How are you?"

Lovely? That's new, she thought. "I'm fine," she said warily.

"I wanted to let you know I'm going to be running a bit late—"

"Ah, geez!" She tried not to whine, but again?

"Now, listen…just listen," he said. "I want you to drive up to the lake by yourself. I'll be along shortly. I know it's a bit much to ask, but I have to wrap up some important business. Then I'll be along. Treat yourself to a relaxing foot soak and a glass of wine or two while you wait. I tossed my bags into the Navigator this morning, so I'm all set. The house will be a little frigid, so if you want to start a fire, please do. If not, I'll take care of it when I get there."

Maggie muffled her sigh of relief. "Okay…so, you won't be *too* late?"

"I won't be far behind you at all, I promise. You'll have to do a quick grocery run for food. There's that little market about a half mile away, if you don't feel like driving into town."

"Oh, yes. Dutry's Market."

"Yep, that's it."

"And, Andrew…I'm sure I don't need to spell it out for you, but we *really* need this time away. There's so much we need to discuss."

"We will have loads of time. I'll see you soon."

***

A few minutes later, Maggie tossed her overpacked bag into the Lexus and drove off. Steering cautiously in the heavy April rain, she played lively tunes that kept her spirits elevated. As corny as it was, the pulsating beat of the songs drove her to fantasize about that damn pole. She'd gotten quite good at her makeshift routines and almost wished she could bring the sleek steel eyesore along with her.

She then remembered the cedar column in the lake house bedroom that had served sadly as an unappealing prop the last time she was there. There was also a column in the living room area. Hmmmm…she began calculating a show-time plan. She found herself bound and determined, once more, to display her revived sense of adventure. Andrew acknowledged that there'd be plenty of time for heavy discussion. Tonight, she decided, would be more about fun.

Maybe I'll start off with the schoolgirl plaid jumper and wiggle my way out of it, she thought, reminiscing about the time she and Andrew had nearly gotten caught doing naughty things inside his Navigator while parked at the Saint Francis Girls' School after the school's annual fund-raising gala.

Or, there's the scarlet see-through negligee with patches of heart-shaped fur. Andrew could meet me in the bathroom for that show, she thought, reliving their very first Valentine's Day—when they'd celebrated predinner and post-cocktails in one of the men's bathroom stalls at Bella's.

Ohhhh, there's also that pink tiger-print baby-doll nightie! Eh, never mind…don't want his mind to drift to Gemma or any other tigresses from Lillian's, she thought, while quickly veering to the right, nearly missing the highway exit.

***

Roughly two hours later, the sky had cleared. But Maggie's attempt at positive thinking and playful scheming had fizzled as she shifted into a more cautionary gear. Approaching the meandering road that led to the lake house, she encountered a sign that read, Watch Your Speed, while another one indicated there was bridge construction ahead. But she ignored the signs, since there were no workers in sight.

Having tenaciously maneuvered along the coiling road, Maggie arrived at the Spencer lake house and was instantly mesmerized by the breathtaking view. The scent of pine. The wispy trees swaying as if to create soothing music. The house jutting out close to the lake. And the simple, free, lifestyle of the residents—paddling their boats to each other's docks, sharing a glass of wine here and there. What could be better than this?

After unloading her bag, Maggie took a leisurely stroll around the house, absorbing the beauty of it all. Sure, it needed a little TLC, but the woodsy flair made it simple yet luxe. Where was the personal touch, though? There were no family pictures on display, no photo albums on the coffee table, no board games, not even a personal coffee mug with a fish or a canoe or even a fun catchphrase on it. The house was quite empty, yet Maggie felt a sense of contentment in its modesty.

She drifted onto the shaded deck and leaned against the coarse railing, thinking about the times she'd spent with Andrew at the lake house. To her surprise, she found herself struggling to recall any sort of meaningful occasion. Aside from her very odd fortieth-birthday weekend and the bizarre friends-giving rescue, Maggie realized that she most enjoyed her alone time at the lake. Sure, there had been plenty of chore weekends before they were married, which were really more about Andrew looking around, discovering new places for sneaky sex. In the utility closet, underneath the deck, in the boathouse— all within a few yards of the working crew. But in all reality, there wasn't a single time they'd ever walked or paddled around the lake, greeting neighbors, exchanging stories, or sharing cocktails. Andrew was right: the lake house *was* more Maggie's thing than his—or theirs.

Without warning, a brutal insight all but slapped Maggie in the face. The memories of Bella's bathroom, the Saint Francis parking lot, the lake house nooks…even their downtown offices. His favorite, in fact, was behind her desk, where he'd become *unusually* vigorous.

That crazy thrill-seeker! she thought. Andrew *wanted* to get caught! He wanted to shake that office door loose from the latch, she realized, envisioning the shit-eating grin he'd flashed after popping his head up above her desk now and again. I married Christian Frickin' Grey, she realized, thinking that *50 Shades* would be a big hit in the self-discovery section at Barnes and Noble, too.

***

The sun began to set, yet there was still no Andrew, and Maggie had become bored reading magazines and scrolling through limited channels on the lake house TV. Having slugged down quite a bit of wine, she'd also become too tipsy to text legibly any longer, and she was way too aggravated to engage in conversation— with anyone! Besides, she was wondering if she'd fallen for the wrong man. There was no way she'd be happy to see him walk through the door *now*. So, in the spirit of all that was afflicted, she polished off the last of the Red Moscato she'd found on the wine rack and decided to whip up dinner for herself—penne pasta with some kind of jarred sauce from the pantry. She'd never made it to the market.

While plowing through dinner, Maggie attempted some self-affirmations. But she felt increasingly mortified. Gradually, Andrew seemed to be treating her as if she were some woman he'd picked up in a bar for a one-night stand… pushing for a dancer's pole that he could now ignored…those damn spiked Louboutin heels…and public bathroom sex. Ugh! she thought. I can't believe I allowed myself to be a make-believe whore!

The alcohol-induced faucet of tears began to overflow. What was he getting out of this ludicrous marriage? Why was *she* still holding on? Her head had swelled with too much of the heavy as she tried her best to sop up the tears. Gradually gaining control of herself, she grabbed another bottle of wine. To hell with talking tonight, she decided. We'll talk tomorrow!

Maggie continued to slam down the wine, thinking about the party-girl getup she'd laid out for what she thought would be a fun evening, had Andrew shown up. She figured there was no need to waste a perfectly raunchy negligee. She struggled a bit to get into the black see-through shorty and coupled it with her scratched up Christian Louboutins. After swinging around on the center column a few times, she became a little dizzy. Her wine splashed onto the hardwood floor as she staggered to the nappy eyesore of a couch. She kicked off the damn shoes that were abrading her feet. As she propped up her throbbing hooves, it began to rain again, and Maggie drifted off to its gentle drumming on the roof.

***

Around 7:00 a.m. on Saturday, Maggie awoke to the horrific squawking of a giant sea gull or some other feathered nuisance out on the deck. She rubbed her eyes in a gouge-like manner as if to hollow out her throbbing head and looked around the empty room, listening for any sign that Andrew might be in the house cooking breakfast, showering, stroking the neighbor lady's hair—anything. She came up empty. She was still alone. She snatched her phone, hoping to hear a very good excuse as to why her husband was a no-show. She opened her hangover-induced squinty eyes as wide as she could to check her phone for messages. "Damn it! I didn't charge the phone!" she screamed, falling back onto the nappy sofa and covering her eyes with one hand.

The house was a bit frosty. So, with a hideous, threadbare house robe covering the black negligee that she could no longer bear the sight of, she struggled to find some warm clothes. Flashbacks of dancing and sloppy glasses of wine tortured her already pounding head. An empty, sticky pasta bowl on the coffee table reminded her why something smelled scorched in the house. She couldn't keep from rubbing an ache that lingered in her gut—the kind that results from a sucker punch of sorts. And even though she felt as if she wanted to throw herself in front of a fast-moving bus, Maggie, like a bloodhound on a mission, did a quick three-minute cleanup around the house and packed her bag. If Andrew wasn't going to make it to the lake house, she'd go home and talk to him there. And if he did show up here, it would serve him right to walk into an empty house. She wouldn't even leave a note.

She threw her duffel into the trunk, jumped into the driver's seat, and had a little word with her car, which had been stalling intermittently over the past few weeks. "Come on now…don't get moody on me today," she said. Finally, the engine turned over. Her usual tenderfoot was quite the lead foot on the gas pedal as she headed home. Her only stop was a few miles down the road for a quick fuel-up and a very strong cup of coffee.

***

By 7:30 a.m., she was driving like a maniac. She ripped her cell phone off the charger to check it for some kind of life. Ahhh, a bit of power! But there was nothing from Andrew. No texts, no voice mails, no anything! Fingers trembling, she clicked on Andrew's speed-dial number as she swerved a little too far off to the right. The crunching stones reminded her to keep her eyes on the road.

I'm gonna nail him down for a chat, and he'd better not drum up some bogus trip and be gone when I get home!

"Andrew," she snapped when her call was answered.

"Yes?" he replied with his usual grogginess.

"Uh, it's Maggie!"

"Oh…oh, yeah, hi."

"Well! Say something! What the hell happened to you last night?"

"Huh? Oh, right. Can we talk about this later? Are you on your way home from the office or what?"

"Andrew! What's wrong with you? I'm on my way home from the lake house!"

"Oh…yeah, I'm sorry. Geez, I had such a rough day at the office. I worked a little longer than I wanted to…just fell asleep, I guess. I'm here in my office suite. So, how long till you get home, then?" he asked, sounding as if he'd come out of his wooziness a bit.

Maggie was silent.

"Okay, so we'll talk later," he said and cut the call.

"Bastard!" Maggie tossed her phone onto the passenger seat, swerving once again off the side of the road. "Damn, I hate these snaky roads!"

With plenty of drive time to think, she mentally rehearsed the topics she'd bring up. Why did Andrew keep dodging when she wanted to plan her resignation? Why was he so seldom home, even when they made specific plans? What could they do to reignite their passion?

"Look, asshole," she began. No, no, that's just name calling, she thought, Hmmm…

"Andrew, how's this life of ours working for you?" she said aloud. No, no. That was too Dr. Phil.

She struggled to muster up the approach she'd suggested to clients in the past during their marriage-on-the-rocks sessions, but she was at a loss. She'd only ever given them textbook solutions that even *she* didn't really believe in.

Maggie thought about Andrew's past. While there really wasn't a whole lot to it, he *was* at one time married to his college sweetheart—Allison. Even though they'd gotten their marriage annulled, had he been paying her alimony? Had the ex been draining him? Is that why he wasn't in a hurry for Maggie to leave her job?

No, that couldn't be the reason. That brief marriage was so long ago. And if there were any kind of settlement involved, the Spencer attorneys would've surely sharked out a deal. Andrew was very private about such information; in fact, he barely spoke of his ex at all, other than to say she'd become quite boring with all her ramblings about wanting children. At the time, Maggie had simply shaken her head in disbelief.

Now, Maggie figured that Allison probably just hadn't wanted to role-play all that freakish nonsense. Maybe she'd been smart to get out quickly, Maggie thought as the next round of reality checks practically knocked her out.

Could she really give up her Louis Vuitton duffel, her Prada boots, her array of designer clothes and handbags? Plus, she'd probably need a new car soon. She'd driven her Lexus for several years, now.

There were many financial perks to being Mrs. Spencer. And how would she face her parents, who thought so highly of Andrew, if the marriage foundered? What would they say to all their friends? Would they become social pariahs at the country club? And, again, what about her desire to quit her job? She'd never be able to switch careers without Andrew taking care of her financially. So many times, he'd said he'd support her decision to resign…but that seemed like a lifetime ago. He'd told her, in fact, that he'd handle that conversation with her father. But as of late, he'd been dropping the occasional reminder of how much her father needed her in the practice. Although she had little to no desire to tell her control-freak father that she wanted out, she'd suck it up and have that conversation just to be gone from there.

She knew he'd lay his famous guilt trip on her, insisting that she was "of great assistance in carrying the caseload *and* taking on more responsibility while he transferred his practice over to Ted Worthington." He'd been peddling that excuse for far too long. On the bright side, continuing to work for her father meant cashing in on a salary that was way more than her quality of work deserved. Oh, what to do? she thought.

The idea of making a fresh career start was completely overwhelming. She let out a heavy sigh, wishing she could turn back time and make better career choices and better man choices. But she couldn't.

*** *

At 9:30 a.m., Maggie, no longer a lead foot, crept down Landis Drive and turned into her driveway, mindful of the head banger of a headache that had resurfaced. Slinking out of her car, she paced a few laps in the garage, gearing herself up to face Andrew, whose car was outside.

"Andrew!" she shouted as she stumbled through the house. The hangover from hell was blurring her vision, turning the place into a maze of big, gaudy furniture, arranged in a confusing pattern. Ugh, I can't believe I picked this stuff out, she thought as she entered the living room.

"In here, babe!" he shouted from the bedroom.

Did he just call me *babe*? Did he suddenly become bipolar?

Maggie crept down the hallway, preparing herself face him. Despite everything, she'd made up her mind to work on their marriage. But resigning from her ludicrous job was a must. She would survive somehow, if she and Andrew split, but she wasn't about to belabor the what-ifs about her job situation. For now, the precise thing she would insist upon was that *Andrew* be the one to discuss her resignation with her father. Dr. Walters adored Andrew—he could sell a load of crap to her parents, and they'd be happy buyers. Besides, her father trusted Andrew, who'd been handling his legal business for quite a while. So, anything he'd pitch in his slick attorney manner would be sure to close the deal.

Nearing the bedroom door, Maggie armed herself internally with a strong negotiating shield. If payment for leaving her dreadful career meant working harder to be Mrs. Andrew Michael Spencer III, so be it. If, by chance, she'd have to muddle through any of the ridiculous role-playing nonsense, she could stomach it. She could feign interest in just about anything, at this point, while devising a new life strategy. Shrewd planning would be her new full-time job.

When she opened the bedroom door, Maggie was rendered speechless. Several bouquets of vibrant tulips were arranged in a vase, scrunched together as one. Alexa was softly playing a cheesy love song.

Oh, God, is he trying to rectify his asshole status? she wondered.

Before she could think any further, a naked, aroused Andrew grabbed her arm, tossed her onto the bed, and stripped off the heather-gray sweatpants. Before she registered any real enjoyment, Andrew rolled over and exhaled. "I'm exhausted," he said, as if he'd just manually plowed several fields and run a marathon afterward.

What the hell was that? Maggie thought. Did we just have sex? She was truly stumped.

Taking in the sound of Andrew's fast-asleep snore, she tried to concentrate on something a bit more calming, but the rhythmic rain had stopped. Again, she focused on the display of tulips, but that unsightly pole dominated her view of the bedroom. Her head-banger headache reemerged as if she'd run smack into the rigid thing, head first. Spotting a crinkled piece of paper on the floor, she got up and retrieved it. It was a receipt for the tulips, time-stamped with the day's date and 8:00 a.m. So, he'd stopped at the Superthrift on the way home from his office.

Maggie moseyed toward Andrew's side of the bed to gather her sweatpants and any other loose garments for the laundry basket. In doing so, she discovered a cocktail napkin. She smoothed it out and saw that it was from Lillian's Tigress Club. Entertaining clients? Why couldn't you just say so, you bastard! She plopped down into the reading chair and began thinking of how she'd spend a big wad of Spencer dough on her first freed-up day, after she resigned from her job.

CHAPTER

9

May Flowers and Timely Messengers

After a very rainy April, Maggie's disposition began to sparkle with the beauty of the May flowers that had come into bloom, creating the perfect picture of loveliness at 1270 Landis Drive. Not to mention, she'd be delivering her resignation by the end of the month. She could no longer listen to her father's guilt trips regarding his practice. He'd already pushed back his retirement date several times, which meant Maggie would have to endure his prickly, controlling demeanor even longer. For his part, Ted Worthington appeared to be in no rush to take over the practice. He was entirely caught up in his daughter's wedding planning and even more so in his wife's activities. She headed several charity organizations and served as a freelance tennis instructor. Seemingly, he kept her on a short marital leash.

Maggie's springlike rejuvenation had apparently rubbed off on Andrew, who'd been quite agreeable lately. He'd been reasonably pleasant and kept his horny paws off her. She was over the moon about her new *arrangement* with him, to which he was oblivious. The arrangement entailed the two of them never having a serious discussion. She kept up with spa treatments, shopping sprees, and anything else that required very little interaction between them. Since Andrew had been practicing the same game plan for several months, Maggie felt justified in embracing the silly cliché, *Two can play at that game.* She had quietly taken her place on the playing field. Sure, they continued to call each other insincere pet names and perhaps give each other a robotic kiss here and there. But she'd become rather numb to his affections—fake or real. She couldn't tell the difference anymore.

However, she did have a slight concern. She'd been experiencing a great deal of nausea and dizziness lately. She'd had an irregular menstrual cycle for all of her adult years and never really paid much attention to its sporadic behavior. But recently, she'd counseled a client with a similar health issue who'd discovered she was pregnant. Maggie had experienced an unusual moment of real sympathy as she attempted to soothe her client's guilt in terminating the pregnancy.

I certainly can't be pregnant, she thought, recalling that Andrew had barely touched her for months. But there *was* that lame welcome-home-from-the-lake-house reception several weeks earlier. Prior to that, there had been just a few random times she'd thrown him a bone, giving in to his appointment-like huddles under the covers.

Nonetheless, curiosity had gotten the best of her, and she'd already purchased a pregnancy test. It was time to face the truth. After a few please-God-don't-let-me-be-pregnant prayers, Maggie entered the master bathroom, placed the Clearblue Digital pregnancy kit on the marble vanity top, and took a deep breath. She chipped a fingernail as she fumbled to get the kit open, and sat on the toilet, confident she'd gotten a top-of-the-line test, which featured a wider wick and a digital countdown to assure accuracy. The result would be spelled out in clear lettering. There'd be no mistaking it! So, she placed the tip of the stick into her urine stream, praying that the test would be negative.

One minute went by. The test was working, according to the digital countdown. Maggie walked away as if to give the little "messenger" some privacy.

Two minutes went by. Maggie sat down in the bathroom again. She didn't want to rush the little messenger. She now waited patiently for her cell phone timer to chime at the three-minute setting. I can't take this, she thought, beginning to tap her foot vigorously as if that would hurry the little slowpoke along.

Ding! Three minutes! She snatched the test from the vanity top as if someone were about to tamper with crucial evidence.

Two seconds later, with great relief, Maggie read the no-mistaking-it results: NOT PREGNANT. She wanted to shout this most fantastic news from the rooftops. And while she was more than elated, she couldn't help recalling her parents' Saint Patty's Day lecture, when they reminded her that she was a bit too old to start a family. She visualized dealing two massive blows to them: Mother, Dad, I'm leaving the practice, and by the way, I'm going to have a baby.

She chuckled at the vision of her father telling her to "run along…go take care of that baby—who's at risk, you know…"

While double-checking to make sure the PT stick hadn't changed its mind, Maggie took the negative results as a very positive outcome—there was *nothing* to keep her from regaining some focus and purpose to her life. She'd be concentrating on finding both tranquility and positivity and getting back to all that gave her a sense of gravity. Did she feel a morsel of shame for *using* her husband? Eh, not really! Besides, he wasn't exactly running full throttle to divorce court.

Still basking in the glory of having one less thing to worry about, Maggie chuckled at the vision of her mother unwrapping a dainty little box bearing baby-blue and soft-pink ribbons—only to discover a positive PT stick inside. She imagined a scene much like Cousin Meg's pomp and circumstance when she'd handed her husband a tiny wrapped box containing *her* positive PT stick as a surprise Father's Day gift. Maggie's chuckle turned into a cackle as she envisioned her father's lack of humor. Surely, he'd lecture her on presenting an unsanitary gift. Maggie hadn't laughed so hard in a very long time.

Maggie sustained her over-the-moon feeling that there'd be no need for "baby talk." And she was thrilled that she would be leaving her father's practice soon. But most of all, she was ecstatic that Andrew had been working long hours and getting home late after entertaining clients. She would simply continue to enjoy his pricey making-up-for-being-a-shithead gifts.

While everything seemed to be rolling along rather smoothly, anticipating her resignation made her uneasy and slightly irritable—enough to drain her of the poise she felt was necessary for mingling with the country clubbers at the annual Mother's Day Brunch. She really wasn't in the mood for pretending to care whose kids were about to graduate from Ivy League schools, who was about to become a parent (or a grandparent), or what the board would decide about next year's dress code. Ugh, major snooze-fest, she thought, yawning.

Maggie decided she needed a little pick-me-up to jump start her much-needed confidence and suppress the anxiety that had taken over. A quick trip to Dillinger's Sweet Treat was in order. She'd enjoy her favorite banana cake with peanut butter frosting. That treat served nicely as solace for any ailment. Besides, she reasoned, her covert pole-dancing workouts allowed her to have such treats.

With her mouth already watering, she threw on some old yoga tights and a hoodie, hoping to sneak by Andrew's study, where he focused on whatever he was pretending to be doing. She also crammed the Clear Blue cardboard packaging and all of its contents into her bag, so she could dump it in the public trash bin near the bakery.

***

As Maggie and Andrew arrived at the Carrington Heights Country Club, her mother was strolling around with her hand above her brow as if watching for their late arrival. But they were right on time. Liz was dressed in a tailored, cream-colored skirt and jacket and a soft-pink blouse with ruffled trim around the cuffs. The other ladies sported expensive linen skirts with jackets that carefully provided color block and layers.

"Andrew! Maggie! Hello!" her mother called as she strolled across the cobble-stone path. She shot a quick glance at her daughter's dress. It was a bit flowy and short, but it suited Maggie's need for comfort quite well. "Join us for some mimosas before we get seated," her mother insisted. "Andrew, dear, I haven't seen you in some time, but I see your lake-house getaway has served you well. You look so very rested!"

Andrew simply kissed her hand and quickly turned away as if to recognize a client.

Damn, Maggie thought. I think I told her that disastrous trip was lovely or something. I hope she doesn't gush on about it. "Mother, did I just see Aunt Fran? Did Dad bring her along for brunch?" Maggie asked, changing the subject.

"Now Maggie, why would he do such a thing? It's really Meg's responsibility to take her own mother out on Mother's Day. And let's face it, dear, ever since her MS has worsened, well, Aunt Fran has become so very high maintenance, you know? With all her issues and whatnot."

"What maintenance? You just have to push her around in a wheelchair."

"Darling, you know that she needs assistance with using the lady's room. It's difficult to understand her, and, well, must I go on with all this in front of Andrew? Now, how about those mimosas?"

"Thanks, Mom," Andrew interjected. "By the way, my parents send their regrets. They won't be able to join us today. They extended their stay in Florida, visiting some old friends."

"Oh, I understand. They certainly maintain a very busy travel schedule."

"I know. It's hard to keep up with those youngsters! Speaking of which, you look absolutely lovely on your special day." He leaned forward to kiss her on the cheek.

"Oh, Andrew! Flattery will get you everywhere," said Liz with a flirty giggle. "By the way, is your trip-planning winding down? Just another month, and it's bon voyage!"

"Yes, well…Hey, is that Everett straight ahead?" said Andrew.

"Yes, it is," said Maggie's mother, looking toward a group of men in gray suits, holding mimosas.

"I'm gonna go say hello to those fellas."

"Take your time, Andrew. Maggie and I can chat awhile."

They watched him walk away.

"So, Maggie, you haven't said much about your Paris trip. My goodness, you've been counting down the months since your fortieth birthday. I'd think you'd have some exciting news on the plans and whatnot."

"Um, yeah. I'd rather not discuss it, Mother, but it's been postponed."

"Oh, poor Andrew with that dreadful work schedule."

Sure, we'll go with that! "So, if you could just not bring it up, please?"

"Of course, dear, and I'm sorry to hear that," her mother said. "Now, tell me. Is this one of those mini disco-club dresses? I know you like trendy fashions, but this *is* the country club. What will people think of such a short hemline?"

Mother, can you just go for one day without this judgmental nonsense? And what the hell's a disco-club dress? "Actually, Mother, Andrew picked this out for me. Today was the first occasion I've had to wear it, and he absolutely loves it on me."

"Oh, that's precious that he likes to pick out your clothes. Like I've said many times before—he's a keeper!"

Yeah, okay, whatever, thought Maggie.

"Biscuit! Over here." Andrew motioned with his hand held high, nodding toward their outdoor table.

"Maggie, did that strapping husband of yours just call you *Biscuit?*"

"Yes, yes he did. He's been calling me that for a while." *Jackass bastard!*

"What an adorable pet name," her mother said as they approached their table. "Andrew, this dress is charming." Liz winked her approval as he pulled out her chair.

"Why, yes, it is," Andrew agreed, but he looked confounded as he studied the dress on his wife.

"Did you buy this dress for today, Biscuit?" Andrew whispered, while he pulled out Maggie's chair.

"Don't blow my little fib," she whispered back. "We'll talk later."

"Mom, excuse us for a minute," he abruptly requested. "I want Maggie to meet Seth Hobson. I just saw him walk into the East Garden. I see Everett making his way to the table," Andrew assured her as he looked toward the gray suits, who seemed to be wrapping up their conversation. "We'll be right back."

"Of course, dear."

"What's up with the dress drama?" Andrew asked Maggie when they had gotten far enough away from her mother. "This one's a bit blousy," he criticized with a scrunched-up nose, while pulling the garment down in the back. "I mean, are your more suitable dresses too tight or something?"

"What do you mean *suitable*? And *too tight*?"

"Well, you've been wearing baggy sweatpants and sloppy old T-shirts, lately. Now, this…this roomy muumuu thing," said Andrew. "You're not…uh… well, Maggie, I just hope you're not pregnant."

Ugly silence.

"So, I'm not going to stand here and discuss fashion with you. As far as being pregnant…are you insane? You haven't even touched me in weeks. How could I possibly be pregnant? And what the hell was that…that…whatever it was we did when I got home from the lake house a few weeks ago? Did we actually have sex or were you just finishing up some cheesy phone sex?" Andrew had tripped the trigger to a barrel full of Maggie's fury.

"Okay! Enough! I know we're pretty far away from everyone, but watch your mouth. Keep it down, for God's sake! What will people think?"

"Who gives a damn what people think?"

"Well, I do! The rumor mill runs pretty hot around here…especially if we're pegged for having marital problems."

"Uh, news flash, Andrew! We are!"

"Oh, stop it. We're just settled like everyone else."

You are truly delusional, Maggie thought, unable to mask her astonishment.

"Furthermore," Andrew continued, "I won't embarrass my parents by giving everyone reason to whisper about their son's *second* divorce."

"Seriously, it was an annulment from, like, twenty years ago. Get over yourself!"

"And by the way, I'm sorry that my quick lovemaking was a disappointment, but I'd been missing you, and I got overly excited," Andrew said. "There's no need for insults. It happens!"

You big fat liar! And never, ever say the word *lovemaking* to me again. "So, to answer your question, no…I'm not pregnant!"

"Well, good! I mean, we're quite settled in our lifestyle, and I've made it very clear that kids simply wouldn't fit in. We've discussed this," Andrew insisted. "Besides, with your female problems, I just assumed that you were safe from becoming pregnant and that you'd take care of any necessary birth control."

Oh, shutty…and who calls it *female problems*? "Yes, we really have no reason to worry about it," she said, thinking back to her morning with Clear Blue. "So, can we please drop the subject?" Maggie felt a chill creeping up her spine.

"Consider it dropped. But do you think you should take a pregnancy test just in case?"

No, it's a done deal…negative! And it was the best news any wife of yours could get! "Andrew, believe me…I'm not pregnant! In fact, I found out this morning."

"Oh! Flo came to town?" he replied, now trying to be funny.

Flo? Seriously, you are the king of cheese…soon you'll be wearing polyester pants and white pleather shoes, Maggie thought, but she remained silent.

"Well, whatever the case," he said, pausing as if a drum roll were sounding. "You're still my little *Biscuit*." He chuckled.

Again, ugly silence. Maggie could not feel her tongue.

"But just to be on the safe side, maybe it's best that I get a vasectomy," Andrew said in his lowest voice as he scanned the crowd, wearing a plastered-on smile. He feigned a slight chuckle as if Maggie had told him something cute. But his quiet laughter bore deep into the core of her soul, scorching it as if she'd swallowed hot coals.

Don't waste your time or a perfectly fine bag of frozen peas by getting snipped for me, Maggie thought. Then she excused herself to go to the ladies' room. "Andrew, I see Seth Hobson over by the ladies' room. I gonna ask if he likes my muumuu. See ya in a bit."

"Ha ha. Very funny, Mags."

***

Maggie stood before the gold-rimmed mirror as tears welled in her eyes, then she splashed some cold water on her face and watched herself sink into distress. She picked up a vanity towel and patted her face dry, leaving black mascara stains behind.

Everything was falling apart, and the broken pieces of her life began pelting her from all angles. Her parents who were impossible to please. She was a prisoner to her own career. She had no good friends, and her own husband was nothing more than a nauseating roommate. She felt as though she were buried in a deep, dark, emotional cave.

A bathroom stall door slammed as she glanced at herself once more in the mirror. She swiftly reached for her phone as if to Google a generic solution for her woes, but she really just wanted to schedule an Uber ride. She rummaged through her purse, but no phone! She suddenly envisioned it resting as a timer on her bathroom vanity. *Damn it!*

It didn't help that she'd caught a glimpse of Harriet Sims, one of the oldest and most well-to-do country clubbers, notoriously known as Carrington Heights's finest gossip and busybody, eyeing her country-club-inappropriate dress. But Maggie made herself impervious to Harriet's silent judgment because she needed a messenger—and the old battle-ax would have to do.

"Mrs. Sims," said Maggie.

"Yesssss, what?" she said as if already bothered by whatever request Maggie might have.

"I've been fighting this awful flu that's been going around. Could you find my parents and Andrew and tell them I'm sorry to have to run out on such a festive occasion, but I'm taking the country club shuttle home. I have to get myself into bed immediately."

"Really? There's a flu going around?" Harriet replied, shrinking back and brushing off her skirt. "Wouldn't it be more appropriate for *you* to alert them? Doesn't your generation do all that texting or whatever?"

"Yes, yes, we do. Unfortunately, I carelessly left my phone at home."

"You do look a little flushed...you'd better run along. I suppose I can find them to deliver that message."

"Thanks, Mrs. Sims." And don't trip over your neck, you old prune!

***

By two o'clock in the afternoon, Maggie had already gotten a how-are-you-feeling call from her mother, which she'd cut short, not wanting to further feign illness. Considering Andrew's typical selfishness, she hadn't expected any sympathy from him, and he hadn't failed to disappoint. What's more, he was most likely onto her subtle drama at the country club, knowing he'd upset her.

She sank into her easy chair in the family room, allowing the dreadful country-club scene to fade while practicing a little introspection. The garage door made its normal rattling thunder, indicating that Andrew would soon walk through the door, calling Maggie some sort of pastry-type pet name, which would completely delete the serenity she'd absorbed from meditating.

"Hi, lovey!" he said, walking through the door with a lily that he had apparently snagged from the May flower displays in the East Garden at the club.

Lovey? "Uh, thanks," she replied suspiciously when he presented the lily to her.

"How's my little cheese danish?"

Aaaaaand, there it is! "Ya, know, Andrew...it's really okay to call me *Maggie*," she said with a huff.

"Oh, now, don't get out of sorts. I'm just havin' fun with you. What's all this stuff?" he asked, waving his hand toward a pile of papers scattered in front of her chair.

"Well, I've been perusing some examples of resignation letters. I printed them out earlier today. God forbid, I'd be so informal as to have a casual chat with my own father about leaving. By the way, did you decide when you're going to approach him about my resigning? Like we discussed?"

"Uh, yeah, about that," he replied sheepishly.

"What do you mean, *about that*?" she asked.

"Well, lovey..."

Oh, stick that stupid name where the sun doesn't shine, along with that wilting lily! Maggie thought.

"I know you've been very patient with my request that you work a little while longer…to help out your father," Andrew said.

Yeah, right! she thought. What's in it for you?

"And you know that I'm on board with you leaving your career, eventually," Andrew continued. "I mean, the Spencer women don't need to work. They're more valuable in their roles within the community."

Cut the scripted bullshit! Maggie thought.

"But your father actually made a good point today at brunch," he said. "As he's already told you, he really needs to rely on someone who knows the business…knows how to handle an overflow of administrative work, is able to assist with new clients as he winds down, can take care of loose ends—"

"Okay, can you cut to the chase, please?" Maggie said. "He's been announcing his retirement for two years now. Is he gonna do it in a few more weeks? Months? When?"

"Now, don't kill the messenger, Mags, but not for another year."

Crickets.

"I'm sorry, what?" she asked, thinking she, perhaps, needed hearing aids or that maybe she'd slipped into a two-second coma.

"Next May, Maggie. Another year. I think he's just having trouble letting go…that's my personal opinion."

"Another year! I'll be a lunatic by then! I'll be a lunatic by June, for God's sake!"

"Oh, stop with the histrionics! What's one more year?"

"Might not seem long to you, Andrew, but that job has been nothing but turmoil for me, and you know it! And some help you are! So, you couldn't give *him* the Spencer-women-don't-need-to-work speech?" she said, imitating an arrogant voice.

"I'm not going to disrespect the man, Maggie."

"Pfff," she replied with arms crossed tightly across her chest.

"And just for the record, it's not my problem that you stayed in a dissatisfying career. Nor that you don't wanna deal with your father. You want out—just tell him. You need to man up, Maggie."

He was right. Maggie couldn't bring herself to tell Andrew that, but he had nailed it. She needed to handle her own resignation.

"Ya know," Andrew said, "I just realized that I haven't spent any time with my own mother today. I hope you don't mind, but I'm going to visit with her for a while and give her the Mother's Day charm for her bracelet. I'm sure she and Dad will have lots to tell about the trip, but I want you to stay home and get some rest. Harriet Sims said you'd come down with the flu or something."

Well played, sly bastard! Did you forget that your parents extended their stay in Florida? "Yes, I do need some rest," she replied. In fact, she was suffering a bona fide headache from hell.

"Feel better. See you in a few hours," said Andrew.

As Andrew closed the door, Maggie wondered what she might find taking place at his office—his private getaway? A few months ago, she'd have been furious. Now, she cared little about his shenanigans, as long as he kept the pricey "apology" trinkets coming.

CHAPTER

10

Juniper Breeze and Magic Mike!

It was the beginning of summer, and Maggie sat alone in her living room, frowning at an old copy of a *What's Up in Paris* guide that Andrew had presented to her a couple birthdays ago. She'd circled several restaurants and boutiques throughout the touristy magazine, rating several of them as a "must return." She'd kept the thing in pristine condition among her favorite stack of magazines, trusting they'd return to Paris for their one-year anniversary. But now the trip was nothing more than a pipe dream. She balled the little dust collector up as tightly as she could and chucked it across the room, not caring where it landed. Never once had the thought crossed her mind that she'd be spending her anniversary weekend alone.

Maggie tilted her face upward as if to escape the numbing emptiness that filled the house. But she couldn't help but zero in on the cobwebs hanging from the ceiling like straggly shredded lace. They'd gathered considerably since the house had gotten professionally cleaned several months ago. She loved the woodsy view from her picture window, but she couldn't focus on anything but those unsightly cobwebs. Her mind spiraled toward all the other things that needed a good cleaning. Be it blemished hardwood floors or her own muddied soul, a cleansing was in order.

She thought, perhaps, a visit with Father Timothy for a long overdue confession would be a healthy way to lift herself out of the emotional quagmire she'd sunken into. Maggie had contemplated reaching out to some old friends, but she quickly remembered how they were completely engrossed with their own lives: Jules and Katie with their kids and Jess, who'd apparently fallen off the grid with all her issues—divorce, therapy, and whatever else had caused her not to return phone calls and texts. She'd lost track of their numerous cancellations throughout the past few years. And the disappointment over just about everything was all too consuming. Maggie needed to talk to someone—someone who wasn't an actual therapist. She needed to unload the heavy stuff, the anxieties and fears that had insidiously obstructed her life.

With Andrew away on his new string of business trips, there was plenty of time at home for arduous reflection, and she'd come to terms with the possibility that she had, indeed, made a mistake in rushing into marriage. Daily, she was reminded that her plush lifestyle came with a very high price. Anyone could hide behind good looks and a prestigious law degree. Furthermore, she had allowed her father to bully her into a profession she hated. Was it all for the inflated salary and the unspoken promise of a mediocre inheritance someday?

It was all too much! Maggie bent forward and ran her hands through her hair as if cleaning the cobwebs from her head. I'm too old to be some wimpy coward, she thought. But how many times had she told herself that before?

She had to admit that most of her angst stemmed from the fact that she'd become too complacent. She had allowed herself to get stuck in an unfulfilling career, and now she was aging and becoming less marketable. She'd also let the idea of getting married cloud her judgment about *who* she married. Reaching that rather authentic self-assessment, Maggie decided there was no real need to talk to Father Timothy. He'd just give the same advice she'd been giving herself.

***

As sundown approached, Maggie thought she'd make the best of her solitary anniversary by embracing the peace and serenity of complete aloneness. Her emotions had worn her out earlier in the day, so a quiet, toxin-free evening on the wrap-around porch had become her goal. She breathed meditatively, imbibing the evening air and inhaling the aroma of her favorite outdoor candle, Juniper Breeze. She reached for the bottle of Riesling that she had iced down to a precise frost and poured herself another glass. Within her restful composure and gentle wine buzz, she actually considered for a hot second how nice it might be, if things were different, to share this moment with Andrew. But that preposterous notion fled instantly…what am I thinking? She waved her hand as if warding off such crazy thoughts.

Having returned to the tranquility of the evening, she marveled at the oak columns that provided the porch with sturdy support, while beautifully displaying elegant string lighting. She had nearly forgotten the built-in hibachi grill that had been a selling point for the house. She'd envisioned dinner parties on this enchanting *Better Homes and Garden* veranda, where guests could gather around the pub-style table. At one time, she and Andrew tossed around the idea of hosting monthly dinner parties, but that never happened—not even once. How festive it would've been to throw a batch of shrimp on the hibachi grill. But then she thought, Huh! We never even learned how to start the damn thing.

Before she could go completely dark and slip into her ugliest thoughts, she heard the slight roar of an engine as Bella's catering van pulled into her driveway. She'd had a gourmet dinner prepared for her one-of-a-kind anniversary party. She pushed aside the emotional relish that was pickling her life. It was time to indulge in something exquisite.

A minute went by, and she wondered, Okay, where is the delivery person? Didn't he see me waving from the side porch?

Another minute went by. Do I need to go hunt him down?

Then she heard an impatient young man calling, "Hello? Hello? Helloooooooo! It's Mark, from Bella's!" He came around the side of the house, spotting her. "I've been ringing the doorbell for like an hour or so! Hope ya don't mind that I came to look for ya."

Yeah, right, fibber! Maggie thought. Can it or you won't get a tip. "Okay, well, I'm right here!" she said, digging into her wallet for some cash. "Tell ya what, can you just put that on the Spencer account?"

"No problem; just sign here," said Mark.

While signing her name, Maggie noticed the ink fading as she reached the end of *Spencer*. "Here ya go. Thanks," she said, and he practically bolted for his van, leaving the defective pen behind.

Maggie spread her meal out on the wicker side table she'd set up for herself. As she began to take her first bite, she heard the van pull back into the driveway. Surely, he didn't come back for that faulty pen! she thought. He can stand out there and ring the doorbell all night—I'm eating!

But then, as Maggie took another bite of chicken parmesan, she was sure she heard some sort of movement from within the house, and she froze in fear. Did that grumpy little bastard come back to rob me? she wondered. Did he put two and two together and realize that I'm alone in the house?

Maggie managed to pry herself from the wicker chair and crept over to the side porch. A board creaked, and she'd felt as though bats were flapping inside her stomach. Then she stuck her head around the corner and spotted Andrew's big Navigator in the driveway.

Ugh! She'd almost rather it be the delivery boy, inside robbing the place. Before she could enter the house to offer a fake "welcome back," Andrew had burst onto the veranda with a slight stagger. "Hi, darlin'," he said.

Maggie detected a slur in his speech. But *darlin'* was better than *Biscuit*, she thought, pulling her miniskirt down a bit. She crossed her arms over her gauzelike, summery blouse, hoping Andrew didn't think she'd dressed for the occasion of his return from Vegas.

"Uh, hi," she said, perplexed. "I didn't know you'd be home tonight."

"Are you *not* wearing panties?" he asked, staring at the hem of her skirt.

"Huh?" she replied, then remembered he'd often asked her that when phoning from a business trip. She hadn't heard that cheesy line in quite some time!"

"Is that a Bella's takeout bag?" he asked, showing greater excitement than he'd displayed two seconds earlier for the absence of panties.

Good. Stay focused on that, she thought, not wanting to participate in panty banter. "Yes! I ordered from Bella's. Why don't you finish it? I'm not very hungry now." Please, eat. Suck in every bit of those nasty carbs till you drop over in a food coma.

"Thanks," he said. "I'm starving. Stopped off at Moby's for a couple of beers with Neil. Wanted to tell him about my trip."

Maggie was not certain she cared. "I didn't think you'd be home till midweek or so," she replied.

"Now, Bisky…"

Gag! That's even worse than Biscuit!

"You didn't really think I'd be gone for our entire anniversary weekend, did you?"

Uh, yeah. I sure did. And I was hoping so! "Well, just help yourself…it's chicken parm. Probably cold by now, though."

"Oh, well, in that case, do you mind heating it up for me while I take a shower? I smell like Moby's."

"Sure," she replied.

"Also, can you open a bottle of cab sauv? I'd love some wine with my dinner," Andrew called out as he strolled off to the shower.

***

Maggie sat and stewed over the sight of microwave steam rolling off what would've been her perfect alone-time meal. She'd completely lost her appetite, so she was more than happy for someone else to enjoy it. In fact, she wanted to make sure it was good and tasty. What would make that chicken parm extra special? she pondered. Taking in the outdoor scenery, there was nothing that remotely resembled a culinary spice that might enhance the flavor. Oh, but there was the soil in the potted plants. Or, maybe she could scrape a little bird poo from the porch railing. He'd never know, she thought, chuckling at that devious notion as she gulped down the last of her Riesling.

The shower stopped. The bats returned to Maggie's gut. With a towel wrapped around his waist, Andrew stepped out onto the veranda. "Ummmmm, smells good!"

You look a little paunchy! she thought as Andrew paraded around in a towel that was losing its tuck. Maybe you need to grind that pole and work off those carbs.

"What's wrong, Mags? Did you get an unsettling phone call or something?" he asked as he grubbed down a few bites.

"What are you talking about?"

"Well, you don't seem to be overly friendly tonight."

Have you not noticed my surly attitude over the past few months? "Oh, well, I'm just tired…don't really want to go into the office tomorrow." And I really don't want to be talking to you right now.

"Well, I think I have something that will lift your spirits. Come back to the bedroom with me," he said, shoving in another bite of the chicken parm.

Ugh! Are you for real? Please don't whip out Magic Mike (as he liked to call his penis) and flaunt it like the grand-prize-winner at the county fair! Panicking, she followed him at a snail's pace.

They entered the master bedroom, and he pulled out a long narrow box from his duffel bag. A sleek, shiny, robin's-egg-blue box. "I know you're disappointed about the Paris trip…"

Eh, not really, she thought as she crinkled her nose toward his bloated gut.

"But I didn't want our anniversary to be a total bust," said Andrew. "Open that up and see how much you mean to me." He extended the box toward her.

Who is this corny imposter? And what did he do with my rotten husband? she thought, scrutinizing his features as if to find the delivery boy, Mark, ingeniously disguised as Andrew. It must be his booze talking.

Maggie hesitantly opened the box and gaped at the most elegant diamond and sapphire bracelet she'd ever seen, sparkling against a bed of white satin. She hadn't even dog-eared the catalog for this ring-dinga-bling! She gasped when Andrew pulled her close.

"So, whatta ya think?" he asked.

"Well, it's certainly stunning."

"Then let's continue this celebration, babe."

I guess I can give him an anniversary quickie, she thought, ogling the megabling he was proudly draping around her wrist.

Maggie now felt like a fumbling green teenager about to be felt up by a master player with all kinds of moves. Is this thing even worth it? she thought, taking another look at the pricey bauble. Eh, what the hell! "So, do you want me to swing around the pole a few times…see what happens from there?" she asked with masked humiliation.

"No! No pole!"

Stand down! she thought. It's not like I was gonna ram it up your ass!

"I thought maybe you could grind on me. You know? Like a lap dance."

Okay. I haven't done that in quite some time, she thought. How bad could it be? After all, Maggie had been quite the performer throughout much of her life. Besides, there was a small piece of her that wanted to show Andrew what he'd been missing.

I'll have to really rev it up, she told herself. That was *her* booze talking. But there was no enticing music…no handy shot of ass-to-the-ground tequila…just a husband whose gut stuck out enough to throw a bit of shade on Magic Mike.

Maggie took a leap of faith, hoping that Andrew wouldn't make her feel any more foolish than she already did. She pushed him onto the bed, hiked her skirt up, shimmied out of her bikini briefs, flung them onto his face, and started her best lap dance. Even though she loathed every second of the performance, she was rather impressed that her pole practice had groomed her into somewhat of a natural tease. And she hadn't seen her husband's face light up with excitement like this since the honeymoon…the lake house nooks… Bella's men's room…her office quickies. Trying desperately to keep her groove on, she pulled out a few dancelike moves she recalled from the YouTube instructor, but she couldn't shake the idea of his warped requests and expectations. She staggered toward the corner of the bed, banging her shin on the sharp-edged box spring.

"Maggie, go down and *speak* into the Magic Microphone," he requested.

"Huh?"

"Never mind…keep going!" he said, not wanting to lose his excitement, but slightly put off by Maggie's lack of metaphor recognition.

As Maggie's mind continued to flood with disturbing memories, these poorly timed recollections began to turn the lap dance into a *flap* dance. She found herself flailing her arms like a drowning victim, praying for a life preserver. Suddenly, she lost her balance and dropped to the floor with a heavy thud. Magic Mike had more or less disappeared.

Andrew reached down to help her up, then stiffened his arm as if to block her. "On second thought, let's just call it a night. We're both a little played out," he said, fake-yawning and patting her on the head.

Maggie became rigid with mortification. She shoved her skirt back down as far as it could go and looked around, searching for a focal point, avoiding the elephant in the room. "Yes, we're both quite exhausted," she said.

"Well, thanks for…whatever that dance was, Biscuit." He chuckled.

Oh, just crawl into bed and take that Magic Mikeroscopic dick with you! she thought while internal steam rolled through her body, trying to make its exit through ears, nostrils—any escape hole.

"By the way, I'll warm up the Bella's leftovers for lunch tomorrow, and I assume you ordered tiramisu for dessert?" said Andrew.

"Uh-huh."

"Oh, hey, Biscuit!" he called as she was already out of the bedroom.

"Yes?" she responded curtly.

"Looks to me like you need a manicure. You don't want to show off a nine-thousand-dollar bracelet on those unpolished mitts, do you? Why don't you go to the spa sometime this week? Get your mani-pedi—the whole package."

Not waiting for a response, he simply added, "Okay, good night, then."

With tears welling up, Maggie stepped out onto the veranda. Her Juniper Breeze candle had already burned out, and the night air had become chilly. There'd be no delight in the outdoors now. She plopped down on a kitchen barstool and dug into the skimpy remains of the chicken parm, but the meal had lost its heat. She'd be sure to leave Andrew a few scraps for his lunch—a couple strands of pasta and perhaps a piece of gristle if she could find one. Maggie had been emotionally shoved back to the earlier part of the day, when she'd been drowning in all that was muddled in her life.

Maggie packed the remaining scraps of dinner into plastic ware and shoved it into the fridge, trying to ignore the tiramisu that stared back at her. Oh, hell…maybe just one bite, she thought.

Several bites later, she decided to tell Andrew that the delivery boy forgot the dessert. She was ready to call it a night as she curled up in her cozy recliner, rehearsing the long-overdue resignation speech that she had decided to deliver the next day.

Reflexively, she raised her hand to bite a nail, and she couldn't help cringing at the snagged cuticles and uneven nail lengths. Ick! I really do need a manicure, she thought. Then she looked down at the diamonds and sapphires, considering their durability, their luster…but they were nothing more to her than lab-created beads. Nine thousand dollars? Really? Well, she decided, slipping the bracelet from her wrist, if she had the courage to stand up to her father, she'd find the strength to stand up to Andrew and extricate herself from this mistake of a marriage. But she'd bide her time until she was set up to live on her own. She'd see what she could get for a diamond and sapphire bracelet when she was ready to cash in.

Final Days in Crazytown

CHAPTER

11

Minding the Heat
in Psychiatric Hell

It was nearing the end of a rather tedious yet profitable summer. The weekend was only a few hours away. Maggie would relax over the next couple days, lounging by the pool and sipping fruity cocktails, while Andrew came and went. But first, she'd have to put a day in at the office… trudging along, just like any other apathetic employee. While selecting a suit, she recalled trying several times over the years to convince her father to offer casual Friday at work. She wasn't suggesting that everyone dress like a slob, but could the staff possibly lose the stuffy suits for a day? He, however, would have none of it. But what did Maggie care? This would be her last Friday at Walters Psychiatric Center. The two-month notice she'd given when she told her father she was resigning would end next week. She'd promised her father she'd work until Thursday—if he needed her. Maggie had seen to it that her caseload dwindled over the summer months, and her father barely spoke to her as she counted down to the last few clients.

Andrew's frequent absences helped soften the blow of her decision to stay married to him. But Maggie was no dimwit. She'd be patient enough to wait for the final straw. The no-shows and the insults stung, but her marriage had thickened her skin. She was resilient. For the time being, she'd continue to sock away money and jewelry—she would be her own cash cow. Yes, she was absolutely certain there'd be something far more despicable than his typical misconduct, but she brushed right past the disgust of it all and turned her thoughts toward the positive—it was time to get that new Lexus she'd been eyeing.

As Maggie prepared a to-go coffee, her phone buzzed, indicating a message from Andrew. It read: *Mags—I scheduled my appointment with Dr. Gilbert. But I'd appreciate if you'd take another preg test. Left one on your vanity…in CVS bag.*

Who the hell is Dr. Gilbert? she wondered. And what's with the pregnancy paranoia? Does he think we've been having sex?

Suddenly, it dawned on her: Dr. Gilbert, the urologist…vasectomy. Took him long enough! But a pregnancy test? She was dumbfounded.

Maggie headed straight for her vanity, in hopes that Andrew's preposterous PT suggestion was a joke. Maybe there'd actually be a pricey bauble inside the drugstore bag. Or a set of keys to a new Lexus! She reached into the bag. It was free of keys. Much to her dismay, a First Response Pregnancy Test stared back at her. *Detects results six days sooner than a missed period*, she read on the package. It was a plain, old back-to-basics test. Two lines for positive and one line for negative.

A few minutes passed as Maggie stared at the pregnancy test resting in her motionless hand. Eh, might as well humor him, she thought. I'll just run tap water over this silly thing!

After the standard three minutes and double-checking for a single blue line to appear in the indicator screen, she whipped it onto the vanity and went into the bedroom to make the bed. How funny would it be if the tap water indicated there was a pregnancy? She laughed until her two-carat princess-cut solitaire diamond got caught in a heap of lightweight summer blankets. She untangled the tiny pieces of fiber that were wrapped around the setting, freeing it from the snagged fabric. She shook her hand vigorously as if to free it from a ring that now seemed to weigh heavily, cutting into her finger. The ring had become a nuisance.

Gearing up for the dreaded workday, she decided that some meditation was in order before she headed for the office. Clearing an open space on the bed, she sat down, bent her knees, and pulled her legs inward. Breathing in… breathing out…relaxation kicked in, and she began ruminating about things that at one time had truly made her happy. Yoga (reminds me too much of how I met Andrew); beach vacations with my girlfriends (eh, everyone's married with kids now); long walks by the water (I need to get myself to the lake house again soon!).

As Maggie eased out of introspection, she perceived yet *another* eyesore in the bedroom. Peeking from behind a small, decorative vase on the side shelf of the armoire was a dusty picture frame that housed a photo of Andrew and her on their wedding day. To her recollection, the picture had always been front and center. She couldn't resist gazing at how stunning she'd looked in her beautiful, but used, wedding gown. The Vera Wang gown that her cousin Meg bought on eBay had been perfect for Maggie's small ceremony. Mother would have convulsions if she knew Meg had said yes to the dress—secondhand! Then passed it on to me! She chuckled and shoved the picture way behind the vase.

***

Maggie arrived at work in a timely manner, already rehearsing her last-minute request for a half-day—a ballsy suggestion she'd thought of when she'd tossed her suit aside earlier for her own version of casual Friday. She felt her tongue become chunky and broad as she neared the doorway to her personal hell.

As she stood in her cluttered office, the thought of spending even one more second in that workplace pounded away at her temples like bagpipe music on top of a hangover. The pressure had gotten to her. She *really* wasn't in the mood to drum up a reason for taking a half-day off. She gathered a few files that housed some admin work she'd been helping out with and headed toward the back stairs for a sneaky exit. She'd just call Margery, the office assistant, once she got on the road.

Halfway down the stairs, the personal files spilled out of her arms, and she scrambled to pick them up, while the usual tension she carried in her upper back penetrated slowly into her throat, practically choking her. She managed to get ahold of herself, only to realize she'd left her keys on her desk.

Upon returning to her office, a shiver came over her. She stared at the couch that had propped up so many crazies—borderlines, sociopaths, and, of course, the ever-popular married couples who were clueless and going through the motions. Maggie's legs buckled, and she landed on the crazy couch. "I don't want to become one of these senseless loons," she said aloud to the imaginary face that seemed to appear on the vacant wall across from the couch—a face with a crinkled brow, heavy glasses, and a slightly red skin tone. "I gotta get out of this psychiatric hell!"

After a few moments of silence, Maggie pulled herself together, picked up her keys, gently shut the door, and fled down the staircase. But she was stopped in her tracks by a bellowing sound behind her. "Maggie!"

Despite her rigidity, she managed to look up at the top of the stairwell, while at the same time shrinking into what she hoped was a magical cocoon. Deliriously, she expected to see some kind of savior standing there, motioning her to a different life, but she was disappointed. "Geez, Dad, you startled me!"

"Watch your language, please!"

Oh, break out the hearing aids, Bozo! I said, *geez!*

"Where are you going?" he asked. "I assume you're coming back to the office; your door is standing wide open."

Oh, that stupid latch!

"You're not running out for your usual Starbucks, are you?" Dad said. "There's plenty of coffee and doughnuts in the conference room. The meeting starts in ten minutes. And why are you not wearing a suit today?" Her father's crinkled brow seemed to push his glasses to the tip of his nose. His tie, she noted, seemed to have an overly tight knot.

"Uh, well…I just stopped in to, uh, pick up a few files I need to purge," she said as her fingers became fidgety. "Is it really necessary that *I* attend this meeting, Dad?" Seriously, dude, what's the point? "I'm not feeling my best today, and I was hoping to work from home." Maggie tried to feign her best green-around-the gills look. This lying crap is completely exhausting, she thought as her face began to glow with a light coat of sweat.

"Well, I suppose. I'll simply have Margery cancel your appointments once again. You don't look well, Maggie. So, run along and just pace yourself with whatever work you might have. I suppose I can give Margery a little overtime to finish anything you don't get to."

Yes, pony up some OT, you miser!

"Hopefully, this is just one of those twenty-four-hour ailments, since your mother and I are expecting you and Andrew for dinner tomorrow evening," he said.

"Yes, I certainly hope it passes quickly," she said. But I wouldn't mind peddling another sick day to get out of the dinner drama.

"Please don't disappoint us by arriving late. The Worthingtons will be there, and they're looking forward to seeing the two of you again. With Andrew working around the clock so Ted can take over the practice, we thought it would be congenial to have a nonbusiness dinner."

Oh, good God, the Worthingtons. What a couple of bores! And I see Andrew has you buffaloed too. Working round the clock? Puh!

"Plus, Ted's a great golfer, you know. Andrew will appreciate that. We'll see you promptly at six o'clock. Well, I need to speak to Margery before the meeting," he said, checking his standard, old Timex. "So, I'll ask you to kindly lock up your office before heading out." With a stiff finger, he shoved his glasses back into place and plodded off to the conference room.

Now standing alone, dabbing the sweat beads from her brow, Maggie felt the sensation of a new pain that was replacing the previous chokehold. Her neck throbbed from looking up at her father as he lectured her from the top of the stairs. Luckily, she had easily lied about her actual plans for the day. She rubbed her neck as if to work out all her life's kinks and started up the staircase to lock her office door.

Maggie took a deep breath when she finally managed to make it to the parking lot of the old brownstone. As she strolled across the parking lot, the heat of the gravel penetrated the soles of her overpriced, casual-Friday flip-flops, searing the bottoms of her feet. Minding the heat, she hurried along to her car, thinking she'd take an early lunch. She remembered one of her clients talking about a diner across town that prepared the most monstrous cheeseburgers with all the drippings and pastries and cakes that were simply to die for. She'd never tried the diner, but now Maggie was in the mood for a change of scenery. She wanted to eat somewhere that she didn't feel the need to order a skimpy salad with a dressing that was 99 percent water. She'd enjoy a little self-indulgence, courtesy of Sal's Diner, before going home "to work."

CHAPTER

12

The Absence of Cheeseburgers

S al's Diner was rather quaint, exuding a sense of nostalgia. The lunch counter was lined with retro swivel stools topped with worn, red vinyl seats and beautifully adorned with displays of cakes and pastries strategically placed at eye level. There was some sort of rapture in the sweet smell of the greasy grill, prompting Maggie to take a subtle whirl on the old-fashioned stool.

She inspected the diner thoroughly, admiring the servers as they scurried around doing postbreakfast-crowd duties—combining the ketchups, filling the salt and pepper shakers, and stocking each table with tiny sugar packets. She couldn't help wondering if they, too, hated their jobs as she focused on their aggressive scrubbing to rid the tabletops of the everyday buildup of grime.

She happened to make eye contact with a server who was taking off her apron and counting her tips. She was rather striking—tall, confident, and fresh-looking, yet seemingly a few years older than the rest of the waitstaff. She didn't quite seem to fit in with the whole diner scene, but she appeared to be a hard worker by the look of her stained apron. Maggie couldn't help over-hearing the strange and comical restaurant language that so often intrigued her back when she dined out after an all-nighter with her college girlfriends.

"Eighty-six Sal's omelet surprise for the late risers and be sure to check back more often with the tables on the far side. Some customers complained about not getting enough service, and the bread baskets—yikes!—They need some serious attention," one server said to another who was just arriving for her shift.

The poised server who spoke with such fervor exuded an uplifting vibe, and this fascinated Maggie. As well, the patrons appeared to be down-to-earth, reasonably normal people, which was quite refreshing. In no way did they resemble the crazies she dealt with on a daily basis. Nor did she detect any egocentric vanity, which was common among the Botoxed housewives of Car-rington Heights who frequented her office.

"Are these yours?" the server asked, pointing to a stack of Labor Day sales flyers left on the counter near Maggie.

"No," Maggie replied.

The server plopped onto the stool and began flipping through them. She then stopped, whipped out her cell phone, and began texting.

"Excuse me," Maggie said.

"Uh-huh," the server replied without looking up.

"Is it too early to order lunch?"

"Nope. I'll let Lucinda know you'd like to order," she replied, still texting.

Nearly a minute rolled by. Maggie felt inclined to tap her foot, bang a saltshak-er, take an attention-seeking spin on the stool—anything to get a cheeseburger. Meanwhile, she simply could not take her eyes off the multitasking waitress, who still hadn't looked up—not even to locate the lunch-counter server.

The server must have felt Maggie's stare. "I'm sorry; do I know you?" she inquired, now looking directly into Maggie's bold emerald eyes as if to scare off a stalker.

"I apologize. I didn't mean to stare, but I feel like I know *you* from somewhere."

"I see. Oh, there's Lucinda," she said, redirecting the conversation. "Lucin-da, this lady wants to order lunch."

The dawdling coworker indicated *one second, please* with her index finger.

"So, I heard the cheeseburgers here are out of this world."

"Oh, yeah, they're crazy," the server replied as she ended her texting session.

I assume she means crazy good, Maggie thought, delighted that the server hadn't had her thrown out of the place for coming off like a creeper.

"So, what brings you in for an early lunch?"

"Well, I cut out of work early and had a craving for a cheeseburger, so I thought I'd give this place a try."

"Good for you—cutting out of work, that is! Total bore, is it?" the server asked.

"Work? Yeah! Among other things."

"Well, it can't be as bad as this shitty job," she asserted, motioning with both hands to encompass the spacious diner.

"Oh, no! My job's a total shit show!" Maggie replied, shocked by the woman's outspoken language.

They both laughed, feeling they'd each met a kindred spirit. The server extended her hand to introduce herself. "Hi! I'm Lindi."

"Nice to meet you," Maggie replied. A lull settled in for a few seconds. "I'm sorry, did you say Lindi? Are you Lindi Wallace, by any chance?" she asked, her heart-shaped face glowing as if she'd hit a jackpot.

"That's right. Lindi Wallace."

"Oh, my God, Lindi! Do you remember me? Maggie Walters?"

"Maggie Walters?" Lindi pondered the name.

"From Penns Ridge Middle School?" Maggie prompted.

"Oh! Yes! Alphabetically seated behind me in like…"

"Every class," both women said in unison.

"Yes, now I remember," Lindi said. "And then, you just disappeared…to Saint Luke's or something?"

"Yes," Maggie said.

"Well, how have you been?" Lindi asked.

"Uh…pretty well, for the most part," Maggie stammered. "And you?"

"Livin' the dream!" Lindi replied, once again motioning at the diner with both hands.

They laughed simultaneously.

"Well, ya look good," said Lindi.

"Oh, thanks. So do you!"

"Thanks. It's hard, though. This aging crap makes it harder and harder to keep in shape."

"Oh, I know!"

"I actually have a start-up yoga business, so that keeps me busy a few evenings a week and of course on weekends. But it's nutrition that I give priority to," Lindi said.

"Your yoga business sounds exciting. Do you rent a studio or something?"

"No, it's actually a personalized yoga business. In other words, I do private parties or private sessions for people who hire me. I got the idea from a physical therapist a few years back. He took a class with me at Yoga Mind, where I started. He contracted me out for his own patients, and my business grew from there," Lindi explained.

"That's fantastic! I'd love to get back into yoga. I guess I've just been preoccupied with…I don't know…life in general." And whatever that big, fat, layered chocolate thing is, Maggie mused, drifting away from yoga thoughts. Yoga, shmoga…I need one of those decadent beauties!

"I'm completely addicted to yoga," Lindi said. "And I'm a lot more zen when I'm out of here."

"Sounds great." Maggie reacted automatically, still fixated on the chocolate cake.

"Here's my business card," Lindi said.

"Thanks," Maggie responded, scanning Lindi's card. "So, do you work the early shift here at the diner?"

"Yeah, weekdays, eight to two, for the most part. Some days I pull a double if Sal's in a pinch and I'm not booked for the evening."

"So, whatta you do for fun?" Maggie asked as if Lindi were a connoisseur of good times.

"Not a lot anymore. But trust me, I used to live a vampire's schedule...I could always sniff out a party or a good time—at any hour of the night. But over the past few years, I've shifted my philosophy toward wellness. I do get burned out from work sometimes, but I'm just tryin' so hard to get some money together to open my own yoga studio and, you know, continue my Yoga-to-Go business."

"That's a great plan, but I have to ask, aren't you tempted to stray from your healthy eating? With all these pies and cakes in your face? And that grease smell! Doesn't it make you wanna plow into a big sloppin' burger?" Maggie asked.

"Oh, I know. They're seductive little monsters! But I stay away from them. Actually, I talked Sal into adding a 'lighter side' to the menu. Not a big seller, but it does okay. The regulars in here...well, they're just not open to change."

Yep...got a father who's quite the "regular," Maggie thought, recalling his insufferable stubbornness.

"Lindi!" a startling voice interrupted. "You left the freakin' walk-in door open again!" shouted a burly man with a sweat-beaded forehead.

"Then get the damn latch fixed, Sal," Lindi retorted.

Maggie gaped at the scene that was taking place in front of her. What was it with men and their broken latches? She felt as if she'd been in the middle of a bizarre but beautiful daydream where she'd bucked her father, who'd been barking something about nonsense behavior or impetuous whims, and told him to shut the hell up.

"Lindi, so nice seeing you," said Maggie as she was getting up to leave. "I'll stop in again."

"As I said, I'm pretty much here eight to two. On a very rare occasion, I'll help out on Saturday nights. I don't like to turn away the late-evening cash that flows in here from the partiers, if you know what I mean."

"Yeah, I'm sure. It would be great to catch up some more."

"Hey, I'll hit you up on Facebook or something.'

"Actually, I'm not on Facebook," Maggie confessed.

"Huh? Not on Facebook?" Lindi asked in disbelief.

"Well, it's the whole client thing."

"Clients?"

"Yes, my father's a psychiatrist. Maybe you remember. Anyway, I work for his practice."

"Oh, right," Lindi said. "Anyway, I'm sure I'll see you again. And yes, it would be great to catch up. I'd love to know what you've been up to—other than playing hooky from your 'shit show.'" She laughed.

A beaming Maggie waved good-bye to Lindi as if she were her new best friend on the first day at summer camp. She didn't want to spoil the moment by laying out the stark realities of all that weighed heavily upon her. That was for another day's conversation.

As she stepped outside, she turned around to take another look at Sal's Diner. She wanted to tell everyone—the whole world, in fact—about her wonderful dining experience at Sal's, although no one had even taken her order!

CHAPTER

13

Fifty Shades of Gray Sweatpants

Saturday morning arrived, and Maggie woke to the alarming sight of Andrew propped up on his elbow, staring her down as if she were a tasty treat.

"Morning, Mags."

"What the hell, Andrew! What time is it?"

"Six o'clock. Sorry if I startled you."

"Didn't expect you till early evening," she said in a groggy morning voice.

"Yeah, well, I need to get some sleep in my own bed," said Andrew, now undressing. "You know how those damn hotel beds can really do a number on your back?"

Oh, shut up! she thought. Aren't we passed the cover-story bullshit? Haven't we moved on to the just-say-nothing-at-all phase of this charade?

"Gotta be rested for the mandatory dinner party tonight," he said jeeringly.

Maggie rolled away from him, staring at the wall, slowly working up the energy to get out of bed. She felt his body heat burning closer and closer until he eventually spooned her, and the stench of God-knows-what nearly gagged her. Ugh, get away from me, she thought. Unless there's a set of Lexus keys dangling from Magic Mike.

It had been a while since he'd given her an I'm-sorry-I'm-a-jackass gift, which by now had turned into a thanks-for-keeping-up-the-charade-as-a-married-couple gift. Since Andrew had become a slacker, lately, in doling out well-earned bonuses, she wouldn't be giving out any please-get-it-over-with freebies.

Maggie lay in bed for a few minutes longer, mulling the lack of respect that stank up the room. Who did he think he was? She could deal with the fact that he'd stopped giving excuses for his several-day disappearing acts. But thinking he could just waltz into an early morning throw-me-a-bone session? Sleep it off, fool, she thought, and when his hand swiped across her inner thigh, Maggie shot out of bed like she'd sat on a hornet's nest.

"What's wrong, Mags?"

"With what? What are you talking about?"

"Are you…embarrassed or something?"

"About what? I thought you needed some rest."

"Thought maybe you were embarrassed that you hadn't shaved; that's all."

Ugh! You are soooo near that last straw! "I have a busy day," she said. "Gotta get moving. Couldn't care less about shaving right now."

"Oh, come on, now! Why don't you crawl back in here and give me some lovin'…I can get past a little stubble."

And the cheese-ball language continues to roll right out of you, she thought, while grimacing at the thought of giving *anything* to the master of smarm. Maggie disappeared into her dressing nook off the side of her walk-in closet.

She pulled on a pair of rogue gray sweatpants and an old T-shirt that hadn't yet made it into her dirty-laundry hamper. She sat on her vanity stool, staring into the mirror at a woman she no longer recognized. Even her hair was messier than her usual bedheaded coif. In search of a brush, she opened the drawer and found a picture that had resurfaced from her wedding-planning days. A picture from *Brides* magazine, featuring an elegant, stylish updo she'd mimicked for her big day. Without the love goggles, Maggie's eyes now bore deep into the model's head as she crumpled the picture and threw it into her overflowing wastebasket.

Remnants of her wedding day continued to torture her as she reflected back, watching her parents beam, feeling elite as the guests ogled her and Andrew, and shamelessly loving the way he'd playfully, *yet falsely*, introduced them as Andrew and *Dr.* Margaret Spencer. What a pretentious asshole, she thought.

"Andrew!" she said, surprised that he'd been standing at the entryway to her dressing area. Please tell me you're not here to do a quickie up against the vanity, she hoped, looking down at his boxers to make sure there was no sign of an excited Magic Mike.

No sign!

"Whatta ya want?" she asked.

"Before I forget, did you do the pregnancy test?"

Oh, for God's sake…hoped you'd gotten over yourself on that idea. "Yeah, here it is." She whipped the little stick at him as a devious smile crept across her face. Once again, she thought how funny it would be if the tap water created positive pregnancy results.

He inspected the PT stick, nodded in satisfaction at the negative single line, and placed it back on the vanity. "Good enough," he said.

Okay, get your hungover ass back in bed, she thought.

"Mags, what's up with the gray sweats? They look like hell."

"They're comfy, okay? And I'm quite proud that I can still wear something from my college days," said Maggie.

"It's gonna get up around ninety degrees today. Why don't you take those ghastly things off…I'd love to watch you primp naked."

He watched her eyes roll in the mirror, and then he turned away. But Maggie could no longer ignore the unbearable bastard. "Andrew! Seriously? What the hell's up with you? Why would you even ask me to do such a thing?"

"What? To change out of those old gray sweatpants and that dingy T-shirt? I just thought you might be uncomfortable on a hot summer day. Now, come on…why don't you take that stuff off and rub up against me?"

I'd rather rub up against a greasy pig that just rolled in shit! "Listen to me! I'm serious. The pregnancy test…why would you ask me to take it?"

"Damn it, Mags! You really wanna get into this now?"

"Actually, I do! What even makes you think for a second that I'd be pregnant?"

"Come on. Do I need to spell it out for you?"

"Apparently! We rarely see each other, let alone touch each other. How could I possibly be pregnant?"

"It's just that I've seen plenty of paternity cases through the years…some of them got pretty ugly."

"And what's that have to do with us?" she asked, highly agitated.

"Well, we've had a couple wine-induced fuck-buddy nights over the past couple of months. Surely, you remember?"

Oh, yeah…those two stupid nights, she remembered. Better known to me as lay-there-and-win-a-prize-night, she thought, toting up the number of bracelets and necklaces she'd soon have appraised.

"So, my point is…"

Finally, a point! Get to it, cheese ball!

"Well, you've gotten a wee bit paunchy," he finally spat out, staring down at the little bit of a belly Maggie wished she could safely saw off. "If you *are* pregnant, I'm not going to be happy about it, but we'd need to get you set up with the best care and all."

She stared at him in disbelief as *Chubba Bubba* rang out in her head. There were no words. Last straw? Indeed.

"Mags, don't get me wrong…you still look like a million bucks. I just noticed a little something when you've been out by the pool. And, of course, when I was lucky enough to get you naked."

"Oh, such bullshit! There's some other reason. It's like you're obsessed with this pregnancy thing, Andrew, and you're getting on my nerves…it's ludicrous!"

"Okay, the truth of the matter is that I've been dragging my feet about the vasectomy. And if you are pregnant, there's no need for me to make an appointment with the urologist."

You egotistical coward! You're nothing more than a scaredy-cat who fears his manhood will be diminished.

"Besides, let's face it. We're just too old and too set in our lifestyle. Starting a family would be absurd at our age. And no offense, but you'd be the laughing stock."

Perhaps *this* was the last straw. "Oh, cut the crap!" Maggie retorted. "First of all, women have babies all the time in their forties. It's not such a foreign concept. So, please don't use that lame excuse. You sound ridiculous. But whatever! You saw the test results. Go get yourself snipped, and then you'll never have to worry about it!"

"Okay, there's no need to scold me…and what's up with your language, lately? It's like you've been hanging out with truckers or something."

"Yeah, well I guess trucker Maggie has reached her limit of BS."

"So, this is what you've become?" he asked. "Bitter and sarcastic?"

"You know, Andrew, I still don't know why you wanna stay in this farce of a marriage. Please tell me why!"

"Let's not go there again. I told you I didn't want to be the talk of the town, nor do I want to embarrass my parents."

"Do you hear yourself, Andrew?"

"We're just going through a phase, Mags. All married couples need to sand out the occasional rough patch."

Okay, whatever, she thought, rolling her eyes.

"So, you tell me," he said. "Why haven't *you* filed for divorce? Am I too much of a sugar daddy to let go of?"

Okay, you got me there! But I'm thinking that the sugar daddy can go straight to hell now! "So, I'm done with this conversation," was all she could say, while brushing by him to take an unnecessary shower at 6:40 a.m.

As the water crashed down over Maggie, she couldn't help thinking that her labyrinth-like life had become paralyzing, rendering her incapable of making wise decisions. *Sugar daddy.* Andrew's final words made the sound of a deadbolt locking in her mind. Although she'd often thought of him as a dumb ass, she sensed his awareness of the game she'd been playing. No wonder the big-ticket bling stopped coming in, she thought.

***

Maggie had never been a guest in her own guest room; in fact, *no one* had ever stayed there. Likewise, there wasn't any linen on the bed—just a big fluffy comforter with matching pillow shams. Nonetheless, she was content to lie on a bare mattress for a bit of meditation.

An eye-catching candid photo of her and Andrew stood on the night-stand. They were embracing while gazing at the picturesque Napili Bay sunset. Maggie could almost feel the serenity of gentle waves and the warm sand as she drifted back to her honeymoon in Maui. She had been svelte then and confidently pranced around in tasteful but skimpy beachwear while partying every single night. There were no schedules, no clients, no parents—and no lies that she was aware of. She picked up the picture frame and tried to blow off the dust that appeared to tint their faces gray. The dust was a bit thick on the glass and clearly needed a good cleaning. Maggie snapped out of her trip down Maui memory lane and threw the picture into an empty drawer.

Such an emotional morning called for something calming, but it was way too early for a glass of wine. Surely there'd be a leftover piece of something gooey in the fridge. Abandoning meditation, she went to the kitchen and flung the refrigerator door open, making condiment jars rattle and knock into each other. Resting in a deteriorating to-go box, a scrap of some kind of tart that Andrew had been hoarding was calling out to her. She took no time to heat the little indulgence but plowed right in to the gooiness. Much to her chagrin, the tart crust now tasted like everything in the fridge, and Maggie gagged at the fusion of flavors. She ate it anyway.

***

Andrew slept most of Saturday afternoon away, while Maggie ran fake er-rands and shopped frivolously. Anything to get out of a crowded house that teemed with deception and lies and way too much Andrew. But now that it was early evening, she had to face the inevitable—the dreaded snoozer of a dinner party at her parents' house.

What would she wear? Her recently purchased Michael Kors mini, which still had the price tag dangling under a sleeve? Or should she settle for her "go to," a forgiving black cocktail dress that had become slightly faded and showed a bit of wear.

"The formal one is probably your best bet," said Andrew, pointing to the more forgiving dress as he stood in the entryway, sipping his glass of wine.

Damn! You're awake. Eh, guess I'd better fake a little kindness. "Yeah, you're right. Mother and Dad would have a fit if I wore too short a dress."

"Why did you purchase such a dress anyway? I have to admit, it's pretty hot-looking, with the sheer sleeves and all. And what is that? Some kind of hardware around the neck?" he asked.

"I wanted something different! Is that okay?"

"No need to get defensive, Mags. Just curious."

Andrew approached her slowly as he sipped his wine. She watched him in the mirror. He had that shady, horny look about him. She'd seen it before when he'd transform into his most irresistible studlike self. He'd become the master of seduction, saying all kinds of corny things like *Mr. Stud muffin's hungry for a love muffin* or *Magic Mike's on his way up*. Maggie's stomach began to churn. How could she ever have thought that crap was cute?

"Here, have a sip or two of wine. You look tense," he suggested.

"No, I'm fine."

"Better yet, I'll get you a glass," he insisted.

She rolled her eyes. Whatever!

As Andrew left the dressing nook, Maggie tried to slip into her black Spanx, so she could smooth her way into the black cocktail dress. Andrew was right. She *had* formed a teensy gut. She supposed this ever-so-slight eyesore was the result of the sweet tooth she'd developed *and* the fact that she'd lost interest in the pole.

"What's that?" he asked as he placed her glass of wine on the vanity.

"What's what?" But she knew!

"That thing under your dress?" He moved forward and playfully snapped the shapewear visible under the unzipped dress.

"Ouch! It's a pair of Spanx, okay! Every woman likes to look smooth." And quite frankly, you could use a little tuck yourself, she thought, as she crinkled her nose at his beer gut.

"I guess a little smoke and mirrors never hurt anyone," he said.

Oh, shut up! "Andrew, if you don't mind, I'd like to get ready without an audience."

"Okay, okay. I'm gone. Gotta get a shower anyway!"

Oh, God…I just can't take him anymore! To hell with the new Lexus and all the bonus bling I'd hoped to earn…I gotta get out of this shit show!

Maggie decided she needed Andrew's generous wine pour, after all. She took a nice, big, calming sip, while staring at his abandoned glass of wine on her vanity. Devious thoughts crossed her mind on how she could sneak into their bathroom and whisk the Ex-Lax from the medicine cabinet. Spiking his wine would give Andrew the runs…It would be the most entertaining dinner party ever!

As Maggie mulled over the endless possibilities of Andrew in the role of dinner-party clown, she heard the shower come to a full stop. She stood up to take another thorough look in the mirror. She was nicely tucked into her Spanx, and her makeup and hair were good, but she detected a new flaw that would require a lightweight pashmina shawl. She desperately needed to hide the tiny bit of bra fat that crept out of the armholes in her sleeveless dress, giving her little underarm pillows. Eww! That's disgusting on any woman of any size, she thought.

While delving into her scarf and wrap drawer, all she could find were winter accessories. Where the hell are my summer pashminas? She couldn't remember. She moved on to her comfort drawer, hoping to find the misplaced summer accessories. She rummaged through what seemed like an endless heap of old sweatpants—all gray. Pewter, heather, slate, ash…and probably fifty more shades or so. Did my pashminas morph into these hideous things and mass produce? she wondered.

"Mags, ready to go?" Andrew asked, finishing the glass of wine he'd left on the vanity.

"Yeah, I suppose."

Maggie wasn't happy that she'd be showing up at a judgmental dinner party, appearing as if she were pilfering the dinner rolls and stowing them in her armpits. Okay, perhaps the wine skewed the image of her arms a bit. Nonetheless, she thought how inventive it would be to craft a pair of those nasty sweatpants into a pashmina, but that would be silly. Gray was *really* not her color!

CHAPTER 14

The Power of Ex-Lax

Maggie and Andrew pulled into her parents' driveway, ready to put on their best married couple pretense at the Saturday night dinner party. Although she didn't go through with it, she simply could not stop giggling over the thought of spiking Andrew's wine with Ex-Lax. The power of one little tablet could launch the best of all shows! It literally would be a shit show, she thought.

"What's so funny?" he asked.

"Oh, just some stunt one of my clients told me about the other day," she said.

"Well, it's good to see you laugh."

Yes, it is good to laugh…and soon, I'll be laughing all the way to the bank.

As they started walking toward the Walters's house, Andrew pulled Maggie aside. "Mags, sorry I called you paunchy earlier."

OMG, an apology!

"I thought more about it…" he said.

Oh, hell…here it comes! What sort of jab is coming my way now?

"I just don't want any wife of mine to be wearing those...those new-age girdle things. Isn't it uncomfortable?"

Save it for the next Mrs. Spencer. "They're called Spanx, Andrew. And could we please lose the talk about undergarments or shapewear or bulges or anything that is completely ridiculous? Seriously, Andrew! Are you still drunk or something?"

He ignored the question. "Back to my point, I think those Spanx things are a little embarrassing."

"Are we talking about you being embarrassed or me? I'm fine with them. It's not like I'm walking around wearing the damn things with nothing over them! Can we just go in now and get this stupid dinner party over with?" The raging fire burning through her soul made her feel like shouting at him.

"Keep it down, for God's sake. Your mother will be rushing out here any minute. And there's something else I want to tell you, Mags."

"Whaaaat?" she asked with a dramatic eye roll.

"Now, just listen to me," he said. "I truly think we still have a chance."

Crickets.

"I mean it," he continued, staring into her eyes.

Oh, you bipolar, cheese-ridden jackass! She no longer fell for his toxic notions. She broke his hold on her and walked ahead of him, wishing he'd turn down the street and get hit by a bus or something.

"I'm serious, Mags."

She ignored him.

"We'll discuss it later, then," he said with a raspy chuckle, kicking up his pace to get ahead.

As Andrew rang his in-laws' doorbell, Maggie charged right past him without waiting for the formal opening of the door, the fake hugs and kisses, and the "so-glad-you-could-make-it" blabber. She needed another glass of wine.

"Hello, dear!" her mother shouted as Maggie bolted right by her to check the wine fridge for a nice crisp Riesling.

"Oh, hi, Mother," she said, taking a few steps back and leaning in with a fake kiss.

"And how's my favorite son-in-law?"

"Fantastic! And you look as lovely as ever, Mom. Are you sure you're not Maggie's sister?"

"Yuck!" Maggie whispered to herself, gnawing angrily on a hangnail.

"Maggie, dear, what is it?" her mother asked.

"I'm sorry...what is *what*?"

"What is *yuck*? It's as if you've been hanging out in a diner or something," her mother replied.

Yes, apparently a truck-stop diner, Maggie wanted to spew out. "I just need to get rid of this mint I put in my mouth. The flavor is a bit much. But speaking of diners, do you remember—"

Her mother's eyes had shot down to Maggie's raw, fidgeting fingertips as they clung to her empty wineglass. "Oh Maggie! Have you been picking at your nails?" she interrupted.

Seriously, Mother, my nails are an issue? Am I not a bit old for this scolding routine? Maggie rolled her eyes, determined to resurrect her earlier wine-induced confidence. Where's the damn Riesling?

"Well, then. Come this way. Your father's entertaining Ted and Rita in the family room."

"Andrew!" Dr. Walters cried, slurring a bit as he placed his martini on the marble coaster and extended his hand. "So glad you could make it!"

Maggie stood in silence as everyone seemed to buzz around her. She was bored already, listening to her mother and Rita chat about their charities and how wonderful Rita's *perfect* daughters were. She stepped back to the sideboard, which offered a nice selection of Maggie's least favorite wines. She settled for the merlot.

Stepping into the dark side, Maggie wondered if Rita and Ted knew about some of their daughters' shenanigans. She chuckled as she pictured herself spilling the beans about Jackie Worthington's visit to the abortion clinic after a torrid affair the contractor Ted hired to renovate their outdoor entertainment area. Or perhaps she would ask Ted and Rita if they knew why Mary's secret nickname was *Mary-go-round* or how Paulina used to brag about "doing" her young swim coach in the country club equipment room when she was sixteen. Of course, these juicy rumors were merely hearsay. But what a bunch of pretentious whores the Worthington sisters were, Maggie thought as her wine buzz took hold.

Suddenly, Maggie could no longer take her father's long-winded stories about God-knows-what. Nor could she listen to anymore golf boasting from Ted and Andrew. She grabbed the half-bottle of merlot that was left and started for the staircase. Andrew, leaving the others to continue with their snooze-fest banter, caught up to her.

"Maggie, may I pour you a glass of wine?" he asked so formally, so lovingly, and so ass-kissingly as he watched her climb the stairs.

"Go jump off a cliff," Maggie said in a loud whisper as she neared the top step.

"What was that?" he asked.

"I'll be down in a jiff!" she shouted down to him, then took a slug of wine straight from the bottle.

***

Maggie entered a room that she no longer recognized, even though it was where she'd spent much of her time as a teenager. She brushed the palm of her hand over the bedspread, sensing weakened strands of fabric that had resulted from neglecting to care for it properly. Was the bedding in between washes? She couldn't imagine her mother throwing any old raggedy bedspread on the bed. At least her long-gone 1990s Laura Ashley floral-print bedding had brightened the room. But now chevrons? Gray? Ick! How jagged and dull.

The wine was getting to her. She needed refocus on mindless, meaningless trivialities. Her thoughts turned back to the Ex-Lax, the extra strength variety. And just like that, she became filled with gut-wrenching laughter. Her only regret of the evening so far was that she hadn't take the chance to spike Andrew's wine. She lay back on her teenage bed, rolling in hilarity at the thought of Andrew having a *most unfortunate accident* that came out of nowhere! Who knew that silly thoughts of a laxative would have the power to make Maggie laugh through all the pain?

Horndogs and Phony Baloney

The dinner party dragged on and on for what seemed like dog years. After much pretentious coma-inducing banter and a few bottles of wine, dinner was about to be served. Liz Walters's famous roast duckling with red potatoes and the amazing sundried-tomato-and-asparagus salad that Maggie had always loved was sure to please Ted and Rita Worthington. Even though Ted and Dr. Walters had projected that all legal matters pertaining to the business transfer would be finalized by next spring, it was time to step up their leisurely pace.

Dr. Walters, however, was fixed on making a sluggish descent into retirement. He would never admit it, but continuing to run the practice into his late sixties was his way of having a postmidlife crisis. Some men tool around in cars that are way too young for them; others tool around with women who are way too young for them. Dr. Walters did neither. His young hottie was simply an old historic brownstone that needed major repairs.

After a few more bottles of wine and a hundred more hours of grueling repartee, Ted Worthington interjected. "I'd like to make a toast."

Really...what for, Ted? Maggie agonized, knowing she couldn't possibly feign being thrilled for anything wonderful going on with one of his snooty daughters. Since she was now pretty buzzed from the wine, she'd have to cross her fingers that no one would detect her half-hearted salute to one of the Worthington sisters—the most wonderful girls on the planet!

"Rita, dear," Ted said, "thank you for giving me the most magnificent daughters in the world."

Aaaand, here we go! Maggie thought.

"Well, yes, Ted...of course *you* had a hand in giving us those perfect darlings as well," Rita replied.

"Ha ha ha ha!" The faux-chuckles around the table were synchronized with Maggie's eye roll.

Oh, get a room, Teddy and Reets! So, is that it? You seriously wanted to give your wife accolades for those skanks? Oh, wake me when this is over, Maggie thought, as she sheepishly looked around the dining room, looking for something to focus on that wouldn't further stir up her bitter resentment toward—well, just about everyone! Maybe she should clear the dishes, water the plants, polish off another bottle of wine—anything, really, to get away from such travesty.

"But seriously, I'd like to make a toast to my lovely wife," Ted continued.

Maggie truly wanted to fake a snore at this point, but that would've made it way too obvious that she was drunk and hating everyone.

"To my lovely wife who will be just as lovely...when she becomes a grandmother in the spring of next year!"

Wow, Paulina! What a fertile Myrtle you must be, Maggie thought, recalling that she and Andrew didn't make it to Paulina's late-June wedding. Hmmm...a shotgun wedding, perhaps? Another fine point to add to your daughter-of-the-year resume!

Everyone stood up to shake hands with Ted and give Rita fake hugs and sloppy kisses. It was one thing to sit back and simulate joyful spirits, but how would Maggie pull off a sincere-enough hug? Waiting her turn in the fake-hug line with dread, Maggie stewed to herself until Andrew interrupted her surliness by taking hold of her hands. He came face to face with her.

If you try to lay a kiss on me, I swear to God I will knee you right in your Magic Mike! "What?" she asked with a boorish attitude, while he gazed into her eyes.

"Isn't this fantastic for Ted and Rita? Look at them. Have you ever seen anyone so elated over such great news?"

Oh, whatta you care? And please drop this stupid act! "Yep! Good for them. Is there any more wine left?" she asked, breaking free from the handholding.

"Don't you think you've had enough?" he asked.

"Aren't you driving?" she replied.

"Well, yes, but—"

"But nothing. Fill me up!"

Gradually, Maggie trudged toward the Worthingtons with the meager serving of wine Andrew had poured for her. She'd be giving them her best fake hugs *sans* the sloppy kisses. She saw her parents smiling with delight over Ted and Rita's splendid news. But all that a fed-up Maggie could reflect upon was getting the hell out of there to discuss some kind of financial settlement with Andrew.

When they returned to their seats, Andrew began rapidly dinging his wineglass with a dessert fork. "Excuse me, everyone. I, too, have an announcement," he declared with his usual bravado.

Oh, please don't embarrass yourself with some trumped-up sentiment for Ted and Rita, she thought. Oh, this would've been a perfect time for the Ex-Lax to work its magic. Bummer!

"Rita, Ted…no worries. My news certainly won't trump your fantastic news!"

"Ha ha…ha ha!" The dinner party once again synchronized faux-chuckles.

"But seriously…" Andrew continued, staring down at Maggie.

Oh, dear God…where is he going with this? Please don't profess your phony love or some other nonsense!

"I believe someone here deserves to be recognized for a hell of career as she embarks upon her final week as a working woman. And since I've been awfully tied up with business, I've decided now is the time to take my lovely wife to Paris on that second honeymoon." He looked tenderly into Maggie's eyes, which held daggers. That Paris trip kicked the marital bucket months ago, she thought.

Maggie's tongue had disappeared. She was now floating on some sort of dark cloud that was about to crash down into a hell of a storm. She just sat in her chair, stupefied and powerless, gaping at Andrew as if she were trapped in a horrific nightmare, and he was the cracked and tormenting demon.

"Oh, how wonderful!" Maggie's mother cried as the ruffles seemed to blow right off her blouse.

Oh, it is not! Maggie thought. So, pipe down, Pilgrim.

"Well, that's fantastic! Second honeymoons are so invigorating! Just ask my little Mrs., here," said Ted, who leaned in to kiss Rita. "Saint Barth's will never be the same, right darling?"

Okay, I don't wanna hear anymore from a middle-aged horndog, Ted. So, shut up now!

"And who knows, Maggie, darling. An early forties pregnancy is very trendy these days. Maybe you'll come back and light your parents' world on fire, just as our Paulina did to ours! Of course, she's only twenty-seven, but a healthy pregnancy is certainly possible at your age," said Rita.

Okay…whatever, Rita. Now it's time for *you* to shut up!

"She's right!" Maggie's mother chimed in.

Andrew and Maggie's father now appeared to be the ones looking for dry plants or dirty dishes—any chore to exclude themselves from baby babble.

Finally, Maggie's tongue reappeared, and she forced a pitiful smile. "Well, thanks for the wonderful gesture, Andrew, but we need to table this topic for now, please." She shot Andrew the stink eye. I'll kill you, later!

"So, when will you be taking this trip, Andrew?" Maggie's mother asked.

"Mother, we'll get back to you on that. I certainly think there's been enough excitement for one evening. So, we're going to say good night, now," said Maggie, while looking down at the remainder of her cheesecake, which she'd have to leave behind. Uncouth or not, she was hoping at least to lick her dessert fork, which had a few tiny morsels lodged between the tines.

"Yes, good night, everyone!" Andrew said after the others had harmonized on their good nights.

Andrew corralled Maggie toward the door, but she forcefully jerked her arm away and then bolted ahead of him. What did Andrew think he was doing? How would she explain the impending divorce after her husband had so lovingly fed everyone a load of crap?

Driving home from her parents' dinner party, she moved further into that ominous storm cloud. She could barely look at her mental-case husband as they rolled along in his Navigator. Most likely, he was in his own encumbering fog, and Maggie longed to return to the previous purple haze of merlot, but it was too late—fury had taken over. Hadn't she come upon her last straw earlier in the day? Could there be *several* last straws to push one over the edge? Maggie's were piling up.

***

Maggie and Andrew made it into their house safely. That is, Andrew was still living. Both remained muted, however. She had tried hard to organize her go-to-hell speech during the drive home, but why bother? An off-the-cuff tirade was inevitable. She trailed him into the bedroom. His arrogant nonchalant demeanor exacerbated her rage.

"What…the hell…is wrong…with you, you raging lunatic!"

Silence.

"Andrew, seriously!" she continued. "You truly need help! You are a bipolar mess! And I want you out of here!"

"Okay, that's enough," he broke in.

"No, I'm not finished. You've been absent from this marriage for more months than I can even remember. And if that's not enough, you're rude and controlling. You waltz in here this morning in the throes of a good drunk, thinking that all of a sudden, I want to pick up the pieces to this sham of a life we have. You're worse than any client who's ever stepped foot into my office. I'm blown away by your ridiculous mind games. And ya know what? It was stupid of us to get married so quickly. Stupid! Stupid! Stupid! I'm ashamed of myself. *We* should be ashamed of ourselves."

"Are you finished?" he asked politely.

Silence.

"Listen," he demanded as he forcefully pulled her close to him. "You wanna know the truth? I just wanted to buy us some more time."

"For what?" Maggie backed away. "What the hell are you talking about? Are you dying or something?"

"No! Now, be reasonable. I was very serious about working things out. Giving us another chance." Andrew pulled Maggie's left hand toward him. "It's been a while since I've seen this on your finger," he said, rubbing his hand over her wedding ring."

"Uh, don't act like it means anything, Andrew…you're not stupid. Neither of us would have wanted to deal with questions concerning the ring's whereabouts!"

"True…but I was hoping you'd at least take some time to think about things. If you wanna be alone to think about it, fine. If you wanna go on a second honeymoon and see if we can work it out together, fine. You get back to me."

Silence.

Maggie took a deep breath and maintained a miraculous composure. "You leave tomorrow morning for whatever trip," she said as she twirled her finger in the air and rolled her eyes, "so, I'll have plenty of time to think about things." Like some of the big fat assets coming my way. "But planning a second honeymoon is a bit much." And it's never gonna happen, you idiot!

"Okay, fair enough. I'll be gone till next Friday…Sunday, at the latest. I think it's best that you finish your last week at the office with some alone time. And just a little FYI, I'm going to push back the vasectomy a bit…just in case you decide to give this another go, I want Mike to be up and running for you!"

And there's the return of the cheese! Blugh!

"And by the way, Mags, with all your female issues, I know there was never a big need for birth control, but, um…do you still have your diaphragm?"

No need to blow the dust off that thing! "It's all good, Andrew," she said, staring him down with disdain.

"Okay, soooo…I think I'll leave you to start thinking about us tonight. I'll stay, as you suggested, in my office suite."

Yeah, yeah! Now get out of here…go to Lillian's tiger place or whatever it's called and get all this horndog mojo out of your system!

"Later, then," said Andrew, while grabbing his prepacked trip bags.

Maggie watched from the living room window until he was out of sight. There were no fake hugs, no sloppy kisses…and she was absolutely fine with that.

CHAPTER 16

Sunday Morning Fat Pants

The God-awful Saturday night dinner party turned Maggie into a hellish hungover mess. She prayed for a lighter headache and promised she'd never drink so much wine again. It was 2:00 a.m., and Maggie's pounding head reminded her that last night's fiasco *really* happened.

I just want to sleep, damn it!

But since she was wide awake, she decided to get some fresh air. A breeze brushed across her face as she stepped outside onto the porch off her bedroom. She tightened her oversized robe and breathed in, exhaled out. Her stomach growled, reminding her that she'd lost her appetite at the dinner table last night, and she immediately thought of the monster burger she'd wanted to try at Sal's Diner. Better late than never, she told herself.

The early morning temperature seemed unseasonably cool, which made it a comfy sweat pants day. To hell with what anyone thinks of these old, outdated things, she thought as she slipped into her tatty heather-gray favorites and pulled out several big bulky sweatshirts. Georgetown University? I thought I'd lost you, she thought, swiping her hand across the peeling letters on the sweat shirt she'd bogarted from Andrew and then patting them down as if they'd reattach to the fabric. Eh, what the hell, she told herself and pulled the imperious heap over her head, wiggling into the arms.

After what seemed like days of careful sweatshirt selection, she crept to her Lexus, shut the door gently, and silently rolled out of the driveway—no sense in disturbing the neighbors at that miserable hour.

***

While driving, she relived a play by play of what led up to last night's grand finale…the whopping tale of a second honeymoon. Such fools, she thought, recalling horndog Ted nearly giving it to Rita right on the dining room table, while Andrew smarmed the pants off everyone but Maggie. She heard the warped sound of slow-motion applause as she congratulated herself for having become "fool" proof.

I suppose Andrew stayed at his office last night, she thought, and that brought to mind the dearly departed late-night hookups she'd had with Andrew when he worked well into the evening during their premarital-bliss phase. She'd bring his favorite takeout from Bella's, a few bottles of cab sauv, and later, she'd nod off in his arms on the suite's futon. In the morning, she'd playfully fold the uprooted, gnarled blankets, while teasing him with yoga positions that required bending over. Her reminiscence stopped when she recalled the ridiculous howling sound he'd make when watching such poses. Blahhh! Let someone else think his antics are cute, she thought. Then she wondered if he had a new office squeeze. Not giving a damn, she told herself—but curious!

In driving across town, Maggie felt the busy energy of nightlife. How did these people manage to look so alive and carefree during the wee hours of the morning? Had she driven into a time warp? Perhaps it was still Saturday night, 7:00 p.m., and she was merely groggy from her interrupted sleep. But no. Once again, she was reminded of staggering home from the dinner party as she watched people stumble to their cars. She took some sort of twisted pleasure in knowing they'd wake up a few hours later to suffer the same head-banging headache she was now hosting. Suddenly, her stomach reared its ugly head again, and she found herself to be quite the lead foot in getting to Sal's for a cheeseburger fix.

***

Pulling into the diner parking lot, Maggie could taste the grease in the air. The gritty aroma of sea-salted french fries intensified her desire for an unhealthy, uninhibited gorge-fest. The solace of the diner smells alone had begun to stifle her hangover. She'd come to the right place.

Inside the diner, she took a seat close to where the waitstaff gathered to chat between serving patrons. She chuckled at their stories of wanting to tell some guy to shove his two-buck tip up his fat ass and wanting to sneeze into the bread basket of a particularly high-maintenance customer. She glanced around, listening closely to bona fide stories. She was enthralled by a rail-thin woman boo-hooing about looking fat in her size 2 jeans, while her companion was focused on his cell phone, which he held under the table, its tiny flashes of light giving away his drifting attention. Is he taking pictures of his junk? Maggie wondered. She wished she had the nerve to approach him—not to counsel him on his absurdity, but to look at the pictures.

These people are wonderfully bizarre, Maggie thought. She was delighted by not feeling so alone and pathetic. "Excuse me," she said, interrupting one of the servers.

"Whata ya need, hon?"

"Any chance Lindi's working tonight? Lindi Wallace?"

"She cut out around midnight. She had to work her other job; I think."

"She has a yoga class? At this hour?" Maggie was perplexed.

"No, no! What am I thinking? I can't keep up with that girl! I believe she went over to the Berlin Loft. Wanted to catch the last set of an old grunge tribute band that's playing...or something like that."

"Oh, I see," Maggie said, rubbing her arm as if someone had removed her feeding tube.

"Well, can I get one of Sal's cheeseburgers to go?"

"Sure, sweetie."

A few minutes later, the server delivered Maggie's order, and Maggie nearly tackled her to the ground in her haste to grab the white paper sack speckled with grease spots. She scrunched the bag under her arm just enough for a tight grip but loose enough to not ruin the goods inside. After throwing some money down, she dashed to the parking lot as though she'd just robbed the place. She slunk down in the leather car seat, savoring every bite of her monster burger, lapping up all the drippings, and wishing there were a piece of chocolate cake with peanut butter frosting hiding in the bottom of the bag.

As she began to drive home, Maggie's hangover tapered off, and she found herself taking a detour to go by the Berlin Loft. She wouldn't be caught dead at a music venue wearing her worn-down, albeit comfy, sweatpants, though. While they masked her cheeseburger-bloated belly quite well, she'd reserved *that* glamorous look for reclusive hangover days.

∗∗∗

As she crawled into bed, she sighed in relief that Andrew hadn't changed his mind and made a surprise visit home. There'd be no stinking up the bed with that weird wet-basement odor that lingered on him after what she suspected were nights out at a dive bar. For all she cared, he could be out with some gemstone-named dancer, hooker, office whore, whatever, as long as that nauseating, cheap scent of wherever he'd been wasn't around to test her gag reflux. Nonetheless, Maggie stayed on her side of the bed. She slowly drifted into the coveted land of slumber, bundled in her Sunday best—a lost-and-found sweatshirt and her favorite fat pants.

CHAPTER
17

Just a Couple of Chumps

Still enjoying the comfort of her Sunday-best couture, Maggie bummed around the house. *Ahhh…*the simplicity of a lazy Sunday afternoon…catching up on reading and sipping her coffee. The day had gotten much warmer than the semifrigid temperature she'd gone out in at 2:00 a.m. It would've been a great day for lounging by the pool, soaking up the late-August sun while enjoying a fruity cocktail. But she was content to stand down from the heat and the booze.

Maggie expected the customary call from her mother, who'd be sure to mention that she didn't see Maggie and Andrew at mass. Occasionally, they'd even have a late lunch together. But there was no call that day. Maggie wasn't sure if she should be thrilled to be free of inane questions about a second honeymoon or if she Mother had put her on an adult time-out for hitting the wine so hard. Either was fine with her—she was enjoying her backed-up stack of *In Style* magazines and her alone time.

Later that afternoon, Maggie became bored with dog-earing pictures in magazines that she labeled *must purchase now* or *purchase after divorce settle-*

ment. She fell back into her easy chair and shut her eyes, attempting to embrace the silence. She didn't get far, however. Her cell phone interrupted with its standard, no frills ringtone, signifying a call from her parents. Should she apologize for Andrew's bogus honeymoon gesture? Or would a simple, "Just kidding!" do? No. She'd be stuck having to dodge the truth about all that was happening with the *fabulous* Andrew and Maggie Spencer.

"Hello," Maggie answered, trying hard not to sound annoyed.

"Hello, dear. I hadn't received a call back from my earlier message. I assumed you were a little under the weather and perhaps silenced your phone?"

Damn, why didn't I think of that! "Oh? I suppose I was away from my phone when you called."

"Well, your father and I would like to meet you for lunch—a rather late lunch by now, of course. If you've already eaten, perhaps you'll have a little fruit plate or something light."

Whatever! And who made you the food police? "That would be fine, Mother."

"We'd like to discuss some things about your future."

Uh, don't they know that I'm a forty-year old woman now? "Ooooo-kaaaay," she replied with a deep inflection.

"Very well, then. It's quite important," her mother pressed.

"So, where should I meet you?" said Maggie.

"Well, there's a new place your father really enjoys…oh, what's the name of it?" her mother hemmed and hawed.

"Actually, Mother, there's this great little diner across town, and you'll never believe who works there—"

"Oh, Maggie, no! Not some diner! Eww—the smell. And the grease-coated tables! Darling, really!"

"Fine," said Maggie, "Where, then?"

"I simply cannot remember the name, but it's that adorable little sandwich shop near your father's office. It was closed for a while but reopened under new ownership. I'm sure you know the one. Your father got great service there last week and said that everyone dresses appropriately. You know how your father doesn't like offensive or suggestive attire."

Of course, not…I'm surprised he hasn't asked the waitstaff to wear ruffles! "Oh, yes. Sammie's. Haven't been there since the new owners took over. So, when would you like to meet?"

"Promptly at two o'clock."

"I'll see you there. But as I was saying, I found a little diner across town, and—"

"Darling, your father is motioning for me…you can tell me your diner story at lunch. See you then."

"Uh, okay, see—"

Click. Mother had cut her off again.

Maggie scanned her phone, checking for *any other* missed messages. But who would be calling? Her college girlfriends, who'd apparently moved into the witness protection program? Acquaintances she'd made through Andrew? Through the country club? Who, really?

She found the voice mail her mother had referred to and a missed call from Andrew. What did he want? she wondered, since he hadn't left a message. Eh, what the hell? she thought, deciding to give him a quick courtesy call in return. But what would she say? She really had *nothing* to say—other than good riddance!

Oh, good…his voice mail. In listening to the greeting, she became sickened by the sound of his high-powered bullshit-attorney voice. It seemed to shatter her eardrum and reminded her of his frequent lies and indiscretions. Her thoughts turned toward everything preposterous about him and their marriage: the stupid pole, the dancers at Lillian's, the fake laughs and feigned interest at social gatherings, Magic Mike, Andrew's overall smarminess, and his absolute and profound degrees of narcissism and selfishness. She left no message.

***

As Maggie pulled into Sammie's parking lot, she observed a Navigator, much like Andrew's, parked in a handicapped space. She picked up her speed and neglected to look at the license plate number.

If Andrew didn't leave for New York as he said he would and was here to discuss some half-baked "plan for the future" with my parents, I'm having him committed, she thought. *And*, I'm reporting his entitled ass for parking illegally!

A long, threatening blast of a horn triggered Maggie to refocus. She applied her brakes and pulled into the nearest parking spot. The check engine light began to flash as she shut off the car, reminding her of the sheer negligence that characterized her life these days.

Oh, this place is probably some glorified stuffy coffee shop, she thought, lumbering toward the entrance to Sammie's. Sure, she'd have to suffer through the border-lacking questions and pushy advice on whatever it was her parents had issues with. But she'd get through it and later take delight in sinking back into her easy chair to devise a fair divorce settlement. There'd also be a woe-is-me vacation after she and Andrew separate, so it would be a good time for Maggie to look into unexplored territory.

Those rewards helped her to at least try turning her thoughts toward the positive. She was well-aware of her bitterness; perhaps her parents had detected unhappiness behind her forced persona at the dinner party. Maybe they actually wanted to hear about it…support her…stop sweeping the pink elephant under the rug. Could it be that they simply wanted to celebrate *her*—for any reason? Maybe for sticking it out in a career she despised, or for deciding to kick her jackass husband to the curb? Or for managing not to kill him? Wouldn't such fine qualities call for celebration?

Maggie stealthily slipped her wedding ring off the keychain, where she mostly kept it, back onto her left ring finger and entered Sammie's. She noticed the bare walls, the murky darkness of the room, and the light that was trying to peek through the massive shades. This was certainly no Sal's! Where was the aroma of coffee? Where were the pies and cakes? What kind of celebratory place is this dungeon? she wonder while scanning the joint.

While the atmosphere was displeasing, Maggie forced herself into a positive place once more. Maybe she'd been in a nightmarish coma for the past several years, and this was the day she'd be revived and sent off to her real world.

She envisioned the scene in full bloom, picturing everyone in attendance at her most celebrated event—her awakening! There was her servant, Andrew, standing tall and proud with a bottle of champagne and a tray full of jewels. There were her *happily* married college girlfriends, whose names she couldn't quite remember, wearing late 1990s sweat pants and cheering her on. There were the plump, raggedy Worthington daughters, trying their best to take spins on the dancer's pole that had been relocated to Sammie's…and there was Lindi, sporting an oversized, comfy sweatshirt that read, *I Love My New Best Friend,* while serving a great big tray of Sal's monster burgers. Oh, and there were her parents. So proud. Her father wasn't wearing a tie, her mother wasn't wearing ruffles, and everyone was clapping and cheering as she pulled a set of keys from the center of an enormous ice cream cake on the hood of a new Lexus.

"We're right here, darling," her mother shouted, waving her arms as if she were drowning.

"Oh, yes. Yes, you are," said Maggie, leaning in to fake a kiss while she came down from that bizarre fantasy. "Hi, Dad," she said as he looked up from his watch.

"Have a seat," her father commanded. "I ordered a round of iced tea," he said, glancing at the waitstaff nook and then back at his watch.

"That's fine," Maggie said. Although, I'd prefer diet Coke.

After the server delivered the tea, Dr. Walters nodded in his wife's direction as if to point at her with his perturbed brow…which really meant, "You handle this one, Liz."

Oh, he has that hideous brow thing going on, Maggie thought. What's the big stink this time? Is Sammie's out of fruit plates? Is this Mother's last day to wear ruffles? What?

Maggie's mother took her cue from her husband, pulled her cupped hands tightly against a mound of ruffles on her blouse, and began, "Darling, we have some things to discuss with you. Your father and I…well, we noticed that you had quite a few glasses of wine with dinner last night."

More like a couple bottles, but we'll go with glasses! "Yes, I suppose I've just been a little overwrought lately, Mother," said Maggie as she glanced at her father, who sported a look of repugnance in his deep-set eyes. She looked away, and her eyes became fixated on his drumming fingers. At this point, she began hoping for a miracle diversion—anything, really…even for Andrew to dash in to discuss some bullshit plan for the future.

"I realize that your caseload has been reduced, tremendously—" her mother continued.

"Get on with it, Liz," her father interrupted.

"Well, Maggie, your father and I had a long chat after mass this morning, and we agree with Andrew."

Huh? He was at mass? What a con artist, that one! "Agree with him on what? What are you talking about?" said Maggie.

"Andrew has been concerned about you lately. He said, and we agree, that your heart's simply not where it needs to be for your role as a therapist. He wants you to get rejuvenated and take it easy…especially as you revisit your planning for Paris," her mother said.

Rejuvenated, yes! Paris, hell, no!

"Everyone thinks it would be best if you only worked half days for the rest of your time at the psychiatric center," her mother continued. "What a dear Andrew is with his concern and all."

Uh, not a dear at all…and I hope this most fabulous idea doesn't mean I have to give him a freebie when he gets back…Nah! Silently, she laughed at that silly thought.

"Your father and I knew this day would come eventually," she said with an insincere frown.

Eventually! Puh! I've been ready to bail out of that shit show for several years! Ever since Dad turned into a micromanaging bully!

"Oh, that husband of yours! I know I sound like a broken record, but he truly is a keeper."

More like a bamboozled idiot, Maggie thought.

"Always looking out for you and your well-being," her mother went on.

"Yes, I would have to concur," her father added out of the blue.

My well-being! Ha! Maggie thought as she motionlessly shook her head in disbelief.

"Maggie, I realize that you're a grown woman," her father said, "and I don't need to tell you…"

But you'll tell me anyway!

"That my long-established reputation in this town is very important to me. My name will still be attached to the practice when Ted takes over. Furthermore, we pride ourselves on our reputation for providing top-notch therapy." Her father eyes were shooting tiny bullets over his heavy rims. "If there is a drinking problem, I can't have that interfere with our esteemed professional status. This is business, Maggie. I realize this is your final week, but I hope you understand the principle behind this demotion."

Do I look sad or something? If so, get those thick, ugly glasses adjusted! I could do a string of cartwheels, right here! I'm sure you'd be mortified by something so outrageous and fun, but I couldn't be happier! Rapture took over as Maggie's insides smiled at the thought of digging her humiliated father out from under a pile of her mother's ruffles. "I don't know what to say!" she exclaimed.

"Calm down, dear. We don't want to make a scene," her mother said, glancing around.

No, Ruffles, you calm down! Maggie tossed an irritated glare at her mother for misinterpreting the excitement.

"Your schedule will consist of reporting first thing in the morning to take care of whatever needs to be done, and then I want you to take the rest of the day for yourself," her father said, rubbing his eyes.

"Sounds good," Maggie said. "I'll see you tomorrow, bright and early."

"Aren't you going to stay and share a fruit plate, darling?"

"No, thanks, Mother." I'm too excited to eat healthy food!

As Maggie left Sammie's, she noticed the light shone through the shades a bit brighter. She wanted to share her "next-to-nothing caseload" news with anyone who had hit the lottery, struck gold, or even successfully robbed a bank. This demotion was the beginning of *her* jackpot! She had somehow received her metaphoric get-out-of-jail-free card.

Maggie sank into the cushy leather seat of her old Lexus, which had oddly taken on a fresh new scent. Who'd have thought the hangover day from hell would blossom into such splendor? She was delighted all over again yet felt slightly ashamed for thinking of her parents as duped dumb asses. From now on, she'd simply refer to them with less fury as a couple of chumps.

Monday's Yada Yadas and Blah Blah Blahs

Andrew had only ever seen Maggie take a few spins on the dancer's pole that still remained erect and untouched in the middle of the master bedroom. In fact, ever since their dreadful anniversary night in June, he'd totally ignored the thing—as if it were a can of forbidden worms not to be opened. But he changed his tune when it came time to cash in on his "U-O-Me" for the reduced work schedule. His foreplay style of howling turned more wolflike as he egged her on, stuffing dollar bills into her lacy thong as she swung around the pole. Much like a gawky colt's, Maggie's knees knocked together as she shimmied the thong down to her ankles and hooked it with the red spiked heel of her left shoe. She tripped as she prepared to fling it at Andrew but got back on her feet and carried on with the nightmarish performance. Attempting to redeem herself and put the sexy back into the flawed routine, she bent over to pick up the thong with her mouth and looked back to check in on Magic Mike's position.

Beep beep beep beep beep! Maggie banged her head on the headboard as relentless blasts of her backup alarm roused her out of a rather unsettling dream. She sat up, slammed the snooze bar, and rubbed her head, already feeling a tiny bump forming. As of late, she hadn't taken much notice of the dancer's pole that he had, at one time, enjoyed. But today, she couldn't take her eyes off the nasty steel rod that seemed to hog most of the bedroom, instigating nightmares.

Big goal of the day, she told herself: call the pole dude. That thing's gotta go! She, too, had been sweeping a big pink elephant under the rug for far too long.

Though her Monday morning started out with a bit of disturbance, Maggie was able to shake it off and clear her mind. Having some snooze minutes left on the alarm, she sank down into bed and thought of all the goodies she'd take advantage of that week.

Ahhh, the frills…total R and R, a mani-pedi, a facial, a massage, perhaps a Sal's cheeseburger or two! What could be better?

Not waiting for the next round of ear-piercing blasts from the alarm, she hauled herself out of bed and into the bathroom, where she had, oddly, left her phone. She had a text message…left at 1:15 a.m. by *Andrew*? She was intrigued.

Dis girl is on phire! Missing you so much, beauty! I know we can work this out. I CANNOT get you out of my mind! XOXOXOXO

Seriously? Drunken ebonics? Alicia Keys would have a heart attack!

Maggie couldn't get past Andrew's sudden change of heart. Not that an abrupt turnaround was impossible, but so much damage had been done! There was no turning back. Was there? She looked into the mirror and scratched her bedheaded coif.

Then Maggie's cell phone beeped. It was Andrew. Ugh! Do I wanna deal with his BS right now? she asked herself.

She answered. "Hello."

"Bisquick! What's up?"

Ooo-kaaay, I was beauty on the text, but whatever! "Yeah, hi," Maggie replied, slightly agitated by the baking mix reference.

"I know it's early, but I wanted to catch you before you went to work."

"Yep, still here."

"So, how'd you like that nice little deal your father offered you?" Andrew asked, practically shouting. "I assume you met up with him yesterday?"

Ughhh, is this where he'll go on with his "give me some lovin'" cheese… or tell me that Magic Mike needs a lift…or present some other slime-ball request. "Yes! How generous," she said. "A light week as the grand finale." Whoop-dee-freakin'-dooo.

"Anything for the love of my life!" he replied.

Oh, pipe the hell down, Maggie silently scolded, annoyed that he wasn't offended by her cynicism.

"So, I wanted to let you know that I might have to stay a few days longer here in New York," he said. "I'm not sure yet, but I wanted to give you a heads-up."

Blah, blah, blah…Not a damn thing has changed with this clown!

"Since we agreed to take some time to think about things, I'm sure my extended stay isn't an issue," he continued. "I respect your wishes, and I'm giving you your space."

Oh, cut the noble crap! And by all means, stay there for an eternity! "I appreciate the space. By the way, what's up with the text? Were you drunk texting around 1:00 a.m.?" Maggie asked with a slight chuckle.

No answer. Did he fall asleep? "Andrew?"

"Yeah, yeah…I'm still here. Just got distracted by a news story. Anyway, so yeah…I was just thinking about you. And yes, I had a few drinks with Tom Stewart and some other guys at the Manhattan Club."

Yeah yeah…yada yada. "Gotta say, the ebonics were hysterical."

"Huh?"

"*Dis* and *phire*…with a *p-h*. You sure *did* have a few!" said Maggie.

"Ha, ha! Well, I thought I might make you laugh."

"I totally laughed out loud." *At you!* "So, anyway…gotta run."

"Uh, okay. 'Bye, Bis—"

Maggie cut the call as a big, toothy grin spread across her face. His extended stay in New York was terrific news! Yesterday afternoon, a demotion; this morning, an extended pampering week!

I'm gonna ride this money train till that jackass is bankrupt, she told herself. "Choo choo!" she shrieked, mimicking a train whistle.

***

Maggie pulled into work a little early. She wanted to avoid a confrontation with her father in case he'd changed his mind about the demotion to part-time. Since it was a late-August scorcher, she'd selected a sleeveless silk blouse to go under the star-neck jacket of her Lord and Taylor suit. The softly muted rose color wasn't one of her favorites, as she favored warmer colors. In fact, Maggie was a fall girl all around and looked forward to the change of seasons that was only a few weeks away.

Minding the heat, she shed her jacket and proceeded into the building through the back door—the one Andrew used to enter when they were dating. She sneaked into her office, plopped her laptop case down, and sank into the roominess of her patched-up desk chair.

Before she could even get organized, a timid knock sounded at the door. "Yes?" Maggie said tentatively, knowing that she didn't have a client until 8:30.

"Ms. Spencer," said Margery in a scared little voice.

"Oh, hi, Margery. Do you need something?" she asked, when her administrative assistant peered around the door.

"No, Ms. Spencer, I don't need anything. Uh, well, I've come to give you this," Margery said, popping into the office and holding out one of the spare ruffled blouses Dr. Walters kept on hand in case of wardrobe malfunctions.

"You're kidding me!" Maggie said.

"I'm so, so sorry. Your father, well, Dr. Walters...he...well...he said that you either needed to wear this blouse or put your jacket on. I told him I'd be very uncomfortable approaching you in this manner."

"No, Margery...don't stress. You're just doing what was asked of you." OMG, he doesn't miss a thing! How did he even see me?

"For what it's worth, Ms. Spencer, I always think you look lovely...*and* professional."

"Ahhh, thanks, Margery, but I won't be needing that ghastly discolored ruffled thing. I'll just throw my jacket on when a client comes in." At least that's what I'm telling you. Maggie chuckled to herself, picturing a client tattling on her for showing bare arms.

"Okay, Ms. Spencer. Sorry to bother you."

"You're no bother at all, Margery. Talk to you later."

Maggie dropped her head in disbelief as she morphed into mortified fashion mess, now fixated on the undesirable rosy color of her skirt. She pulled up her first crazy's profile and recalled that this client had some real hang-ups about body image, aging, blah blah blah.

The intercom buzzed. "Ms. Spencer?" Margery said.

"Yes?"

"Ms. Pierce, your eight-thirty appointment, is a little early. Are you available?"

Yep! Let's roll this nonsense right along! "Yes, Margery, that's fine. Send her up, please." Maggie did another quick scan of the woman's profile.

Sidney Pierce...hmmmm. Dealing with husband's adulterous behavior... taking 50 milligrams of something daily...serious identity issues...yada yada, blah blah blah.

"Sidney, hi! Come on in," Maggie said in her most caring voice as her client more or less plowed through the door. "Go ahead and get comfortable, please," she said, though her client was already reclining on the couch and propping her legs on the magazine table.

"*Comfortable*! There's no comfort in my world! I can't take this crap anymore. I don't know why Mitch has to be such a dick; you know? He's sleeping with one of his students at the university. And she's hideous! I mean what the hell am I? I'll tell you what I am...I'm over the hill compared with that *girl*." Sidney was up and pacing as she ranted. "When we got married ten years ago, we decided not to have kids because he already had two by his first marriage. Plus, he said he didn't want me to become all stretched out and saggy. Now this...this *millennial* he's seeing is about half my age and twice my size."

Ewww…I bet she's a real cow! Maggie thought.

"I mean, what's going on here? I bust my ass at the gym. I keep up my mani-cures, my pedicures, my hair appointments, my facials…I need some answers, right now!" Sidney said.

Okay, Crazytown. Sit down and shut your pie hole. "Sidney, have a seat. Let's start there," Maggie demanded with a bit of justified arrogance. "What I want you to do is take out the journal I gave you. Let's look at the pros and cons you've listed for yourself. Let's practice some self-affirmations and let that be our focus for right now," she suggested.

"I don't have the damn thing with me. And I'll tell you something…I had nothing on the con list, so I'm not sure why Mitch has such a problem staying faithful to me."

"Well, then, let's try something different today. I want you to look at me, pretend I'm Mitch, and let me have it! I will fire back to you in the manner in which he might respond. In other words, we'll role play, okay? Let's begin."

Sidney collected her thoughts for a moment and then said, "You're incon-siderate when you stay out all night and don't even give me a courtesy call."

"Well, I can't stand your bitching," Maggie said in a pretend man's voice.

"Of course, I'm a bitch! You're a control freak! You always pick on me…you tell me I'm fat…you watch me like a hawk," Sidney replied.

"Well, that's because I'm sleeping with other women. It's okay for me to step out, but you can't. I *have* to watch you…I *have* to know that you're not doing the same hideous thing to me that I'm doing to you," Maggie responded.

At that, Sidney's Botoxed face changed completely. It now sported lines and divots that Maggie had never seen. "Huh? Mitch would never respond like that."

"I know, but he should if he were being honest. That's indeed the reason he's watching you so closely. Sidney, men oftentimes become the accuser after they've done repugnant things. You see, if they have someone to share the guilt with (even if there's no real foundation for it), they don't have to carry the burden alone. It's too painful for them, yet they'd never admit it. The male ego is too big. It's a bigger concept than even *they* can imagine." Maggie heard a victory bell in her mind as she spoke. "I want you to really be careful with your temper in the next couple of weeks, and when I see you next, I want you to tell me why a woman like yourself is staying in such an unhealthy relationship. *That* will make up your con list, and we'll go over it with a fine-toothed comb," she said with fire in her eyes.

Sidney looked like she wasn't sure if she had just been slapped in the face or hit the Powerball, but her gears were grinding, and she needed to put it in neutral for the day. So, she parked herself back on the couch, feeling the sting of a lecture that had rendered her motionless.

In the meantime, Maggie couldn't take her mind off Sidney's cheating hus-band. Not that she had sunken so low as to actually pursue a full-bore affair, but she *had* contemplated the idea—as payback to Andrew. She began to loosely scheme a feasible plan with Cheating Professor.

"So, tell me more about your husband, Sidney. The good stuff." What's he like in bed? You know…stuff like that.

Sidney's voice trembled as she made futile attempts at answering in a coherent manner. She twitched as she muttered little words, such as *good-looking* and *intelligent.*

Eh, not bad! Maggie thought. "Well, okay then, Sidney. I can see that this is hard for you today. It's important to think about the positives as well as the negatives," Maggie said. I am just so full of shit.

"Well…thanks," Sidney said uncertainly.

"Margery will see you at the front desk," Maggie said, giving Sidney a "hurry along" smile and a "you're dismissed" nod. Okay…one down and a ten o'clock to go!

Maggie continued to entertain herself by conjuring up more ways she might seduce Professor Pierce as she waited for her next appointment. Maybe she'd strut into his office wearing that silly schoolgirl getup she had foolishly purchased for an adventurous night with Andrew…or perhaps she'd suggest free pole-dancing lessons for Sidney, but first give the professor a private show. Ha ha…I'm ridiculous! she acknowledged.

Maggie quickly switched back to proficient therapist mode and followed protocol by keying in professional notes from her session with Sidney Pierce. And although Maggie despised her career, her favorite thing to do after a session was to record private notes about clients in a secret journal. She'd often look back at her humorous "prose" and have a good chuckle, which helped get her through the doldrums of a typical workday.

Her journal notes on Sidney Pierce were titled: *The Narcissistic Housewife of Carrington Heights and the Nutty Cheating Professor.*

"Oh, damn! That stupid pole," Maggie reminded herself loudly as she snapped out of her comical writing zone. She had more serious matters to deal with—like calling Greg from Oasis Pole Expressions. De-poling her bedroom was now a top priority. How would they ever sell the house with that *uglification* standing erect and unmovable? She continued to search through her cluttered desktop for pole guy's business card.

"Ms. Walters!" Margery interrupted through the intercom.

"Yes, Margery."

"Your ten o'clock is here."

WOW, time sure does fly when you're not with crazies. "Send her up, Margery." Okay, who's this nutcase coming to see me? I haven't even reviewed the history.

"Hi, Ms. Walters," said a mousey girl with a faint voice.

"Oh, hi…" Maggie did not remember her. "Please come in."

"Thank you."

Maggie was clueless. "Forgive me, please. I've been a little under the weather lately. So, can we start by reviewing your last session with me?" Maggie asked while continuing to scroll through her laptop in search of the client's file. She then subtly flipped through her private journal notes to see if there was any hint of who this woman could be. But there was nothing.

"I hope you feel better soon," said the client, staring down at the chipped hardwood floor. "I have the journal of pros and cons that you had me work on."

"Oh, wonderful!" said Maggie, practically leaping across the desk as if to tackle an opposing coach for his playbook. "Let's start there."

Maggie looked at the client's journal, hoping to find some hint of a name. Something. Anything that would prevent her from looking like a total jackass! But she had no such luck. The woman's journal entries consisted only of cons:

too skinny (Boo hoo…what a problem! Maggie thought.)

controlling parents (Yep, all too familiar!)

not many friends (Hmmmmm.)

no hobbies (Hmmmmm.)

controlling, cheating husband (Ha! Wanna compare?)

Wait, was this Maggie's journal? As she continued to read the list of undesirable qualities, Maggie's thoughts drifted to her own mess of a life. She ran her hands through her hair, pressing tightly as if to squeeze out the sickening tension that was knocking heads with her emotional box of pain, which once again stabbed her in the gut.

"Uh-huh," said a rather detached Maggie, while listening to the client.

"Blah, blah, blah," the client went on.

"Yes, yes," Maggie agreed…to something? To what?

"Blah, blah, blah," the client prattled.

"I see," said Maggie…*still* clueless.

Finally, the client interrupted Maggie's troubling thoughts. "Are you okay, Ms. Walters? Should I come back another day?"

"Yes. Yes, perhaps another day would be best," she replied.

"So, should I schedule another appointment at the front desk?" the client asked.

Yes! Uber-efficient Margery will have her data on file! I'll check with her later for client Whoever's info. "Yes, that would be fine. As you know, we are in the process of transferring the business to Dr. Ted Worthington. So, if you need to update any information, Margery will be more than happy to assist you."

Maggie immediately slipped into a state of neurosis and entertained the fantasy of taking on a random affair.

"I hope you feel better," said the unknown client.

"Thank you," Maggie replied, feeling no desire to record anything in her comedic journal about client What's-Her-Name, who seemed to be in a sad, sad situation—one that Maggie was all too familiar with. There was no way she was going to poke fun at this young lady, who was completely harmless.

Perhaps that was why there were no notes in her private journal about this client. Maggie had a heart for the underdog…it reminded her of the reason she'd become a clinical therapist in the first place. And she was completely ashamed of her work ethic in negligently deleting this client's file. There was no other explanation for such unprofessionalism. I need to get the hell out of this toxic lifestyle, she thought as she swiped an irritating strand of hair off her forehead, thinking that Andrew couldn't get home soon enough, so she could start the process of reinventing Maggie. Step one: file for divorce!

Maggie's earlier zest had left the building, and she was all too ready to free herself from the drudgery. She hadn't even come up with a pampering plan for the rest of the day yet. Instead, she found herself crestfallen, as numerous issues stirred within her. She sobbed gently, careful not to smudge her mascara. She wasn't sure if tuning out the sad-sack life of client No Name had made her feel so deflated or if it was the knowledge that she'd become entirely negligent within her career, disregarding everyone else's problems, while boo-hooing her *own* status. Or was she merely ashamed of entertaining the fantasy of a hookup with Professor Pierce?

I gotta get out of here, Maggie thought as she gathered her things and patted her eyes with a tissue. This place makes me crazy!

She quickly changed gears and exulted in the fact that she was headed for one of Sal's monster burgers and whatever cake du jour might be spinning around in the rotary case. And, she was looking forward to chatting with Lindi about any old thing, really—burgers, cakes, middle school…yada yada, blah blah blah. Anything but deception, parents, husbands, or clients!

CHAPTER

19

It's Complicated…and Layered!

Maggie shook off her rather disturbing Monday morning with crazy Sidney and client No-Name as she arrived at Sal's for a gal-pal lunch chat with Lindi. She strolled into the diner with great confidence, unconcerned about bare arms, micro-managing fathers, or complicated relationships.

"Maggie!" a booming voice shouted.

"Hi, Lindi. How are you?"

"Great, thanks! How was your weekend?"

"Not bad. Not bad at all," she responded, losing eye contact with Lindi.

"Whatcha do?"

"Uh, you know…just dinner with my parents. Nothing exciting, really," Maggie replied, wanting to steer the conversation away from her mess of a weekend. "And you?"

"Work, work, work!" Lindi replied.

"No fun stuff?" Maggie asked.

"Actually, I was able to make it over to the Berlin Loft. They showcase some really great bands over there. But Saturday was grunge tribute night. There was an awesome band called Kobain. Not sure if you've heard of them?"

"I have, actually! Kobain with a *K*, right?"

"Yeah! So anyway, these dudes are a real good time and still rock like they're in their twenties or something."

"Wow! Good for them," Maggie replied with great interest but still wondering why her mouth wasn't wrapped around a big juicy monster burger by now.

"So, you're a fan?" Lindi asked.

"Fan of?" Maggie replied, thinking that she'd soon be a nonfan of Lindi's unless a big fat plate of comfort food were to magically appear.

"You know...old grunge."

"Oh, yeah. Definitely." Now take my order, please!

"Funny...I pegged you for something so different, I guess."

"I might look all professional, but...well...let's save those stories for another time." Please, as much as I want to chat with you, right now I need a burger in me!

"I'll look forward to that. So, do you need a menu?"

Finally! Thought you'd never ask! "Yes! I'm starving!"

Lindi slid a menu across the counter in Maggie's direction. "By the way, how's your sweet tooth today?" she asked, stooping behind the lunch counter to pull out the most amazing work of art. "Betty Ann, our pastry chef, made this buttercream ruffle cake! How awesome is this?" said Lindi, beaming at the tall cake, coated with layers and layers of tan and white ruffles.

"Oh, wow! That's beautiful!" said Maggie, ready to dive right in. "Sort of looks like a wedding cake."

"It is. Sal's letting her promote her side business in here. I think he has a thing for Betty Ann," Lindi said on the down-low. "We're selling this one by the slice."

"Looks great, but I've been indulging a bit too much, lately...I'll pass on the sugary ruffles today."

"Speaking of ruffles...I have to ask," Lindi said.

Maggie panicked for a nanosecond and looked down to make sure she hadn't put on the wouldn't-be-caught-dead-in ruffled blouse her father had sent with Margery.

"Do you remember when we were like twelve or something, and your mother came into the school looking for you for some reason? You were embarrassed by her ruffled blouse, and you asked if she'd killed a Pilgrim."

"Oh, yes...yes, I remember." Maggie chuckled. "And my father grounded me for being disrespectful. But, yes, my mother was the ruffle queen. Layers and layers of ruffles! Still wears them!"

"No way! I personally thought she had great style," said Lindi.

Ya think? "Yeah, she's always well put together," Maggie said, now quite hungry and feeling the urge to smash the ruffled cake. "So, it was great, running into you last week. I can't believe it's been, like, twenty-five years or something!"

"Yeah, I know…wish we had more time to catch up today," Lindi said.

Bummer," Maggie thought. I'll have all the time in the world…after I eat!

"But anyway, you're hungry. What can I get for ya? I have another thirty minutes on my shift…I'll take care of your order."

"Great; thanks."

"Oh! I forgot!" said Lindi as she extended a different menu in Maggie's direction. "Here's Sal's healthy menu. Judging by how great you look, I figured you'd probably want to take a look-see."

Awww, so sweet of you to say that, but I want the real deal…carbs, sugar, fat!

"I must admit," Lindi said, "Sal's healthy-alternative selections aren't too bad. And he's completely stoked that they've been selling. I, personally, recommend the grilled-turkey Reuben on multigrain bread. It's layered with a low-fat Swiss cheese, a bit of fat-free Thousand Island dressing, and, of course, a heap of overpowering sauerkraut. Lots of probiotic power in that sandwich! And he toasts it in the oven with a little mist of spray butter instead of all that sinful frying. Sal's been getting on the other girls to push it…and it's truly not bad." Lindi leaned in to assert the last bit of her sales pitch.

"Oh?" Maggie feigned interest. "Well, that does sound good…I'll have one of those." She secretly would have preferred a sloppy cheeseburger and crossed her fingers that a few fries would make their way onto the side of the plate. After all, it was pampering week!

A few minutes later, Lindi slapped down Maggie's lunch. "Here ya go. Enjoy!"

"Thank you! It looks great!" She sank her teeth into what she'd always imagined cardboard would taste like, hoping that it would morph into one of Sal's monster burgers. This is like…like sawdust meshed with fermented cabbage gone bad or something.

"How's everything?" Lindi asked a few minutes later.

"Fabulous! Great choice! And what a nice little treat on the side. What is that?" It's disgusting!

"It's Sal's black bean salad. Isn't it to die for?"

Well, more like to die *from*. Maggie tried hard not to grimace as she nodded her head affirmatively.

"I'm not sure how he makes that, except there's some sort of light vinaigrette in it. That much I know. But I shouldn't be talking about his recipes. He'd be outraged!"

Pretty sure his recipe secrets are safe! Maggie thought, chewing.

"Here he comes now…I'll talk to ya in a few minutes. My shift is just about over."

"Lindi! Make sure the back-room tables are set up for the dinner crowd," Sal said. "Last week, we got hit and needed to seat people in there."

"Okay, big boy!" Lindi growled back.

Amazing, Maggie thought, chuckling slightly. She could picture herself talking to her father with a new flair.

"Oh, hey, you!" Lindi shouted to a rocker dude with tousled hair coming into the diner.

Maggie looked over at him. Oh, my! Who's the Dax Shepard-lookin' hottie?

Lindi leaped into the arms of the mysterious guy, and he swung her around, laying the hottest kiss on her that Maggie had ever seen.

"Sorry if this is too nosey, but who is that?" Maggie said to the young server who'd just come onto the scene to replace Lindi.

"I'm pretty sure that's Dagger, Lindi's boyfriend. He's the lead singer of Kobain. He's all she talks about lately."

No wonder! Maggie thought, unable to stop staring at the two of them embracing and having a sidebar conversation.

"'Bye, babe," Lindi said a few minutes later when Dagger gave the cool-dude fist bump and then blew her a kiss as he left the diner.

Lindi watched him walk through the parking lot, then turned toward Maggie. "Can I getcha anything else?" she asked.

Maggie had been so gratefully distracted by Lindi's love scene that she hadn't taken more than a few bites. "I think I'll take the rest of this to go." And chuck it in the trash when I get home.

"Okay, hold on a sec," Lindi said, reaching under the counter for a to-go box.

"So, Lindi, aside from your business plans, tell me what else has been goin' on," Maggie asked, eager to get girlfriend chummy.

"Well…you know…just plugging away with my Yoga-to-Go. And like I told ya last week, I'm really lookin' to someday open a yoga studio. That's really all I have goin' on right now," said Lindi.

Hmmmm…don't wanna tell me about the boyfriend, I see. "Well, I hope it all works out for you," said Maggie.

"Thanks! I appreciate that. So, we need to schedule a cocktail date, then we'll have some real time to catch up. Right now, I gotta run," Lindi said abruptly, while waving to the server taking over her shift. "I'll see ya soon, I hope."

Maggie's gut tightened the way it always did when disappointment took over. That's it? No asking me what I'll be doing this weekend?

"Later, Sal!" Lindi called into the kitchen.

"So, what are you up to this weekend?" Maggie blurted in an ask-now-or-be-lonely-this-weekend fashion. "It seems so far away, I know, but I hear it's supposed to be beautiful."

Lindi had one foot out the door. "Really? I heard something about rain."

"Oh...maybe I heard wrong." Maggie, you dumb ass, she chastised herself. Just ask her to go shopping or something!

"You know what?" said Lindi, now back inside the diner and sporting a serious thinker face, "I have a couple shifts I'd like to unload. I might just call in a few favors. I've been wanting to check out this loft that's coming available for a yoga suite. In a town called Laurelton...a big lake community. Lots of year-round vacationers who aren't afraid to drop some serious cash. At least that's what I hear," she said, winking and rubbing her fingers together, indicating the big-spender potential.

"Yes, I know the area well!" Maggie said. "My in-laws have a house on Keasley Lake. There's also that big ski resort in the neighboring town."

"Oh? You're married? Didn't know that," said Lindi, looking at Maggie's ring-free finger.

Oh, shit! Don't wanna get into all that nonsense. "Well, it's...it's complicated right now, Lindi."

"Sorry to hear that," said Lindi, picking up on Maggie's reluctance. "So anyway, I'd like to check it out. Not sure I wanna dive right into a purchase...I was just lookin' to maybe rent for a while. I don't know...it's such a big step. One of my personal yoga clients gave me an inside tip. He's a physical therapist. Do you know Donnie Hayworth—Hayworth Physical Therapy?"

"Oh, yes. I drive by it often."

"So, he has a house on Lake Ellis...the adjoining lake, I believe."

"Yes. It *is* Lake Ellis," said Maggie.

"Anyway, Donnie's good friends with the owner of this loft, who's moving out west for whatever reason. He's been tellin' me all about this place for some time. Says I should check out the area and at least consider it. Not sure why I've been draggin' my feet, but I wouldn't mind snooping around to get a feel for the area and what sort of business traffic runs through there. Would *you* maybe wanna go with me? Check the place out? Especially since you're familiar with the area? I hear Laurelton is very artsy and quaint."

"Yes, it is. And, yes! I'd *love* to go with you. In fact, we could stay at the lake house," Maggie offered.

"Oh, that would be great!"

"You'll love the area," said Maggie.

"Oh, good! Glad we're doing this!"

"Me too! There's tons to do. Lots of outdoor festivals like wine tasting, art shows, jazz bands. They even have a mini fashion show in the fall and spring. With Laurelton only an hour or so away from New York City, there are a lot of local designers in the area. And you might be interested in this: there are several cafes and bistros that feature farm-to-table dining. So, there's a very clean-eating mentality among the residents," Maggie said as if she were Laurelton's publicity rep.

"Wow, no wonder Donnie gave me a heads-up on this place! Hey, I'm sold," said Lindi.

"Oh, great! Can't wait to get there!"

"Hold on, Maggie. I don't wanna get in your business, but will your in-laws mind? You know…using the lake house? With things being complicated and all."

"Not at all," said Maggie, eager to nail down the invite. She hadn't been on a girl trip since the beach excursions with her college girlfriends, who, for all she knew, had kicked the bucket by now.

"Seems like everyone's having issues with men lately," Lindi said.

Really? You practically porno'd your hot rocker boyfriend in front of the whole diner. Eh, whatever…it'll be fun to boy bash!

"Speakin' of rotten dudes," Lindi continued, "would you mind if we meet up with my friend Jillian for lunch sometime over the weekend? She lives about forty-five minutes north of Laurelton, but I don't think she'll mind driving down to meet us. I feel bad because I've had to cancel on her a couple times. She has a real told-ya-so situation goin' on," Lindi said. "If you'd like, I can just meet her myself…don't wanna burden you."

Boo! No Debbie-downers, please! "Oh, that's fine. We can meet for lunch."

"Don't worry. I won't mention you're a therapist. She'd be talkin' your ears off."

"Oh, no! Can't have that," said Maggie.

"So, you have my business card," said Lindi. "Give me a text, so I can save your info. And b-t-dub, I'll drive, since you're takin' care of the lake house."

"Oh, okay. That works."

"Well, hey…gotta head out. Talk to ya later!" said Lindi as she headed for the door.

"Oh, okay. See ya!" Maggie sipped the last of her diet Coke and simply could not erase the permanent smile that stretched across her face. As she got up to leave the diner, the vibration of her phone deep inside her bag startled her. Oh, hell, she thought. It's probably my flaming jackass of a husband. She hesitated for a moment, hoping Andrew hadn't come home early…hoping that he was, perhaps, stranded in New York…or held hostage…anything, as long as she could at least get her girl-bonding getaway in before serving him with a proposed divorce settlement. She ignored the call, allowing her phone to vibrate its way to the bottom of the bag.

Maggie had driven a few miles away from the diner and still felt an incredible surge of happiness. In a few days, she'd be shedding the burden of an aggravating career and reconnecting with an old friend—a no-nonsense, low-maintenance friend. Someone who couldn't care less about a slight paunch, professional office clothing, social status, or any other kind of hooey! Her week of pampering had reached an all-time high, yet she hadn't stepped foot into a salon, nor eaten a Sal's monster burger or a piece of that goopy chocolate thing in the dessert case. Thinking she'd soon get back into her toning routine—next week, after the divorce chat—Maggie decided there was no way she would deprive herself of a few well-earned indulgences. She made an illegal U-turn and drove back to Sal's.

***

Maggie skulked into the diner in hopes that no one would notice that she was making her second visit of the day. Could she simply order the whole cake that was displayed? Not the ruffled one, but the one that dripped with peanut butter frosting and featured pockets of extra fudge tucked into the three layers of mind-blowing chocolate. She stood mesmerized in front of the display case until a semishrill voice interrupted her trance.

"Hi, sweetie! The cakes are to die for!" said a pudgy, middle-aged woman wearing a food-stained nametag that read *Betty Ann.* "Weren't you just here a few minutes ago?"

Aaaaaaaand, it looks like Betty Ann the baker is also the cake police, Maggie grumbled to herself.

"Hi. Yes…so I was wondering if I could purchase the entire triple-layer chocolate cake right there," Maggie asked, pointing to it.

"Oh, my! Someone's got a sweet tooth!"

Shut your pudgy face, Betty Ann, so I can get out of here and stab a fork into that bad boy, Maggie thought, practically drooling over the raised swirls of frosting. "Well, actually, it's for a dinner party. Is this going to be too complicated, or what? If it is, I'll just be on my way. No worries," Maggie said.

"Oh, my, no…it's no problem at all. Let me just box it up for you."

"Thanks," Maggie said, eagerly tapping her strappy-sandaled foot on the grease-laden diner floor, anticipating the satisfaction and delectability of her weeklong sugar fix.

"Here ya go, sweetie," said Betty Ann, holding a sturdy cake box. "And I believe you forgot this," she said, handing Maggie the to-go box with her lunch leftovers.

"Oh, my. Thanks for saving it," said Maggie. Is there a trashcan in the parking lot? she wanted to ask.

"Have a great day, now," said Betty Ann.

***

Maggie rushed into her house, heading straight for the kitchen to grab the nearest sharp object to slice through the chocolate layers of deliciousness. She could no longer wait to take pleasure in her little infused piece of heaven. Besides, she'd had two bites of a healthy yet unsatisfying sandwich—this little treat was well earned. She kicked her shoes off a corner and dropped her keys and bag in the middle of the kitchen floor, careful not to tip the bakery-boxed cake.

Maggie was about to stab her fork into the mound of fudge-drenched heaven when an avalanche of self-doubt poured over her. She threw her fork down and pushed the cake away from her, struggling to block out her horrendous behavior as of lately. The weightiness of playing Andrew for a fool was crashing down on her. Who was she? she pondered.

Maggie took a deep breath and picked up her fork. But her triple-layered afternoon delight had all but vanished. One bite left. Where had it all gone? Had she even fully enjoyed it? Taking that last bite of the "heavenly monster," she tried her best to turn off the switch in her cluttered mind. She did not want to think about how she'd clean up her fabrications or reset her life on the right track, so she simply burrow her way back into bed for an afternoon nap. As she swaddled herself with an eyesore of mushroom-colored sheets, the *eww* factor prompted her to kick off a few layers of bedding that had been, at one time, very appealing and solacing to her.

***

After a long nap, Maggie awoke to the sound of nothing. No neighborhood traffic. No birds chirping. She was well rested and turned her thoughts toward planning what she'd wearing on her girls' weekend.

Ambitiously, she began to try on all sorts of outfits. "Crap!" Maggie shouted at a pair of jeans that showcased her slightly bloated belly. I'd better lay off the sweets and revisit that pole, she thought, recalling how beautifully toned she'd been several months earlier. She decided to throw random garments into the oversized duffel bag, packing it full of clothes she'd probably be able to wear and clothes she hoped to get into by the end of the week. She remembered reading up on the keto plan—some faddish diet that resulted in quick weight loss. Eh, I'll sleep on that idea, she thought.

Maggie plopped down onto her shambled bed and began to assess the day. I'm so glad Lindi invited me to a GNO weekend, she thought, glowing over the beginning stages of a new friendship. Her mind turned quickly to the litany of Andrew's lies and duplicity, which sufficed to justify her *own* outlandish conduct. Although she was eager to get back into her toning routine, the obnoxious dancer's pole did have to go. She'd find some other way to tone. Besides, how could they sell the house with that silly thing taking up floorspace in the bedroom?

Maggie decided to Google the guys from Oasis Pole Expression and put these de-polers to work. But the phone interrupted her mission.

"Maggie, dear."

"Oh, hi, Mother."

"Were you expecting someone else?"

"Nope."

"Nope? Now Maggie, there's no need for such informality," her mother scolded.

Of course not, you bore. "So, Mother, what can I do for you?"

"Well, darling, I called earlier, but you didn't answer. I merely wanted to check up on you to see how your day was…with a reduced case load and such."

Oh, that call was from you. "Thanks, Mother. I appreciate that. I had a wonderful day, in fact. I ran into an old friend a few days ago, saw her today, and we made plans to go up to Laurelton this weekend."

"Oh?"

"Oh? What do you mean by *oh*?" Maggie asked.

"Maggie, I suppose I'm just an old-fashioned gal, but a weekend away… with a girlfriend? Aren't you *well* passed the college-age years? Is that really what a mature married lady should be doing?"

"I don't see anything wrong with it, Mother, but let's move on. You asked about my day, and I wanted to let you in on how great it truly was. It's been a long time since I've…" Maggie stopped. There was no need to open this particular can of worms with her mother right now. What was she thinking? Having a normal mother-daughter conversation where true feelings flowed freely?

"I know it's been a long time since you've seen your college girlfriends, darling. And what does your friend's husband think about this little excursion? Which friend is it, by the way?"

Maggie recalled being cut off when attempting to discuss how she'd run into Lindi Wallace at the dinner party Saturday night. She decided to go with, "You don't know her."

"Okay, well then, when do you think you'll return? Your father and I would love to have a family dinner when both you and Andrew can make it."

Ughhhh! I'd rather chew off all my toenails. "I'll get back to you on that. I need to check in with Andrew, actually."

"Very well, dear. I'll speak with you later this week."

"Good-bye, Mother." Click.

Needing a diversion, Maggie rummaged through the clothes that didn't make the trip bag and were strewn about on the floor. Was she really surprised that her fun-girl clothes were a little tight on her jiggly thighs? *If I continue down this path, my ass will spread from coast to coast,* she thought as she patted her bloated tummy.

Maggie plopped down on the bed, completely vexed. Although she'd had a wonderful day, for the most part, it was hard to shake the life she'd gotten caught up in. And her mother's judgmental airs certainly didn't soothe away the frustration. She crawled back into bed, hoping to nap until Friday, when she'd be well on the way to a carefree, blissful weekend. But she was still in Monday, riddled with anxiety about carrying off the good-wife routine for just a few more days.

CHAPTER

20

Tuesdays with Corey

Maggie's Tuesday morning was more like a Snooze-day morning. She had tapped the snooze bar on her alarm clock several times, not wanting to report to her charade of a career—one that had been nearly phased out. Awww, just a few hours of hell, she thought as she rubbed her tender temples. Her stomach began to growl, reminding her that she hadn't eaten dinner last evening. Instead of turning toward the kitchen for a supersized coffee, she reached for her phone to make a call to the local fitness club.

"Good morning. Carrington Heights Fitness Club," chirped an irritatingly upbeat voices, whose owner Maggie pictured as a superfit, model-type girl high on life.

"Yes, hi. I'm calling to check on membership fees at your gym," Maggie replied.

"Will you be a first-time member here at C H Fitness?"

"Yes."

"Okay, we have a first-time membership package of fifty dollars a month for the first three months. After that, the fee will go to sixty-five dollars a month. We also have a family plan, which is really the best deal."

"No, no…it's just for me. But do you offer, perhaps, a one-week guest pass or something? I'd like to see if your gym is a good fit for me."

"Well, I can check on a temporary membership, but there's not a lot we can do for you in a week," the chirpy woman said.

"I understand," said Maggie, feeling her snark index rising, "but I'm still interested in that plan if you can work up a deal."

"Super! Then what I'll do is talk to the director about a special rate for you. We're all about wellness here at C H Fitness. Let me just put you on hold for a minute. Our fitness director has just arrived."

Maggie zoned out, wondering if the whole gym thing was really necessary. Oh, why don't I just use the pole for another week, she thought, deciding to end the call. Too late!

"Ma'am…thank you for holding. Our director has simply prorated the fee for a week, which would come to $16.25."

Caught off guard, Maggie said, "Thank you so much for doing that, and would it be possible…" She hesitated. "To make an appointment for today?"

"Oh, certainly. We'd be happy to set you up for a tour and plan your exercise routine according to your needs. I'm very pleased that you're taking these steps toward wellness. Let me just get your name, please."

Calm down, Bubbles. You're way too excited about your scripted greeter job. "Okay, so I'd like to make an appointment for three o'clock this afternoon if I could?"

"That would be fine. Can I get your name, please?"

Maggie drew a blank. Suddenly, she couldn't remember her own name.

"Ma'am?…hello? Ma'am, are you still there?"

"Uh, Samantha…Samantha Jones," Maggie said as a sudden sickness consumed her. For the first time ever, Maggie resented that lovable tramp from *Sex and the City* for having such an easy, roll-off-the-tongue name. What the hell is wrong with me? Really? Samantha Jones?

"Fabulous, Ms. Jones. And my name is Melissa. You can ask for me when you arrive. I'll see you around three. Have a fabulous day!"

Click.

Damn it! She'll wanna see my ID, I suppose…ugh! I'm out of control, thought Maggie. She called the gym back in order to cancel her appointment but quickly cut the call when she heard way-too-energetic Melissa's voice once again. *Damn!* Maybe I just won't show up, she thought. It's not like she'll be able to track down Samantha Jones. Ha ha!

But she'd at least pack a gym bag for the day. Maggie was eager to move the morning right along and strolled to her closet to pick out the day's office attire. I guess this camel-colored thing will do, she thought, rolling her eyes as the gauzy, colorless blouse slid over her shoulders. She'd be sure to change into something with some sort of style dignity for lunching at Sal's.

***

Maggie became irritated on the drive to work, running up against a detour that would inevitably delay her arrival time. She called Margery, the office assistant, to report the circumstances, so her father wouldn't have a cow. While driving on the unfamiliar roads, she began to zone out, recalling a time when she and Andrew joked about his running late for one of her father's legal meetings after a session of what *they* called "naked-yoga-therapy" in Maggie's office. He'd clowned around, imagining the excuses he'd offer. *"Hi, Sir. Sorry I'm tardy! I just had your daughter nailed to the wall."* Or, *"Sorry I'm a bit wobbly, Sir…your daughter just gave me the most staggering blow job!"*

Maggie laughed, remembering how Andrew would meticulously pat himself down with baby wipes in order to rid himself of any lingering scent of sex. She smiled at the thought of what they'd once been together. How much fun they'd had. How playful and daring they'd been throughout their engagement. So much exhilaration! But she'd been duped. She'd drunk his Kool-Aid, just like everyone else.

A heavy sigh rolled out of her as she chalked these thoughts up to *once upon a time, not so long ago*, when suddenly, she was alarmed by the sound of a road worker's shout.

"Hey, lady! Pay attention!" he bellowed. "Don't you see the stop sign I'm holding?"

"Oh, get back to work, you doofus!" She wasn't sure where the word *doofus* had come from, but she'd be sure to use it for Andrew too—after all, he was knee-deep in Dupesville, so Doofus seemed quite fitting. A devious grin swept across Maggie's smug face.

***

Arriving late, Maggie marched straight into her father's office to double-check that Margery had notified him that she would be tardy. "Dad, hi… good morning. I assume Margery told you I'd be late."

"She did," replied Dr. Walters, his stoic face buried behind a file.

Damn! He's pissy. "Okay then…have a nice day," she said as she turned to leave.

Maggie's gait resembled that of a wildebeest escaping a cheetah that was eyeing her. She made it to her office and slipped inside, closing the door quickly and catching her breath as if she'd escaped a hungry carnivore.

She had some time to prep a bit for her next client, so, patting her slightly sweaty brow with a grainy tissue, she sank into her rickety desk chair and pulled up her incoming client's history so there'd be no embarrassing episodes like yesterday's meeting with the who-the-hell-are-you client.

"Okay, so who's this joker?" she asked herself, browsing her client's chart. *Sessions to be held on Tuesdays…Corey Heckinger…DUI charges.* Oh, the hot guy, she remembered. Let's go Margery…buzz me and send this dude up, so I can blow out of here as soon as possible.

"Ms. Walters," Margery interrupted.

"Yes, Margery?"

"Your appointment has arrived. Shall I send him up?"

"Please do. Thanks, Margery," Maggie replied. "Great! This hour will fly by!"

Barely a minute had passed, and a young gentleman was standing in the doorway. "Hi, Ms. Walters," he said a confident voice, which startled Maggie. "Sorry if I alarmed you…your door was open."

Of course, it was…defective piece of shit! "Hello," Maggie said, doing a double take on her client. Yep! Hot guy! "Yes, the latch isn't very reliable, but come on in and have a seat."

My God, he's on fire! Maggie thought, noticing several shades of red on her face in the tiny vanity mirror on her desk. Am I really this horny, or is he absolutely breathtaking? "Will you excuse me for just a few minutes?" she asked, needing to visit the water cooler, which, at that moment, was her trumped-up code for visiting the ladies' room in order to get herself together—and undo one tiny button on an otherwise nondescript blouse, so her sexy lace bra might peek out just a bit.

Maggie returned to her session with Hottie, holding two cups of water. She apologized for the slightly humid air, while offering him a beverage. She then shut the door firmly and headed back to her desk to look further into her client's file. She saw that he was a bartender in a downtown bar, who apparently never heard of a cab or Uber.

"How are things going?" Maggie asked in a sexy voice.

"Fine, I guess…I just feel…I don't know…kind of dirty. Like I'm a criminal of some sort."

Dirty…yes, you thug. Nail me right here…behind the desk…till the door shakes loose.

Maggie couldn't take her mind off of the way he said *dirty* and wished she could tell him about her dancer's pole—possibly invite him to one of her "performances." Perhaps he'd get all horned up and then throw her around on his *own* dancer's pole. I mean, he's a bartender…he would understand lies and deception and one-nighters, she reasoned.

"Don't even think such nonsense. DUI charges do not discriminate. I mean, everyone's gotten a DUI or two. In fact, I got one in college," said Maggie.

"Really?" he asked in a shocked voice.

Okay, Maggie, shut your pie hole. Who cares if some young bartender thinks you're cool? "Well, you know…I really shouldn't talk about it," she replied.

"Of course, Ms. Walters. I understand."

"So, tell me, what would you like to discuss today, Corey? What's on your mind?"

"Well, I'm not really good at this…this therapy thing," he replied.

That makes two of us, Maggie thought.

"I'm just trying to own up to my mistakes," he said.

"Well, that's a good start."

"These sessions have to be quite boring for you," Corey said. "I mean, really, what's there to talk about? I'm only here to go through the motions as part of my DUI sentence."

We can go through any motions you want, you hot piece of…"Well, it's good to just talk about whatever's on your mind. Like work, for example. Oh, forgive me, I can't remember the name of the bar where you're employed."

"Zina's. It's quite the hot spot, as I guess *your* generation would say."

Watch it, boozer! You don't wanna be on my shit list, Maggie scolded silently. "Ha ha, how funny you are! My generation!"

"Oh, sorry, Ms. Walters. I didn't mean anything by it."

Okay, okay…I'll let that one go by. "So, continue. Zina's. Hot spot. Got it!"

"Yeah, so the money's pretty good there. Plus, I'm taking some online classes through—"

"Oh, yes, Zina's. I *do* know that place," Maggie interrupted.

"So, as I was saying…" Corey blabbed on, while Maggie drifted into a wacky daydream in which she, as her younger self, and Corey were making beautiful babies. But then her fantasy took a turn for the worse as it grotesquely shifted to having Andrew's babies! The vision of a baby boy, born with a girly magazine in his hand and smoking a cigar…and a girl, born topless with a little baby thong full of twenties.

That's some scary shit! A disturbed Maggie thought as she snapped out of her daymare.

"Well, hey, I'll look forward to seeing you out some night," Corey said.

Maggie looked at the session timer. Time had elapsed with Hot Guy. "Uh, yes, I'll look forward to seeing you as well," she said, clueless as to what or where he was talking about. As she straightened her posture, she caught an ugly glimpse of the beige dreadfulness. It didn't quite pull off the sexy, unbuttoned modification she'd hoped for. A cloud of mortification shrouded her as she felt Corey's eyes become glued to the hideous blouse, which now choked any sort of cool flirtation.

"So, I'll see you next Tuesday at this time?"

"Um, well…"

"Oh, never mind. I totally forgot that this is your last week," said Corey. "Well, thanks for everything, Ms. Walters."

"You're welcome, Corey. And by all means, call me Maggie."

Maggie led her steamy client to the door with a playful smile. As he left, she threw herself onto the crazy couch. She needed to come down from her "Corey high" and put herself in check. Why was she even thinking about hooking up with a client? She'd heard that this sort of thing happened quite often. But she'd be violating the code of ethics...she'd lose her license to practice. And although she'd turned into a highly irritated, snarky girl over the past several months, *she* would leave the profession on *her* terms—not due to some scandalous dismissal. Besides, she'd have to get out of her current mess with Andrew before entertaining the thought of another potential disaster.

Maggie pulled herself up off the couch to double-check her calendar, reconfirming that there were no more clients on her schedule. Ah, yes! I'm out of here! she rejoiced as her heel caught on a wrinkle in the area rug, causing her to sink down onto the crazy couch once more. She brushed her hand across the worn fabric, which, just a few minutes ago, had rested beneath Corey's seemingly rock-hard glutes. She couldn't resist another few sinful seconds of mischievous fantasizing. But she reminded herself once again that she had no business getting down to *that* kind of business with anyone.

Now steady on her feet, Maggie slipped out of her drab blouse and into a lightweight summer top, then she headed toward the door. She stopped and looked back at her old office, which screamed for a coat of paint, a pop of color and soothing designs in a new area rug, and a desk and chair from the current century—serious renovations! She was in complete disbelief that any sort of arousal could be stirred up within these cold, sterile walls that she'd called her workplace for several years. Now, it had been reduced to nothing more than a room full of craziness, and she was the lead crackpot. Nonetheless, it was refreshing to learn that Andrew hadn't completely numbed her ability to feel an attraction for another, even if her Tuesday sessions with Corey were over.

CHAPTER
21

Having Her Cake…
and Eating for Two

Maggie's adrenaline-charged Tuesday morning had rolled right into lunchtime. Her session with Corey had managed to increase her appetite, as the shameful yet playful thoughts returned, driving her straight into the arms of a monster burger.

"Hey, Maggie," a woman called from across the diner.

"Hey, Lindi," Maggie said.

Lindi slapped a healthy-side menu in front of Maggie, took the seat beside her, and began counting her tips.

Ewwww, I forgot about this light menu nonsense she's pushing, Maggie moaned to herself, still craving the monster burger. After all, she *could* order it without the roll—for the sake of keto or paleo or whatever was on trend. But why bother? She'd be heading off to her dancer's pole workouts after lunch… what not treat herself?

"So, you're just coming from work?" Lindi asked.

"Yes…and if you don't mind, Lindi, I'm going to pass on the light side today. My appetite's much bigger than that," Maggie replied. So, take that list of sawdust items out of my face.

"Oh, no problem! I'll give you a few minutes." Lindi extended an original Sal's menu to Maggie.

"No need, I know exactly what I want. I'll have Sal's famous monster burger. And a diet Coke."

"Okay…I'll get that right back to Sal. So, did you have a bad day or something?" Lindi asked, while setting a fountain diet Coke in front of Maggie.

Can't a girl just stuff her face? "It's a long story, but the truth is…well, I'm just a mess right now. All this crap with Andrew…"

"Andrew? Is that your husband?" said Lindi.

"Yeah, but things are pretty much over between us…it's been over for some time."

Lindi was silent.

"And, of course, working for my father isn't exactly easy," Maggie said. "At least this is my last week. Did I tell you I resigned? I mean, I gave notice like two months ago…I can't believe this week has finally come."

"With all due respect, Maggie, I just can't imagine cozyin' up to your father, telling him my life problems. I mean, I'm simply going on memory of him from years ago, but he didn't exactly seem like a people person. Sorry. I guess that was harsh."

"No, no…I get it, but he's truly a professional. And keep in mind that he's more in charge of the diagnoses and treating mental illness…not so much listening to *life problems*. He's really built quite a practice over the years," Maggie said, feeling an unfamiliar well of admiration. "But, yeah, he can certainly be difficult. And I'm sorry to have dumped all this on you."

"Oh, no worries. Life has its shitty side, for sure," said Lindi.

"And speaking of life problems…yesterday you mentioned your friend was in a mess of a situation or something?" said Maggie.

Lindi cocked her head to the side. "Oh, yes. Jillian. Which reminds me, I haven't heard back from her yet. Maybe I shouldn't have put out an invite…not really up for the whole guys-are-dicks conversation. What was I thinking? I gotta do the right friend thing, though. I'll follow up with her this afternoon."

Please don't! Maggie said silently. Three's a crowd, ya know? Let that invite die on the vine.

"Well, hey, we'll have lots more time to chat over the weekend. Right now, I gotta head out. I have a ton of things I need to get done," Lindi said as she pulled a cake from Betty Ann's secret cabinet.

Maggie was shocked to see that the cake was shaped like a penis, and *He's a Dick!* was written on it in thick, swirling, cream-colored letters.

"Uh, okay," Maggie stammered, thinking she wouldn't mind having a slice of penis cake in celebration of her soon-to-be separation.

Lindi caught Maggie eyeing the cake. "Isn't it awesome? I'm getting together with a couple girlfriends. We're having penis cake to celebrate a breakup."

"Oh?" said Maggie.

"Long story...talk later. Lookin' forward to the weekend!" Lindi shouted as the diner door closed behind her.

That's it? Maggie wanted to shout. Don't you wanna tell me about Dagger or some other dude who's a dick? Don't you want to know about my hot client that I'm not legally allowed to discuss? Don't you wanna discuss your troubled friend Jillian, even though I'm not really interested? Maggie wanted to lure Lindi back into the diner. She wanted Lindi to give her the full-friendship service. Instead, she had to settle for a big, fat helping of neglect. So, she flagged down another server and ordered a side of waffle fries with cheese to go along with her monster burger.

***

Feeling heavy and tired from her mammoth-sized lunch, Maggie sat for quite a while at the diner, perusing her email, scanning her Twitter feed, and checking the weekend weather forecast for Laurelton. But she was distract-ed...What's up with Lindi? she wondered. I can't seem to nail her down for more than five minutes.

Maggie stared at the diner door as if Lindi were about to come back into Sal's after running an errand across the street or something. She tried not to take Lindi's tendency to distance her personally; after all, Maggie was accustomed to that behavior; people had treated her that way for her whole life. Why would Lindi be any different?

Prying herself from the diner stool, Maggie plodded to her car. She then drove aimlessly around town, lost in thought and feeling strangely smothered. When Maggie nearly ran a red light, she came to an abrupt stop and was forced to check out her surroundings. Unexpectedly, she'd come upon Carrington Heights Fitness.

"Damn! Eh, maybe it's a sign...might as well check the place out," she said, turning left in the direction of the fitness club.

Driving into the parking lot, she noticed hard bodies and a few softies going into and coming out of the gym. She suddenly glimpsed a familiar body that had mesmerized earlier. A tight, mouthwatering body. One that stirred up an arousal that Maggie hadn't experienced in well over a year. Corey?

She whipped her car into a handicapped space in order to get a closer look. Was she really seeing her hot-body client walking into the gym she was content to blow off? Her focus was interrupted by a beeping cell phone. I'd better take his stupid call, she thought, so he doesn't keep trying to reach me. "Hello."

"Mags, baby!" bellowed a buzz-killing voice.

"Uh, hi," Maggie stammered, still watching Corey through the gym's enormous windows.

"Are you enjoying your light workload?" he asked.

"Uh huh…sure am." *Who's that Barbie doll Corey's talking to? I bet it's that Melissa pest,* she thought as Andrew rambled on about something.

"So, I just wanted to tell you I'm really looking forward to coming home," Andrew said.

"Uh huh, yeah, sounds great. See you then."

"Mags? Sounds like you're a little distracted. Where are you?"

"Uh, yeah, I'm in traffic. Not a good time to chat, really," Maggie replied as she slowly backed out of the handicapped space.

"Aren't you connected to your blue tooth?" Andrew asked, a tinge of reprimand in his voice.

"You know I hate the connection on those things. Half the time I'm asking people to repeat themselves…it's annoying. So, is there anything else, Andrew?"

"I'll just check in with you over the weekend. You sound a little testy."

Because you're an irritant! What are you not getting, dumb ass? "Okay, but you can just send me a text." *No need to be a buzzkill on my girls' weekend, as well!*

"Anything for you, darling."

Ugh…someone hand me a barf bag! "Sounds good. Again, the traffic is unbearable. Gotta go."

Click!

She paused for a few minutes, then took another look at Corey through the gym doors. *Well, I did schedule an appointment,* she reminded herself as she shut her car off. Maggie checked her face in the visor mirror, ogling her new shade of lipstick, nude pumpkin, which had plumped her lips into a bodacious smile.

As she approached the glass doors of the gym, Maggie caught a glimpse of her distorted reflection, making her frame look smaller and better toned. Her confidence soared. And her feet no longer felt as if they were clopping along like a heavy Clydesdale—they were now snappy and spry.

"Hi, I'm Maggie Walters. I have a three o'clock appointment," she said to the young woman at the counter, still unsure of how to clean up the little name fib from earlier.

"Hi! And welcome to Carrington Heights Fitness Club! Thank you for stopping in today," said the woman, whose name tag read, *Melissa.* With a puzzled gaze, she scrutinized the appointment screen.

"Is there a problem?" Maggie asked, hoping Melissa would answer with a resounding, *No, not at all!*

"Well, I'm not sure. The only three o'clock appointment is for a Samantha Jones. Oh, geez…" Melissa said, smacking her forehead and rolling her eyes.

"Ha ha! I must've gotten pranked! Samantha Jones…too funny! So, if you'd like to take *that* appointment, I can fit you in. Obviously, Samantha Jones isn't going to show." She chuckled. "My mom was such a huge fan of *Sex and the City*. Wait till I tell her about this!"

Okay, no need for a meek age jab, Maggie wanted to say. "Yes! I *will* take that appointment." And thanks for helping me out from my very own fibberoo, millennial greeter girl!

"But I *am* concerned that someone isn't following protocol here. You said you called in? Scheduled an appointment *here?*"

What are you now, the gym cop? "You know, I bet I called another gym. I had several brochures spread out in front of me this morning. Everything must've gotten jumbled up. It's my fault. I'm sure your staff is right on task. Now, can I get to that appointment?"

"No problem. I mean, we all make mistakes," said Melissa.

"Yes, we do," said Maggie with a fake chuckle in her tone. "So, will *you* be taking me on the tour of the facility?" Maggie scoped the place in hopes of being assigned to anyone else.

"Actually, I have to leave shortly. I'm going to hand you over to Chase," said Melissa.

Once more, Maggie shot a look around the gym to see if Corey was anywhere in sight. He was not.

"Ms. Walters, this is Chase," said Melissa. "Chase, Ms. Walters is a new member."

A deflated Maggie saw that Chase, while very striking and fit, was a Corey doppelganger. She'd have sworn he was the very client who'd given her quite a charge earlier that morning. But, of course, there was no sign in this man's eyes that he'd ever seen Maggie before.

"Nice to meet you. Why don't we get started," he suggested, opening his right arm as if to put it around Maggie, while pointing her in the direction of the ladies' locker room.

"Oh, uh, excuse me, Chase!" big-time nuisance Melissa interrupted, while Maggie stomped off toward the locker room.

"Yes?"

"Ms. Walters is expecting. I forgot to mark it on her chart. You'll need to set her up on the Mommy and Me program and see if she's interested in the Eating for Two nutrition guide."

Maggie, still within earshot, stopped dead in her tracks. Does she think I'm deaf? Maggie wondered. Her ears blowing steam and her face an infuriated fire-engine red, Maggie whirled around. "*Excuse* me, Miss?" she said with forced dignity.

"When we spoke this morning…oh, gosh. No! Never mind. I'm looking at another client's information. I'm so, so sorry, Ms. Walters."

"Chase, can we just get on with this, please?"

"Absolutely. I'll be right outside the locker room when you're ready," he replied, while he shot a stern look toward Melissa, whose head now hung in mortification.

"Thanks, Chase. I'll be right back," Maggie said as she sashayed into the locker room for a quick change. She wondered if she could make an escape through the locker room exit door without triggering an alarm. Although incensed and considerably embarrassed, she decided to honor the gym appointment.

She pulled out her ruched tank and her workout capris with the mesh side panels. She contemplated the exit door again, until she checked herself in the mirror, becoming ecstatically pleased with the fit of her sports tank. The miracle of ruching allowed the flaps of overlapping fabric to disguise any sort of out-of-tone jiggles. She took a deep breath. Okay, Corey impersonator, let's get this phony show on the road.

"I'm ready," she announced as she stepped out of the locker room.

"Okay then, let's get started, Ms. Walters."

"Oh, please call me Maggie."

"Will do," Chase said with a heartfelt smile.

Chase was lacking Corey's charm, and after much scrutiny, Maggie decided that his features were way off. His physique was quite similar to Corey's, however, and Maggie chalked the case of mistaken identity up to emotional wackiness. Nonetheless, she felt like a giddy schoolgirl who was seeking help with homework from the cutest boy in class. She had no clue what Chase was trying to explain to her—all the fitness equipment: body masters, free weights, abductors, adductors, yeah, yeah, whatever—who gives a shit?

CHAPTER

22

Wednesday's Agenda: Camouflaged Lectures and Words of the Day

M aggie awoke to the beautiful sound of a Wednesday-morning alarm. A soft, mellow tune from her cell phone setting soothed her ears instead of that ear-splitting siren of an alarm she'd been waking to. Her eyes became focused on her two-day-old bag packed with goodies for her trip, but sadly, it was only midweek.

I can't wait until the weekend! Then, reflecting on Lindi's emotional detachment, she thought, I hope Lindi doesn't turn out to be a dud.

In order to get things rolling, Maggie dashed straight to the bathroom for her morning shower. As the water gushed over her, she eased into a pampering meditation. She got lost in the luxurious sensation, which triggered a reminiscence of naked-yoga-therapy in Andrew's office, followed by a hot, steamy shower. At the time, she had been enthralled by the personal amenities in the small but luxurious bathroom off his cozy overnight quarters. Now, however, she now considered his office suite nothing more than a sleazy hideaway nook. But those showers, she had to admit, were the best! Sneaky and exhilarating, for sure! That part of their romantic life seemed so long ago. Andrew's hands would follow the curves of Maggie's body, which led to bending her into the downward dog position that first attracted him.

She wanted to continue her trip down memory lane, but another memory interrupted: the ludicrous howling noise Andrew would make as he positioned her in *his* favorite pose. His impression of what a horny dog might sound like had become loathsome and trite…and downright maddening.

Ingratiating jackass, she thought as the shower spray reduced itself to a pathetic drizzle and then to a drip. Sighing, Maggie dried off from her dud of a shower and pulled on the necessary-for-work beige baggage that was sure to ward off any kind of high self-esteem.

***

Maggie grudgingly arrived at her office, having just a few minutes to sip her mocha macchiato. Waiting patiently for her only client, she dutifully reviewed the profile and recalled this woman's fascination with dating much younger men, who'd often dump her for someone closer to their age.

And she's paying me for a lecture on how stupid she is…eh, another doofus! Maggie remained baffled by the emergence of the word *doofus,* but it triggered some much-needed laughter in her life. It would be her word of the day!

She decided to buzz Margery to see if, perhaps, her client was lingering in the reception area. She wanted to get this senseless show on the road.

"Margery?"

No answer.

"Margery, are you there?" Maggie said into the intercom.

Maggie left her office in a bit of a tizzy and headed straight for her father's office to see what was going on. As she approached, she heard voices. They were familiar voices she used to overhear on the telephone and behind closed doors while growing up. She was skulking by, hoping to catch some clear dialogue, when the door was flung open.

"Oh, Maggie, that beige color is not becoming to you, my dear," said an older woman with hideous, deeply set wrinkles and thinning hair who, nonetheless sported a lovely figure draped in the most exquisite designer fashions.

"Ms. Devon," said Maggie.

"I'm sure your father will fill you in on poor Margery. Toodles."

What a bitch! "Dad, where's Margery? Did something happen?"

"Margery is fine, Maggie. She retired without a major announcement to anyone but me. She wanted to keep it quiet. You know, she's a humble lady who doesn't want all the pomp and circumstance. Besides, Ted would like to remain loyal to *his* office manager once he takes over. I simply thought it would be best to nudge Margery along. I've provided her with a handsome severance package, of course. She was quite pleased with it. Eloise was kind enough to step in for the final months. She's very proficient, and she certainly knows a great deal about *this* practice. She's truly the best person to manage the office—especially now that *you're* leaving the practice."

"What! Why would you hire Eloise back? She's…she's mean!"

"Maggie, I won't have you speak that way about a woman who helped me build this practice to what it is today. She has been sorely missed around here for all these years. I'm thrilled that she's come back to the area, and I'm sure her son's family is overjoyed by her return."

"Uhhhh, okay, are you high or something?" Maggie growled under her breath. They probably can't wait for her to kick the bucket!

"Furthermore, it's *Ms. Devon*. You know she prefers everyone to address her that way. Please don't stir up unnecessary turmoil, Maggie."

Maggie's mind drifted to a chunk of summers, years ago, when Ms. Devon would tag along on their vacations, working privately with her father on some "caseload," while her mother read a book on the beachfront terrace. Maggie's resurfaced aggravation impelled her to crack her knuckles, mimicking the sound of twigs snapping during a windstorm.

"I had hoped that with a lighter schedule during your final week, your mood would've changed for the better," her father said.

"It has. I'm going to my office now."

"Very well, Maggie."

Doofus.

Maggie continued to her office, ignoring her father's not-so-subtle lecture. She then noticed that her office door was standing wide open, and her client had already situated herself on the couch.

"I must see you for a moment!" Ms. Devon barked, seeming to appear out of nowhere and startling Maggie.

For God's sake, Rip Van Wrinkle Face, stop lurking! "Yes? What is it?"

Ms. Devon closed Maggie's office door firmly to prevent the client from overhearing their conversation. "Maggie, you *must* tell that young woman in your office that she simply cannot come into a respectable place of business so…so scantily clad."

You are kidding me, Baldy! And who says *scantily clad*? Hmmm…*clad*… that's kinda funny, though! "I'm sorry, what?" Maggie replied, still dazed by the brash request.

"You *must* refuse to provide service to anyone so disrespectful to this establishment as to come here dressed like some…some common streetwalker," Ms. Devon replied in a hushed voice.

Streetwalker? I suppose that's old slang for *prostitute*? "Uh, okay, Ms. Devon…let's not discuss this right outside my office. If you don't mind, I'm going to see my client, now." Maggie hoped that Ms. Devon would just disappear…into traffic…into a storm drain…into anything, really.

As Maggie walked into her office, she took a better look at her client who, indeed, maintained a rather slender, taut figure for a forty-something. She was wearing a tight white tank top that clearly displayed her braless, semiperky breasts. Rounding out her attire was a *very* short denim skirt, which allowed for an unavoidable peek at a barely there thong. Maggie would be sure to request that housekeeping spray down the couch with sanitizer later.

"Hi, Nicole."

"Hi, Ms. Walters. And please call me Nicki," the client said.

"Oh, yes, that's right. You prefer Nicki…got it!" *A little old for the teen version of that name, aren't you? Oh, God…I sound like my ridiculous judgy mother!*

The client nervously began to explain her presence in Maggie's office. "That wrinkled lady let me in. In fact, she insisted. I'm so sorry."

Wrinkled lady…ha ha! "It's not your fault. Don't worry about it. I'll speak with her later." *But you do look rather slutty…no wonder Wrinkle-Dinkle wanted to shove you out of sight.*

***

While Nicki whined about her latest breakup—he'd left her for someone new…someone younger…same old, same old—Maggie stared right through her, occasionally nodding and agreeing to God-knows-what while her thoughts drifted to the various functions that had included Ms. Devon long ago. The woman's very existence had always created such tension. Everyone, except her father, seemed to be on edge when she came around. And that obnoxious, doofus-like son of hers, Thomas! "Thomas is going to West Point," wrinkle-clad Devon would brag. "His father would've been so proud of him," she'd gush, while feigning a bit of grief over her late husband.

Yeah, yeah, Wrinkle Dink, you probably killed him, Maggie thought facetiously.

As the client continued to babble, weaving her tale of woe, Maggie's eyes glazed over in frustration, anger, and a bit of shame as she thought about the numerous fabrications that had infiltrated her *own* life—those of her clients, her father, Ms. Devon, Andrew, and herself.

Seriously, Jabber-wacky…enough! You need to wrap this nonsense up and get out of here, Maggie thought, not wanting to face her *own* noise anymore. "Excuse me, Nicki…our time has just about expired. But here's what I want you to work on. I want you to do these meditation exercises," she said, handing her client a beautifully designed pamphlet she'd picked up at a seminar a year earlier. "And please, please practice your self-affirmations. I want you to think about all that's good. Your job, for example. You seem to be a very efficient office manager. Your boss constantly rewards you with bonuses, right?" Maggie asked, glimpsing a note in the client's file.

"Yes…very true. And the gifts! A Louis Vuitton bag, a new iPad…oh, the list goes on. He says he's helpless without me!"

Seriously, Nearly Naked Girl, those gifts usually come at a price. I should know! Maggie thought. "Helpless without you? What a great compliment. Your best affirmation would be to think about how much you're appreciated every day. And you seem to really enjoy your job, right?"

"Yes, very much!"

"Do you know how many people truly hate their career choices? They get stuck in dead-end jobs. They're too afraid to try something new. Geez, Nicki, I don't even want to open that can of worms." And you're looking at one of those worms right now…feeding you loads of advice that I can't even seem to follow myself, Maggie thought, heaving a sigh and trying her best to suppress tears. She glanced at the time once more.

"Yes, I suppose your right, Ms. Walters."

"Practice your affirmations. Do that for yourself," Maggie instructed as she stood up to see Nicki out. "Now, don't forget…you'll be seeing Anne Kramer next week."

"Oh, yes. Best of luck to you, Ms. Walters."

"Thank you very much. I appreciate that. You can see Ms. Devon on your way out to schedule an appointment." Damn! Ballsy Devon will ask if I spoke to her about a dress code. Ugh! "Hey, Nicki, I have one more question for you. This is a delicate matter…but I think it's something you should consider. Uh, does your boss approve of your…um…your very stylish fashion sense?" Good one, Maggie.

"Oh, I don't dress like this at work! Oh my, no! Ha ha ha! In fact, that's the one part of the job I truly dislike—having to dress so dowdy…and old. The workplace really sucks the life out of fashion, doesn't it?" Nicki asked, eyeballing Maggie as if to confirm that she'd gotten the "frump memo" as well.

"Yes, yes, it does! I don't know about you, but I've always been told that people attract certain types of…of others, according to how they dress," Maggie said, not finding it within herself to come right out and tell slutty-clad Nicki that perhaps a more respectable appearance might attract a more respectable man…and maybe she really should tone her nonprofessional garb way down.

"Well, I don't want to attract any old, frumpy men…that's for sure!"

Okay, doofus…you're so *not* getting my camouflaged lecture, Maggie thought as she all but shoved Nicki toward the door. "Ha, ha. Well, no, we wouldn't want that! Buh bye, now, Nicki. Have a great day!"

"Thank you," said the client as she struggled to walk in her high-fashion stilettos with lucent heels, which reminded Maggie of stripper pumps. Ah, yes, those ridiculous, tacky…*clodhoppers*, Maggie thought, cringing at the thought of archaic Devonlike vocab popping into her head. Ha ha…clodhoppers!

Now alone in her office and preparing to call it quits for the day, Maggie took another glance at her ever-so-fascinating client's profile. She'd noticed prior notes on a rather despicable, yet intriguing, disclosure. Nutcase Nicki had actually worn one of those sympathy pregnant bellies in order to keep her young boyfriend from dumping her.

Good God, what a hot mess! Wonder where she got that thing? Maggie said to herself flippantly. *That* would mess with Andrew's head!

CHAPTER

23

Crickets, Carbs, and Shit-Lists

That beige color is not becoming to you, my dear," Maggie mocked in her best Ms. Devon voice as she stomped through her house, irritated because an accident had detoured traffic away from Sal's side of town. Wednesday afternoon was now on Maggie's shit list.

She'd thought about calling her mother to discuss the return of Ms. Devon, but she wasn't quite up for the possibility that her mother might turn the conversation to somehow scold her for bringing up the topic. And she was equally disinclined to listen to her mother's subtle judgments on the impending weekend trip she'd alluded to the other day.

Abruptly, Maggie's phone beeped.

"Hello."

"Maggie, dear, I was just calling to check in on you. How have you been? Has your tension diminished a bit with having a lighter caseload?"

How sweet of you, Maggie thought. Now let the hammer drop! "I'm fine, Mother. I've had a very good week, in fact."

"I'm *sure* you miss Andrew, darling, especially since you have a bit more time on your hands."

Nope! not at all…in fact, I couldn't care less if he stayed in New York permanently. Now, go drink some more of his bullshit Kool-Aid.

"Well, dear," her mother said, "since this has been a bit of a pampering week for you, I thought you'd be delighted that I arranged for the two of us to join Rita and her daughters for tea tomorrow afternoon. Your sessions will be through by noon, won't they?"

Aaaaaaaand, there's the hammer! "Yes, I'm freed up by noon, but that won't work out for me," Maggie lied. "I have some appointments lined up that I simply cannot cancel." And how deluded are you? When have I ever shown interest in hanging out with those women? And I don't even like tea!

"Oh, dear, really? Nothing can be postponed? It's awfully difficult to get every single one of us together for a mother-daughter tea."

"I'm afraid not. I have to see Candace for my hair appointment. I'm having a mani-pedi done as well. And you know how hard it is to get into her salon. I wouldn't dare cancel."

"I thought you just had your hair done last week," Mother said.

Okay, you got me there, Sherlock.

"Perhaps I'm just confused," Maggie's mother continued. "Well, then, of course, by all means, get yourself all dolled up for Andrew's return this weekend. Have you two lovebirds done any further planning for the Paris trip?"

Someone hand me another barf bag…a whole value pack, in fact. "Uh, no, Mother."

"Well, I'm sure it will be wonderful."

"So, Mother, you'll never guess who I ran into at Sal's Diner."

"Whose diner?"

"Sal's. It's across town, near the old Center Street Marketplace."

"Oh, yes…now, Maggie what on earth would you possibly be doing over there?"

"A client told me how wonderful the food is, so I thought—"

"Yes, well that's fine, dear. I'm sorry to interrupt you, but Janice has just arrived, and we need to discuss a few things."

"Okay, see ya later, then." And thanks for cutting me off—once again!

"Now, hold on, dear. I might as well tell you…Andrew has hired Janice as your cleaning lady. He wanted me to get her into the house without your knowing, but I can see that it's not going to be easy."

"Oh, wow, that *is* a surprise. I know we've talked about hiring a cleaning lady for some time."

"It's all part of his pampering, dear. He knows how unsettled you've been lately."

Maggie scrunched her face into a give-me-a-fucking-break scowl. "Yeah, so the best time for Janice to come by would be Friday afternoon or Saturday morning. I'll leave a key for her," said Maggie.

"So, you'll be gone from the house during those times?" her mother asked.

"Actually, I'll be gone all weekend. Won't be back till Sunday evening. Remember? I spoke briefly of the trip to Laurelton the other day."

Maggie heard nothing but crickets in the silence that followed.

"Oh, Maggie, are you meeting Andrew and keeping your romantic trip a secret?" her mother finally said. "I think it's precious that you two still act like newlyweds!"

Stand down, flamer! "Uh, no, Mother. That's not what's going on at all. It's just a little getaway…for me."

More crickets.

"It's part of my pampering week," Maggie said.

"By yourself? I don't understand."

For God's sake, Stepford wife, get with it! "No, not by myself, *for* myself. The trip is for *me* to get away and do something fun."

"Oh?" Maggie's mother replied perplexed. "I'm sorry. I simply don't remember that conversation."

Okay, whatever. "Well, I haven't called the office yet to clear my Friday work schedule. It's just some final paperwork. I don't have any clients scheduled, so I'd appreciate if you wouldn't say anything to Dad. I'll let him know tomorrow."

"Darling, you know I don't get involved with office matters. Not to worry."

"Sooooo, as I've been trying to tell you, I ran into Lindi Wallace…an old friend from middle school. We've somewhat rekindled a friendship, and she asked me to go along to check out a potential business opportunity for her."

"Lindi Wallace? Oh, that name rings a bell."

"Like I said, she was a friend from middle school."

"Hmmm…no, I don't recall her as one of your school chums," Maggie's mother replied. "What is the nature of her business, dear?"

"She's a yoga instructor, and she—"

"Oh, yes. Lindi Wallace. Rita simply goes on and on about her Yoga-to-Go class. I believe that's what she calls it. She's a private instructor for the Worthington gals…does sessions right in their sunroom once a week."

Interesting…didn't know that. The Worthington daughters will be a great topic for gossip during the ride to Laurelton, Maggie thought deviously.

"Well, if this is all part of your pampering, I hope you'll find time to relax. And don't worry, I won't mention your trip with the yoga girl to Rita," said Maggie's mother.

"Why? What's the big deal?" And BT-dub, she's *not* a yoga girl, you snob!

"Oh, darling, it would be awkward to explain why my married daughter is going on a single-girl excursion."

"Okay, whatever, Mother."

"No need for attitude, Maggie. I'm just not comfortable with having that conversation. And I really must go now. Janice is waiting patiently."

Yes, please hang up…I'm completely over-the-top aggravated! "Will you tell Janice I appreciate her coming over? I'll leave a key with Dad when I go into the office, tomorrow."

"Very well, dear."

"Good-bye, Mother."

Click.

Tea with the Worthington bitches? Ha ha! *Right!*

Maggie's appetite had gone into overdrive. She briskly opened the freezer, hoping she'd find a frozen pizza. Yes! You little carb-loaded savior!

Maggie turned on the oven, ignored the preheating nonsense, and threw her pizza in to bake. She took a seat in her living room and stared out into the woodsy backyard, which had been a big selling point when she and Andrew were shopping for a house. A discontented face was reflected back at her in the window as she stewed over the lengthy sixteen minutes of baking time the pizza required.

"Why isn't the timer dinging yet!" she shouted. Impatiently, she marched back into the kitchen and stared through the oven glass. The cheese had barely melted, but she was full of hanger. So, she yanked the half-baked feast out of the oven, sat at her marble-topped bar, and chowed down. Yum, this is the best pizza ever, she thought as she bit into the barely chewable frozen center.

A few minutes later, Maggie schlepped her carb-infested self into the bedroom for an afternoon nap. Not having followed through with her firming and toning plans, she became highly provoked by the dancer's pole, standing firm and obnoxious in the middle of the room. On must-do list: get head out of ass and call pole guy before weekend, she told herself. I can't have Janice over here while the pole is still here. What would she think of me?

Maggie slammed herself onto the bed, both hands rubbing her temples, which were pounding *again*. After a few deep breaths, she began to talk herself down from anxiety-ridden thoughts. After all, Janice wasn't judgy. She'd never disclose anything that was none of her business. Besides, she could leave Janice a note, instructing her *not* to clean the bedroom.

Maggie's anxiety dissipated as she reminded herself that the weekend was only a few days away. She decided it would be best to nap in a pole-free room. Besides, the sunroom couch was always so comfy. She simply needed an hour or so to get out of the carb-coma. As her tension continued to ease, a slight sense of humor resurfaced. She looked toward the Echo device, "Alexa, wake me when it's Friday."

"I can only set a one-time alarm within the next twenty-four hours," Alexa replied.

Oh, take a joke, Alexa. Don't *you* get on my shit list.

Crickets.

CHAPTER
24

Thursday's GSD Agenda

Maggie was early to rise, and her Thursday morning mindset proved to be sharp and focused—she'd already drafted an agenda/to-do list and was primed and ready to Get Shit Done! She'd be leaving the next morning for a wonderful weekend away with a fun-loving, salt-of-the-earth kind of woman. Clearly, Lindi seemed to be pulled in different directions…and *perhaps* had shards of intimacy issues. At least, that was Maggie's premature diagnosis. But all in all, Lindi's blithe spirit was quite refreshing. And most importantly, Maggie was eager to welcome a judgment-free weekend. With such comfort and ease less than a day away, she could *surely* plug away for a few hours in crazytown, *right?*

Maggie curled up on her sunroom couch with a steaming cup of coffee and swirled in her favorite mocha café creamer. It was a beautiful summer day; the sky was an exotic Maya blue. But her weather app called for scorching temps, which made for the perfect kind of pool day. Maybe Lindi would like to hang by the pool this afternoon, she thought. What better way to discuss the weekend agenda? Lunch at Sal's, followed by some poolside banter and cocktails.

"My agenda!" she said, suddenly remembering it. "I need to get to it."

She reached for the iPad that lay on the magazine table in front of the couch, exposing her to-do list and various goals for the day.

At the top of the list was a reminder to call the office to reschedule Friday's paperwork.

She called.

"Walters Psychiatric Center," Ms. Devon screeched.

"Uh, hi…Ms. Devon." Maggie stammered as if she were choking on a disgusting piece of fruitcake.

Dead air.

"Ms. Devon, this is Maggie calling."

"Maggie who?" Ms. Devon asked snobbishly.

Ughhhh! "Maggie! Maggie Walters!"

"Oh, Maggie, please, *please* refer to yourself by your full name. How would I know whether or not you're a client?"

Maggie rolled her eyes so hard she felt a blood vessel break. Whatever, Wrinkle Face! "So, I'm calling because I won't be in on Friday to finalize paperwork. I will be going out of town, and I'd be perfectly willing to come in on Monday to wrap things up. So, if you'd kindly let my father know, I'd be very grateful."

"No clients tomorrow…Oh my, Maggie! What have you been reduced to?" Ms. Devon said.

Oh, shut up, you old hag! "Okay, so thanks for doing that," Maggie said through a forced smile.

"I'm not sure why you couldn't just see me in regard to this matter when you arrive at the office, Maggie."

Because I don't want to look at you, Wrinkle-mania!

"But yes, I will take care of this for you," Ms. Devon continued. "Margery certainly had folks spoiled around here."

Back off Margery, or I will absolutely punch those sagging crow's feet right off your face! "Yep, she was the best! And *everyone* misses her tremendously! Toodles," Maggie said mockingly and quickly cut the call.

Maggie paraded herself right into her father's office when she arrived at work that morning, eager to accomplish the second task on her list: give Dad a house key for Janice.

She knew he'd most likely let her know that Ms. Devon "didn't appreciate her attitude over the phone." But she didn't care. She was leaving for a long-overdue girls' getaway…a refreshing trip, sans the typical day-to-day drama.

"Good morning, Dad, I wanted to drop off my house key for Janice. Mother said she'd see that she gets it."

"Yes, your mother mentioned that Andrew had hired Janice. *And,* Ms. Devon told me you'd be out of town this weekend," her father replied, while perusing some paperwork.

Aaaand? That's it? No lecture? Good. Task number two completed.

"You know, Maggie?" her father said when she was *almost* out of his office. Aaaand, here it comes!

"I'd really like it if you and Ms. Devon could get along."

Maggie took a deep breath. "Yep. That would be great for office morale. But we can't…I've tried. So, have a great day. I'll see you next week," she said, while her father gazed in disbelief that his daughter had become so ballsy.

The third item on Maggie's to-do list was to call the pole guy. Maggie checked the time. It was 9:05 a.m.; apparently her Thursday morning client was running late, so she decided to get on with the humiliation of asking for someone to remove the senseless dancer's pole.

She called. And she was thrilled to be connected to voice mail.

"Yes, hi, Gregory. This is Maggie Walters, uh, Maggie Spencer. I was hoping to reach you in order to set up a time for someone to remove the dancer's pole you installed back in January. We are, uh, selling our house, and I'm not sure that it would be a good idea for the pole to be such a…a fixture. Will you please return my call so we can arrange for the removal? Thank you for your time."

She cut the call.

Whew…that's over with. Soooooo embarrassing!

While Maggie was slightly stressed by doing such an awkward task, she also felt a great sense of accomplishment. She was plowing through her list. Gettin' shit done is awesome, she thought. Her discomfort was lessening with every bold checkmark that appeared on the list.

"Ms. Walters," came a nasty voice on the intercom.

Ugh! "Yes, Ms. Devon?"

"Your nine o'clock has canceled, and Dr. Walters said he'd arrange for Ms. Girard to take your later appointment. You are dismissed."

Maggie scrunched her nose…dismissed? What the hell's wrong with you, Wrinkle Dink? "Very well, then."

Click.

Maggie thought about sticking her head into her father's office to thank him for the early dismissal. But she was too afraid of the possibility that Wrinkle-puss Devon had mistaken his instructions.

The fourth item on her to-do was the have lunch at Sal's. Could the day get any better? Maggie was now near the end of her to-do list. Lunch at Sal's was no real task at all. And surely, he'd serve a *very* early bird lunch to his newest loyal customer.

While Maggie was packing up for the day, her phone beeped. Ugh, hope it's not Andrew! But an unknown number appeared on her phone. Oh, perhaps it's Gregory from Oasis Poles, she thought.

She took the call. "Hello."

"Hi, Mrs. Spencer?"

Ugh! Guess I asked for that bullet, she thought. Maggie rarely used her married name, having kept *Walters* for professional reasons. Oddly, it was one thing that Andrew never really nagged about.

"Yes, this is she," Maggie replied.

"I'm returning your call about removing the dancer's pole."

"Yes, thank you for getting back to me. When do you think you'd be able to remove it?" she asked.

"Not sure…my guys are pretty busy."

Seriously? How busy can dancer-pole installers be? "Well, you see, I'll be putting the house on the market within the next couple weeks, and it needs to be gone," Maggie said.

"I understand, ma'am. We'll do our best to get there. Don't usually have too many cases of buyer's remorse with these things," Gregory said.

"Ha ha," Maggie said, faking laughter. "So, I'll be hearing from you soon, then?"

"Since you're in a pinch, ma'am, why don't I take care of it myself…Monday morning…around eight-thirty."

"Monday would be perfect!"

"All righty. Sorry it didn't work out for ya," replied Gregory.

Yeah, yeah, don't rub it in, doofus!

Click.

Maggie walked from her office, thinking that today's lunch might be her last meal at Sal's—for a while, anyway. Although she was enjoying her week of pampering, which was mostly burgers and naps, she knew that in just a few days, Andrew would return, and she'd be making some all-around life-changing decisions. But for today, as a gettin'-shit-done reward, the monster burger was screaming, *Grand prize*!

CHAPTER
25

The Good Wife

Maggie was intrigued by Lindi's Thursday morning "call-out" from work, as reported by Lucinda, the counter server at Sal's. Maggie hoped Lindi hadn't come down with something, only to bail on the trip. Surely, Lindi would've texted if something had come up.

Agonizing thoughts rolled through Maggie's mind while she sat poolside with her bagged lunch from Sal's. She scrunched her face at the monster burger, which had seemingly lost its heat and the waffle fries that no longer crunched. Such dissatisfaction led her to consider texting Andrew, like a *good* wife, to let him know she'd be staying at the Spencer lake house that weekend.

Nah, to hell with it, she thought as she spit the last of her soggy fries back into the bag. Besides, her focus was on tomorrow. Friday. Departure day. The big day! But was it? What did Maggie really know about Lindi, other than she was a smoking-hot forty-year-old woman who appeared to have great confidence, yet seemed to be a little out of place in life? Although, Lindi had a great start-up business, perhaps she needed to be a little more ambitious. Was she really serious about it? And *supposedly*, she had decent savings…but how did she manage to put money away? Were diner tips really that great? Or was she up to something shady on the side?

Perhaps, she's one of those high-paid escorts…with a body like that, I bet she does have quite a beefy savings account, Maggie thought for a split second before reprimanding herself. Oh, for God's sake, Maggie, the sun must be getting to you!

As Maggie soaked up the warmth of the blazing sun, she began to mind the heat. She jumped into the pool and then hopped onto a raft, and the turmoil slowly seeped from her body as she reclined. She took a deep breath, then exhaled, drifting aimlessly on the gentle currents in the water. She'd forgotten how great it felt to truly let go and relax the mind.

***

A lengthy raft float was the panacea for Maggie's earlier emotional commotion; and so, she decided to take the task of finalizing trip plans into her own hands. Why couldn't *she* be the one to touch base with Lindi? Sure, it was Lindi's idea to take the trip, but even if she canceled, what was stopping Maggie from a relaxing jaunt to the lake house? In spite of her feelings for Andrew, she absolutely loved Keasley Lake and the very cozy feel of the lake house, which begged for some long-overdue TLC.

While retrieving her phone, she saw that she had missed a call from Andrew. Eh, he'll call back if it's important, she thought.

She then sent a text to Lindi, careful not to sound put-off by Lindi's failure to prioritize the trip planning.

Hi, Lindi…just checking in on where and when to meet you tomorrow morning. Thanks.

***

Maggie had gotten quite a bit of sun already that day, so she decided to call it quits. In wet flip-flops, she clomped into the sunroom, where she tossed her phone aside and walked away. She was fairly well packed for her weekend. She would just needed to take care of toiletries in the morning. And she wanted to do a sweep of outdated food products, since the trash would go on Friday morning.

As she pulled the trash bag from the kitchen receptacle, there it was! The cake box that had so beautifully housed Betty Ann's layered masterpiece was nothing more than an oil-speckled pile of paperboard containing dried-up cake crumbs.

After several minutes of ridding the kitchen of anything that could possibly stink up the place, Maggie decided to check her phone. She was prepared for the possibility that Lindi, in all her aloofness, might not have replied. Maggie, who couldn't quite shake the ants in her pants, was willing to accept that and take the trip anyway. What the hell, she told herself. I need to get out of here!

Much to her surprise, however, Lindi had called and left a voice mail. It's not like her to leave a vm, Maggie thought. Something must be wrong.

Maggie tapped into her voice mail and listened to the message closely.

Hi, Maggie. It's Lindi. Had to leave a voice mail, too much for text, really. So sorry to just now be checking in, but I ended up driving to Collinsville this morning…where Jillian lives. She can't meet for lunch over the weekend, so I thought I'd hang out with her today and spend the night at her place. She's a bit of a mess. So, I'm sorry if I've inconvenienced you…now that you have to drive. I would totally understand if you bailed on the trip. Okay, see ya!

What the hell? Maggie thought. What sort of dud has Lindi turned into? Maggie was slightly put off by Lindi's lack of enthusiasm, but she wasn't going to take it personally. She immediately texted Lindi to let her know the lake house address and tell her that she would, indeed, be there by 10:00 a.m. Friday. And what a bonus, Maggie thought, that Debbie Downer, Boo-hoo-Jillian, or whatever her name was, wouldn't be around to spoil the trip!

Maggie fell back into her easy chair and let out a sigh of relief as if she'd just run a marathon in those silly Louboutin heels. To think that her whole world had changed tremendously within a week's time, and it would only get better once she cut her ties with Andrew. With that horny flamer off her back, everything would be so uncomplicated. Even confronting her control-freak father and judgy mother will seem effortless, she told herself lightheartedly, as a cheeky grin formed on her slightly sunburned face.

Maggie's phone vibrated then, interrupting those entertaining thoughts. The caller was Andrew. Reluctantly, she picked up. "Yeah, hi," she said.

"Hi, babe."

Ick. "What's up?" she asked.

"Do you *really* wanna know?" he answered in his predictable smarmy manner.

Please, let this not be a Magic Mike conversation, she thought, remaining silent.

"Oh, come on now! Be a little more playful, babe," said Andrew.

"Just kinda busy," she replied.

"Really? With what? You're supposed to be relaxing this week. You've been pampering yourself, haven't you?"

"Of course, I have."

"What are this past week's indulgences gonna set me back?" Andrew asked, jokingly.

Oh, you have no idea…but we'll discuss it on Monday, she thought, deviously. "Ha ha…you're funny, Andrew."

"Well, I just wanted to check in on my girl."

Eww.

"And I have to confess," Andrew continued, "I spoke with your father about some legal matters earlier today, and he alluded that you were going to the lake house. Of course, I pretended to know what he was talking about. So, were you thinking of going there this weekend?"

"Uh, yes. I was, actually."

"I think it's great that you're treating yourself to a weekend away, babe, but I was just a little shocked that you hadn't touched base with me about it. Besides, it looks like business will wrap up earlier than expected—possibly by late Friday morning. Thought we could do dinner at Bella's or wherever *you'd* like to go. Then maybe go to my office for dessert…you know, the way we used to."

Too late to recapture your nauseating romance tricks, she thought. "Sounds fun, but I really want to get away. I need this break, and you know I love the lake house, Andrew. I hope you understand."

He paused. "I do understand. And if this trip will provide further solace, then that's what I want you to do."

"I appreciate that. And by the way, I was going to call you today to let you know of my weekend plans. You just beat me to it," Maggie lied.

"Of course, you were. Like any good wife would. I love you, babe. I'll just see you on Sunday, when you return."

Ugh, cut the sap, jackass. "Yep, see ya then."

Maggie took a good long look around the house, assessing it the way the soon-to-be-hired Realtor would. She was glad that Janice would be in over the weekend to clean.

Ah, she remembered. Gotta leave her a note about the master bedroom. She did *not* want Janice to see the dancer's pole. But then she thought, To hell with it. Andrew might be home…he can deal with it! But as much as she tried to relax and focus on the lovely scenery from her sunroom windows, she became troubled by the trees that needed a good trimming. I wonder if Janice does pruning? she thought.

***

A few minutes later, it occurred to Maggie that there was no reason for her to stick around in a house she'd grown to despise, and that a Thursday afternoon commute to Keasley Lake would be better than winding through Friday-morning traffic. So, she scurried off to the master bathroom to pack her toiletry bag. She stuffed it into her Louis V. duffel and took one last look at the ridiculous dancer's pole and the muddy-colored sheets on a hulking, empty bed. That's one lonely pole and a hell of a big bed for one person, she thought.

Then, out of the goodness of her heart, she decided to do something nice for Andrew. Something he'd enjoy. She dug out a few of the tawdry magazines he'd buried in the drawer of his bedside table and fanned them nicely around a bottle of cab sauv. On her way out, she stopped in the doorway with duffel, purse, and keys in hand, and simply smiled back at her little welcome-home-honey gift. Ahhh, I really am a good wife, she thought.

Weekend in Hell

CHAPTER 26

A No-Frills Friday

Maggie couldn't remember the last time she'd slept so late. It was 9:15 Friday morning, and she had awoken to the sound of nothing. No alarms, no traffic, nobody. The lake house…cozy and serene with a gentle cross breeze coming from the open, screened windows. Since she'd arrived Thursday evening, there'd been plenty of time to freshen up the stuffy cottage, which hadn't been occupied since that disastrous weekend in April when Andrew was a no-show.

Lighting candles and fluffing blankets and pillows with a "mountain fresh" dryer sheet gave a crisp, clean welcoming fragrance to the place. Maggie glided through the cottage, taking in the soothing tranquility and calculating all that she would change—once the cottage became hers in the divorce settlement! This was her house. She belonged here.

She brewed a fresh pot of coffee in the regular, slow-working coffeemaker, then poured herself a cup with no café mocha frills…just a plain old cup of joe with a little cream and sugar she'd picked up last night at Dutry's Market.

It had only been a week since she'd gotten reacquainted with Lindi, an earthy, free-spirited kind of friend, she mused. Sure, she'd had great times with her college pals long ago, but she recalled that even *they* were all about what to wear, who to meet, how to look…*blah blah blah*.

Wanting to breathe in the morning dew from the lake, Maggie, drifted toward the deck, wearing the threadbare robe that had somehow become part of the house. As she got closer to the french doors, she was startled to see the figure of a woman in the lotus position on the deck. Lindi? Here already?

Maggie didn't want to disturb her friend, who was clearly deep in meditation. Then Lindi began to shift into various poses that were quite impressive, prompting Maggie to think, I bet she'd good on the pole. She heard the light humming of very Zen-like music coming from what appeared to be a tiny portable speaker. Wow! Maggie thought. So poised and peaceful. Can't believe she's the same sassy girl who runs the show at Sal's!

***

In order to give Lindi her privacy, Maggie drank her coffee on the little side porch, where her view was that of willowy trees and the outer edge of the driveway. She recognized her own car, of course, but did Lindi drive a Mercedes? Maggie craned her neck as far as possible to check it out.

A sleek black Mercedes? Not brand new, but not exactly vintage. Hmmmm, Maggie thought. Lindi has to be an escort or something.? Maybe Sal's is a cover business for some sort of shady enterprise.

Again, Maggie had to talk herself down from such foolish thoughts. After all, why would Lindi have to work at the diner if she were a high-paid escort? Maybe business is slow, she thought. Maybe the younger girls are taking clients away? Maggie chuckled to herself at the thought of Sal and Betty Ann, the baker, running a secret escort service. All jokes aside, she was ready to spend some serious time getting to know her easygoing friend—whoever she was.

As Maggie sipped her coffee, she began to devise a more solid plan for approaching Andrew on Monday morning. Sure, she'd see him Sunday night, and he'd most likely want to be all touchy-feely and discuss how lonely Magic Mike has been. She, in turn, would gag and tell him she wasn't feeling well or some other trumped-up story. Monday would be her day to break the news, and she knew exactly what she wanted when they divided the marital assets.

So, the lake house will be my new home, she thought. Obviously, I'll take half the sale of our Landis Drive home. I won't push for a new Lexus, but I will need some money to do a few repairs around here…Of course, I'll insist on taking the small inheritance from my grandfather. Oh, and the jewelry! He shouldn't have a problem with that.

Maggie's settlement thoughts were interrupted by the beep of a keyless entry. She stood up and leaned out over the porch railing. "Hi, looks like you found the place," she said, waving.

"Yes…it's so peaceful here!" said Lindi, throwing the last of her yoga equipment into her trunk.

"Sure is! C'mon in…I have fresh coffee and pastries in the kitchen. We can chat on the deck, if you'd like. The lake looks beautiful!"

"Yes, it does. I'm so glad it didn't rain, after all!" Lindi said.

***

After Lindi dropped her overnight bag in the spare room, she joined Maggie on the deck with a cup of coffee.

"I hope you don't mind that I was doing a little stretching and meditation on your deck. I was gonna hang out by the lake until you got here, but you must've driven up last night."

"I did. I figured there was nothing keeping me home—so, why not beat the morning traffic? But had I known you'd be here early, I would've gotten up sooner."

"No worries. I typically start my day off with some form of yoga, and I could no longer take Jillian's excuses and nonsense reasoning about what's goin' on with her. Had to get out of there. That's why I'm early."

"So, how *is* your friend?" Maggie asked, making idle chitchat and not really wanting to waste more than five minutes on sad-sap Sally or lost-my-lover Jillian or whatever her name was.

"Yeah, what a hot mess, that one. I *do* feel for her…gave her a shoulder to cry on. But she doesn't listen to anyone's advice…only wants to hear what she wants to hear. Bet you see a lot of clients that have that same mentality," said Lindi.

Maggie nodded. "So, what's her deal, anyway?"

"I suppose I can tell you…since you don't know her. So, she allowed herself to get pregnant. Guess you could say she trapped this guy."

"Whatta ya mean, *trapped*? Did she stop using birth control or something?"

"Yep! That's exactly what she did…and she admits it. I just think she's young and dumb…and got hooked up with some married dude who said he'd leave his wife for her, or at least that's her version of the story. I guess she thought she'd rush that load-of-crap promise along. And…whatta surprise! Her plan backfired!"

"How do you even know this girl?" Maggie asked. "No offense, Lindi, but she doesn't even sound like the type of person you'd be involved with. You seem to be a no-nonsense kind of woman, who wouldn't put up with someone so…so high maintenance—and scammy."

"Oh, I know. This damn bleeding heart of mine. Well, she was a receptionist at my salon and picked up a few shifts here and there at Sal's for a little extra money. She met some big hotshot businessman from New York, *allegedly*," said Lindi, giving air quotes to *allegedly*. "He came in with a bunch of horny middle-aged men after a late-night show at Lillian's."

Ughhhh, Maggie thought. Of course he did!

"So, he wined and dined her," Lindi continued, "and she eventually relocated to Collinsville, so she'd be closer for their weekend hookups. He paid her rent and spoiled her with nice things, just to have a young hottie on the side. But now, here she is a year later, newly pregnant, and he's still with his wife. I know…shocking, isn't it!" she said in a sarcastic tone. "I tried to warn her about scum like that."

"What about the baby?" Maggie asked, genuinely caring and now wearing the therapist hat.

"She's not sure what she's gonna do. According to her, he said he'd help support the child but has no intentions of leaving his wife. Something about a change of heart…blah, blah, whatever. I'm sure the truth is somewhere in between. And for all she knows, he might already have kids. But she doesn't know that for sure, since he's never spoken of any. I met the dude once. He's just a slimy, arrogant jackass, in my opinion, so I wouldn't doubt he's kept most of his real life from her. In fact, I'm surprised he even told her he was married. Anyway, Jillian said he has no interest in pursuing the relationship, but he'd take care of them. In other words, his generous child support will be more like hush money."

"Oh wow! That *is* a hot mess," said Maggie, thinking, for an instant, that this dude made Andrew look like husband of the year.

"Yeah, it sucks, ya know? Jillian looked up to me…like I was her big sister or something, but I just couldn't get through to her. Told her not to get involved…told her how I learned the hard way…how I felt so cheap and used and brokenhearted."

Hmmmmm, Lindi's finally going to get personal, Maggie thought.

"But anyway, enough about all that. This is just so…so WOW!" said Lindi, abruptly changing the topic as she opened her arms to the view. "The lake, the cottage, everything!"

Annnnnnd, we're back to the mystery. "Yes, it is. It's my very favorite place to be." Should I tell her it's soon to be all mine? she wondered.

"But ya know what I noticed?" Lindi said.

"What's that?"

"Well, the layout and design of the place is beautiful, and I love the rustic feel. But there's nothing personal about it. Like, why are there no pictures on the shelves or side tables? There's no welcome sign. I think I saw maybe two books on the bookshelf, and they looked like real snoozers. As awesome as the place is, it just seems like it needs a little life."

Yes…and I will soon give it that! Maggie thought, sipping her coffee.

"Don't get me wrong," Lindi continued, "the view alone would keep me here year-round."

"Yeah, my mother-in-law is certainly no decorator, and I always wondered why she didn't have someone at least stage the place. Or have the same decorator who did her own house add a little style to this one. But quite frankly, I like that it doesn't reflect anyone's life. It makes me sink into true simplicity when I'm here." Besides, soon it will be all about me!

"Yeah, I can see what you mean. So, anyway," said Lindi, changing the subject again, "I was thinking I would go check things out in Laurelton and meet up with this James Krendall guy for a business lunch."

"Oh, yeah. He's the commercial real estate guy." I still don't feel close enough to ask you where you're getting your money. And if you *are* an over-the-hill escort…well, you go, girl!

"Yeah, so, I figured I'd get my business out of the way, then we can do something fun tonight and go to a festival or whatever's goin' on tomorrow. Whatta ya think?" Lindi asked.

"That sounds great! It'll give me time to do some more things around here. I think I might even do a little shopping…get some personal items to throw around, since this will all be mine very soon," said Maggie as she edged closer and closer to letting Lindi in on what was *really* going on in her own life. She shamelessly hoped to hook Lindi into a deep, personal conversation.

"Oh good. I saw several shopping plazas on my way to and from Jillian's. Are you heading up that way?"

Aaaand, no hook! Let me try this again. "Oh, I'll probably just sit on the deck and do a little online shopping…spend a big wad of dough on my husband's credit card, which will totally piss him off when he gets the bill."

"So, tell me about that," said Lindi.

Aaaand, she's hooked! "Eh, he just became such a douche after we got married, ya know? He used to be so fun and romantic! Now, he's turned into this cheesy, cheating slimeball. I can't even stand to look at him. And these stupid pet names and one-liners he comes up with…it's like he read a book called *Cheesy One-liners for Arrogant Assholes.* And what kind of women fall for that?"

There was silence. And Maggie heard herself for the first time as a real therapist.

"Well, I guess *I* fell for that," Maggie continued. "I was one of those dumb-ass women who thought it meant something to marry into a prominent family."

"It sounds pretty shitty, Maggie. I was hoping to avoid all this emotional chow-chow about relationships. Penis-cake night was enough for me," Lindi said with a slight giggle. "But it sounds like you need to get some things off your chest."

"Yeah…and I could go on for days. But what about you and your band guy?" said Maggie.

"Ah, Dagger. Yeah, he's great. But he's not really the marrying kind, ya know? But then, neither am I. I'll always be a girl-about-town. We *do* love each other, but we've been in and out of this relationship, or whatever you wanna call it, for a few years now. We were mostly apart over this past year, but we're pretty hot and heavy right now…we'll see how long it lasts. I *do* love him, though," said Lindi, looking down at her coffee as if she'd see an image of Dagger's face smiling back at her.

"So, what are you gonna do?"

"Don't know…I just don't know," Lindi said.

"I have to confess something," Maggie said.

"Oh?"

"Yeah, I've been…well, kind of stringing my husband along…allowing him to think I might be willing to give our marriage a second chance. All this time, I've been running up his credit card and stashing all the jewelry he's gotten me over the past couple of years and having it appraised. He's been a real cash cow, and he's oblivious to it. And the thing is, I really don't have a lot of remorse. I mean, sometimes it gets to me…now and again, I suppose. But most of the time, I just recall all his late-night visits to his office or his nights out 'entertaining clients' or his trumped-up 'business trips'…even the way he calls his dick Magic Mike and how he pressured me to install a dancer's pole in the bedroom. I just don't even know who I am anymore. But I'm so glad you and I reconnected, Lindi. Thanks for listening to me…I probably overshared."

Lindi's eyes reflected the weightiness and exhaustion of a subject she really had no intention of discussing. "Sorry you married such a douche, Maggie. But hey, as much as I hate to drag myself away, I really do have to get ready for my business lunch."

That's it? All you can give me is a cold shoulder? "Yes, yes. Let me show you where the towels and things are in the bathroom," said Maggie. "And, if you're back in time, the lake residents start happy hour around threeish…we can just sit out on the dock while people come and go in their boats, sharing a glass of wine here and there."

"I'll play it by ear. Who knows what this Krendall dude has to offer? I could honestly use a little craziness tonight. I wonder if he's a partier?"

Maggie was confused by Lindi's sudden desire to crank up the crazy with a guy she hadn't even met yet. Maybe she shouldn't have grilled Lindi about Dagger or smothered her with marital issues. Damn! Why couldn't I just keep it to a no-frills kind of weekend? Maggie asked herself.

CHAPTER
27

Sipping and Drifting
into Crazytown

With Lindi off to take care of business, Maggie thoroughly inspected the lake house. She scrutinized every little nook and cranny that needed repair, cleaning, or decorating, making a mental note of it all. She didn't want to jump the gun in taking ownership of the lake house, but she thought it would give her a boost to order some new furniture. Of course, she'd stick to the plan of charging it to Andrew's account. She could simply ask the neighboring residents, Joan and Howie Connors, if they'd watch for the delivery. So, she decided, a little Friday afternoon shopping would, indeed, add to her lake-house-high disposition.

She glanced at her phone and discovered a missed call from her mother. Ugh! But Maggie decided that even her judgmental mother could not get under her skin on such a beautiful day. So, what was one little return call?

"Hello," her mother answered.

"Hi, Mother. I wanted to give you a quick call before I get into my weekend."

"What exactly does *getting into your weekend* mean, dear?"

Oh, for God's sake...what was I thinking in calling her back? "Well, I'm gonna do a little shopping, maybe have a late lunch at Nell's—"

"Oh yes, Nell's. You've spoken of it before. Not sure that Andrew's mother is overly fond of the place, but I hope you have a better experience."

Oh, who cares what that nitpicking snob thinks? "I've always had a good experience there," Maggie replied defensively, "so did you need something? I had a missed call from you."

"Well, your father spoke to Andrew the other day, and he promised the two of you would come for dinner Sunday evening. I'm sure that Andrew has already communicated this, but just in case he's gotten too tied up with business, I wanted to make sure you knew. You *will* be back from Laurelton early enough to make it for dinner, won't you?"

Hmmm, Maggie thought. Actually, this could work. She'd be spending less time alone with him at the house. "Yes, that sounds fine, Mother. I should be home by late afternoon."

"So, are you having a relaxing time?" Maggie's mother asked with a slight edge in her tone.

"Yes, I am...very much so."

"Now, you said Rita's yoga gal went with you, correct?"

"Yes, Mother. Her name is Lindi. And she's not some kind of servant to Rita."

"Oh, Maggie, I know that. Please don't assume I meant anything by it. Aside from that, I'm still a little confused by your weekend getaway...without Andrew."

"Don't be," Maggie snapped.

Silence.

"So, Mother, are you and Dad doing anything fun this weekend?" she asked with a sarcastic grin.

"Actually, your father and Ted are going to be working through business matters this weekend with Eloise Devon. Do you remember her?"

Maggie choked on her own spit, which tasted rather like vomit. "*That* wrinkled-up bitch! Who could forget her?"

"Maggie! What has gotten into you? I've never heard such nasty language coming from a well-polished lady."

Well-polished? Do you even know me anymore? "So, Dad told you that he hired Eloise back?"

"Yes, of course he did. Ms. Devon does a fine job. And apparently, Margery just isn't as sharp as she used to be. I think that's why he suggested an early retirement. She was going to retire by the holidays, anyway."

You're just full of excuses for that man, aren't you? "Whatever. But Margery was the best!"

"I know you liked her, dear, but your father knows what he's doing. He's closing in on the end of his career, and he just wants Ted to carry on the firm with the reputation he's worked so diligently to build. He firmly believes Ms. Devon will help with the transition, and she understands that Ted will be bringing his own office manager on board as well as some of his clinical staff."

"Well, just so we're clear…I will never like that woman. And isn't she like a hundred by now?"

"Maggie, please! Have you been drinking?"

"Not even a single glass of wine yet."

"You're embarrassing yourself with this…this teenage jargon of yours. It sounds as if you've been hanging out at a mall or something. Ms. Devon *is* a little older, yes, but she's very wise."

I gotta hang up right now, *Mrs. Stepford.* "Well, hey—I have to go, Mother."

"Very well, Maggie. We'll see you and Andrew at six o'clock Sunday."

"Yep."

Click.

***

By three o'clock, Maggie had gotten over her mother's state of denial. An afternoon of planning and shopping for what she hoped would be her new home had boosted her spirits again. She considered the shopping spree a parting gift from Andrew. It was time to start happy hour with the remains of a bottle of Tanqueray she'd found in the liquor cabinet along with an unopened bottle of tonic.

She suddenly felt the gurgle of an empty stomach and remembered she hadn't made her way to Nell's for that late lunch. The buzz of a few boats motoring around on the lake suggested that some of the neighboring residents had begun their happy hours as well. She didn't want to miss out, so her lunch would now consist of a handful of Ritz crackers she'd found in the pantry. Nell's would be there tomorrow.

With crackers in one hand and cocktail in the other, Maggie strolled onto the deck, taking a seat on a cushioned lounge chair. She rolled up her shorts a bit to get a little afternoon sun on her legs, as a modest breeze softly rippled the lightweight cotton of her loose tank top. Ah, what a beautiful day, she thought, flicking cracker crumbs from her thighs.

"Hi, Maggie!" Joan Connor shouted as she and her husband prepared to take their boat out.

"Hi, Joan…hi, Howie! Not working today?"

"No, we left Connor's Place in good hands for the rest of the day. Haven't seen you in quite a while," said Howie. "Where's Andrew been hiding himself? Is he up for the weekend too?"

"He's not, actually," said Maggie as their boat headed toward her dock.

"Never seen anyone work so hard," said Howie.

Oh, Howie, I hope you're just making chitchat and that you, too, haven't drunk the Andrew Spencer bullshit Kool-Aid. "Well, it's good to see you. Will you be back around this way in a bit? I have my friend Lindi up for the weekend," said Maggie. "She's in town taking care of some business." *And I hope she blows off a night out with Krendall.*

"Oh, wonderful! A girls' weekend," said Joan. "We'll catch up with the two of you later, then."

"Fabulous! Have fun!" Maggie shouted as they drifted away.

***

Maggie returned to her deck with a second cocktail, made with the last of the Tanqueray, and a bottle of Riesling resting in an ice bucket. She sank down into her deck chair, wondering how Lindi's business meeting was going with James Krendall. As much as Maggie *wouldn't* want to be in Lindi's late-start-at-life situation, she also admired her. After all, she knew what she loved to do and decided to go for it. *Takes a lot of guts,* Maggie thought.

As she poured herself a glass of Riesling, her mind further drifted into thoughts of the ever-so-secretive Lindi. Why could Maggie not scratch beneath the surface of this enigma? *Hmmm...* She continued to sip her wine and waved to a few more boaters as they passed by, thinking that they, too, might stop back around for a dockside party.

***

By 4:30 p.m., Maggie had emptied the bottle of Riesling and opened a new one, but she was starting to mind the heat. Where had the gentle lakeside breeze gone? *Damn, if I weren't going to be a resident soon, I'd jump right into the lake naked,* she thought, chuckling. But who was she kidding? That was something Lindi might do—not her. Nonetheless, she needed to take a dip. She went inside to change into her tankini and took the opportunity to text Lindi and put her on pizza-pickup duty.

Hey Lindi...Hope you're having a productive day! Was wondering if you could possibly pick up a pepperoni pizza, extra cheese, from Gia's.

Maggie's thoughts turned slightly dark, as she hoped her food-run request would guilt Lindi into returning to the lake house for a later-than-planned happy hour.

***

Maggie drifted back onto the deck with a much-needed bottle of water and two empty glasses in anticipation of some early evening Riesling. She saw that Joan and Howie still had their boat out, and she was slightly miffed that Lindi hadn't even so much as texted her back. How inconsiderate, Maggie thought. If she'd made evening plans with Krendall, could she at least deliver the pizza?

Still minding the heat, Maggie rushed down the splintering wooden stairs to the dock and jumped into the lake. It was instantly refreshing and sobering! Ahhhhh, she thought. Might as well open that last bottle.

When Maggie climbed out of the lake, she wasn't sure if it was the sun or if she'd sipped her way into a bit of craziness, but she'd become slightly woozy. She reclined on the cushiony lounge chair. Her mind began to race in several directions as zany thoughts seeped into her conscience. Was Lindi, perhaps, James Krendall's escort? And what about this supposed backer? Was she "escorting" *him* as well? The Mercedes? How? And this Jillian person? Was she even a *real* person? Sal's has to be some kind of shady business. How would this diner waitress *Jillian* meet up with rich business men? Or was Lindi really Jillian? Was Lindi pregnant! Was she meeting up with adoptive parents and calling that a "business meeting?"

Maggie's mind continued to spin out of control. Then a boat horn blasted in the distance, yanking her back to real life. Fearing she'd return to that craziness, she lay still, and eventually, she relaxed, listening to the rippling water. All was quiet again, but she heard the faint sounds of stones crunching in the driveway.

Oh, good. Lindi came back. I'm starving!

As the door to the cottage opened, she shouted over her shoulder, "Hey, I'm out here. C'mon out…I just opened a bottle of wine."

"Uh, hi, Biscuit."

Had Maggie drifted back into Crazytown?

CHAPTER

28

When Shit Hits the Fan

Maggie's mood went from high to low within about two seconds as she whirled around to see Andrew standing at the french doors. There he was. All smarmy-looking and pleased with himself. Proud that he'd decided to surprise Maggie on a Friday night at the lake house. Invading her privacy. Ignoring her request to be alone for the weekend.

Ohhhh, noooo. "Hi, Andrew," said Maggie with a hint of displeasure in her voice.

"Well, hi there. Expecting someone else?"

"Actually—"

"You were expecting *me*, weren't you? I just had a feeling that tonight was a good night for us to talk…it's so romantic here at the lake house."

Please leave, Maggie thought. You're killing my buzz.

"And look at you," he continued, "with a fresh bottle of wine. Not my cab sauv, but I took care of that," said Andrew, reaching into the wine carrier, pulling out an already opened bottle. "So, looks like I'm just in time. Will you hand me that other glass, babe?"

She handed the wineglass to him. "So, as I was saying—"

"I just love it here," he interrupted as he leaned back against the deck post, taking in the scenery. "Why have we not come here more often?"

Grrrrrr...drop the act, you phony bastard!

"And this weather!" Andrew rejoiced. "Doesn't get any better than this. That lake is just beautiful...makes it cool enough to enjoy a hot summer night. And if it gets to be too much, well, there's always skinny-dipping," he said as he dipped his finger into Maggie's wine and put it to her lips. She could smell his boozy breath.

EWW! EWW! EWW! You stink, she thought. And get that dollar-bill-smelling finger away from me! She gently brushed his hand away from her face.

"So, anyway—" Maggie began, *again.*

"Hold on...just hold on. We can talk later," said Andrew as he rushed toward the french doors and reached inside his overnight bag. "I thought you might want to take a peek at this."

A satiny textured gift box...from somewhere. She opened it. A gorgeous string of sapphires. Had he forgotten he'd already gifted a similar wristlet a couple months ago?

Well, this thing can go right along with the rest of the bankroll jewels. "Thank you." Ching-ching-a-ding!

"You're welcome, Bisky."

Annnnnd, the stupid pet names are back!

"Now, let's take this wine inside and have our *own* happy hour."

"Andrew, I think we've both had plenty to drink," said Maggie, slipping into her mesh swimsuit cover-up.

"Oh, come on...let's not spoil the moment."

Damn it, Lindi! Where are you? Get your ass over here! Maggie thought. I'm just tipsy enough to let this jackass feel me up...I don't want him to take away my new bling!

"Andrew! I'm trying to tell you something!"

"I'm sorry, babe. I'm just so wanting to have a special night with you. I'd say it's long overdue."

"Andrew! I have an old friend staying here with me," Maggie finally blurted out. "She's in town on a business thing. She'll be back soon."

"Oh? Is it Jess? Out on a *business thing*, is she? Is that what women call it when they're out doing nasty things?" said Andrew.

No, dumb ass! That's what you call making business arrangements. "It's not Jess...it's an old friend from way back. You don't know her."

"Okay, well, I'd love to meet her," said Andrew. "Hope she doesn't mind the hubby hanging out tonight."

Uh, I mind, jackass!

"But, she's not here now," he continued. "So, let's take advantage of our time alone. Go on over there and do a little shimmy on that cedar pole," Andrew suggested as he stripped down to his boxers and sank into the couch.

"Seriously, Andrew? It's full of splinters," she said, scrunching her face at his wine-buzzed request.

"You don't have to grind it, Bisky."

Call me that one more time, and the shit's really gonna hit the fan, she thought. At that moment, Maggie was certain she'd made the right decision to divorce Andrew. He wasn't husband material. He was an arrogant control freak whose behavior had been excused all his life, as he was Andrew Michael Spencer III, Esq.

"Let's go, babe. Give me a show. Or should we head straight for the boathouse? You know, the way we used to?" he reminded her as he raised his glass of wine.

"This isn't exactly what I had in mind for our reunion," she said with a killer sneer on her face. "Besides, it's a little stuffy in here…let's just hang out on the deck."

"You're right. It *is* a little stuffy," he said, ignoring most of what she said. "Let me turn on the fan. Now, come on! Take that mesh thing off…slip out of that granny-looking swimsuit and do a little dance for me," Andrew insisted, standing just a hair's breadth from the fan.

Odious jerk! I hope Magic Mike gets caught in that fan!

As Maggie shook her head in disbelief that her husband could outdo his master-level assholery, she heard the sound of stones crunching in the driveway again. Yes! Finally! Lindi would be the much-needed interruption.

"Is someone pulling up in the driveway?" Andrew asked as he quickly pulled his pants back on.

"Yes, I told you I wasn't alone," Maggie said as Lindi stopped right inside the door with a steaming pizza box.

"I almost did a U-turn when I saw the Navigator…but I wanted to clear some things up with Maggie," said Lindi with arms crossed and head cocked to the side.

Huh? Maggie slipped into serious bewilderment.

"Thought you were spending the weekend with Jillian," Andrew said. "How is she?"

"Oh, don't even pretend to care about her! How do you think she is?"

"Calm down…no need to get all excited. And you can back down off your high horse. Jillian's nothing more than a common gold digger. *You* know the kind. And she knew what she was doing when she went off the birth control. We've already had this discussion," said Andrew.

He turned his head in Maggie's direction, hoping she'd miraculously lost her hearing for a few minutes.

She had become comatose. What the hell was happening? Her thoughts had put her in a chokehold, while an epiphany smacked her right in the face.

"You are *such* a liar!" Maggie screamed. "You're Jillian's…whatever!" Maggie couldn't say the words. "Bet you wished you hadn't wimped out on the vasectomy! No wonder you went on with all that crap about pregnancy tests and that too-old-to-start-a-family nonsense. You'd already knocked up some gold-digging tramp!"

"Now, hold on, Maggie," said Andrew.

"I'm not holding anything, you bastard. How many more times must you humiliate me? Is this where our money's been going? Is this the reason you've not wanted me to resign?"

"Damn it, Maggie, listen to me!" Andrew shouted.

"So, I'm the mysterious, uninformed Mrs. Spencer?"

Lindi tossed the pizza on the coffee table and walked out to the deck for some much-needed air.

"Mags, let me just say this—" said Andrew.

"Okay, Andrew. Go ahead," Maggie interrupted. "Tell me some lie that will completely explain and justify all of this! Go ahead!"

"Look, babe. I'm sorry I haven't been honest with you, and I guess it's time to come clean," Andrew said, shooting a look of contempt toward Lindi through the french doors. "I had a little bit of an affair…but it's over. So completely over, and I really mean what I've been telling you for the past week. I truly want to start over…I do. Please believe me." He reached out to her with open arms.

"A *little bit* of an affair?" Maggie extended a stiff arm, telling him to back off. "What does that even mean, Andrew? You are truly insane! You have this 'affair' bitch pregnant, and you're acting like it's nothing. What the hell is wrong with you!" she shouted. "I bet you've been seeing her from the very beginning of us!"

Lindi now stood in the doorway, looking at her friend, with no words to say except, "Actually, it's been on and off for about three years now."

"What? What the hell are you talking about?" Maggie asked as mass confusion overwhelmed her.

"You got the wrong girl, Maggie. I'm the affair bitch. I'm so sorry. I put it together earlier when you mentioned the office suite…and the dancer's pole… and, well, Magic Mike," said Lindi. "I just couldn't stay here with you. I felt so ashamed. And I…I had to come back and talk to you about it tonight. But I can see that we need to talk about this later. I just can't stay here." With that, Lindi glared at Andrew.

Maggie was coming unglued. Her one-time trophy husband, her new trophy friend. Who were these people? What kind of nightmare was this?

"Seriously, Andrew? Some aimless diner waitress has been scamming you? Was she your escort at one of your trumped-up 'guys' nights' or something? Is *this* where our money has gone?" Maggie extended an arm toward Lindi. "At least the dancers at Lillian's aren't users. I'm sure they're pretty up front about what they charge."

"Maggie, you're not making sense, and you're a little crazy right now," said Andrew.

"You're damn right I am! Do you even know how humiliated I feel?"

Maggie's shit had hit the fan.

"You're drunk, Maggie," said Lindi, who'd now become less apologetic and more antagonized. She was ready to shoot back with vicious jabs and a sharp, forked tongue. "I know you think you're better than people like me or Jillian, but you're not. In fact, you're quite pathetic. You say you hate your job and that you're just going through the motions like everybody else. Well, that sounds a whole lot like what an escort probably does. And who are you calling a *user*? What was it you called Andrew earlier today? An *oblivious cash cow*, I believe? Why don't you take some of the money you've been stashing and get a fuckin' life! And get some friends, why don't you! While you're at it, lose that needy, desperate thing you have goin' on! No doubt, that's how you got together with this one," Lindi said, pointing at Andrew.

"Okay, ladies...enough with the cheap shots. Let's just all settle down," Andrew suggested as Maggie curled herself into a ball on the couch.

"And you!" Lindi now zeroed in on Andrew. "You're the biggest asshole I've ever known! And I'll be giving back every single penny I've *earned* from you!"

"Saffy, wait. Let's all work this out," said Andrew.

"Oh, go to hell! And don't call me by that stupid dancer name," she demanded. "Ya know what? At least Jillian's loser was up front about his marriage. That's a hell of lot better than your bullshit story." Lindi stormed out of the cottage, slamming the door behind her. Then she opened it and stuck her head in again. "By the way, I want my Louboutins back! I assume they're still shoved under the office futon, where I left them last New Year's Eve!"

Lindi's shit *and* all of her early morning Zen had hit the fan.

Having gained a little composure, Maggie now stood up, glaring at Andrew as if to launch a thousand daggers. She was speechless as the magnitude of what he'd proven to be penetrated her mind.

"Babe, listen, please," Andrew said.

"Shut up. Please, just shut up. And don't call me *babe*, don't call me *biscuit*, don't call me *anything*!"

"Maggie, let me at least—"

"Soooo, the shoes! I crammed my feet into another woman's shoes and painfully strutted around like some whore! Was I the butt of everyone's jokes at the New Year's Eve party?"

"Maggie, now come on. Nobody knew about our business."

"You mean *your* business! And what's up with *Saffy*?" she had to ask. "Let me guess...short for Sapphire?" she asked, remembering the pricey bauble he'd gifted her *twice*. Oh, you ass wipe…the bracelets were probably for Lindi, she thought as she sank down into the couch again.

"I just want you to know that I knew her before us," said Andrew—as if that made a difference.

"Who cares! Leave *now!*" she screamed as she picked up his bottle of cab sauv and whipped it toward him, missing, but hitting the fan, which crashed to the floor.

Andrew slung his duffel over his shoulder and swaggered out the door.

CHAPTER

29

Waking up Crazy on a Saturday Morning

Maggie awoke to the mother of all head-banging migraines. She peeled herself from a damp couch, which had served as a sponge for her wet swimsuit...and for her gushing tears. And while the lake house had always been devoid of any real signs of life, it also appeared to be stripped of all its dignity on this dismal, late-August, morning. The cedar poles had never looked so full of splinters. The couch had never felt so tacky. The hardwood floors appeared to have lost their glossy tint. And Maggie had never felt so crazy.

She was now completely sober and staring at an untouched, stone-cold pizza on the coffee table. She was alone...forced to face her demons, sort it all out, and make sense of everything. She rubbed her eyes as if to gouge herself into a new life—one where no one would know her; one where she could make a fresh start; one that had no mirrors.

Oh, God! This is what crazy looks like, Maggie thought, gazing at her hideous reflection in the bathroom mirror. She gasped at the gnarled mass of hair that rested on top of her head and covered her eyes immediately.

A knock sounded on the french doors, interrupting her self-loathing and startling her into a slight panic. Certainly, Lindi wouldn't have the nerve to come back for round two. And surely Andrew wouldn't show his face again. But who?

"Maggie! Maggie, it's Joan," her neighbor called, peering through the door.

"Oh, hi, Joan," she said, relieved, but unable to look her in the eyes as she opened the door.

"I'm sorry if I startled you, Maggie. I just wanted to stop over to see if everything was all right. Howie and I were sailing by last night, hoping you and your friend would be out on the dock for a late happy hour. And we…well, we heard some shouting. We noticed your car was the only one in the driveway this morning, and I wanted to check on you. Are you okay?"

"Oh, Joan. I really can't get into it. But, yes. I'm fine. I'm an emotional mess but otherwise fine."

"Oh, sweetie. If you need me for anything, will you call me, please?"

"I will, Joan. Thanks."

"Howie and I are going into town for breakfast. Would you like to join us?"

"Oh, thanks, Joan, but no. I'll find something to eat," said Maggie, eyeing the sealed pizza box on the coffee table.

"Well, could I bring you something back?"

"No, but I really appreciate the offer."

"Okay, Maggie. Again, call me if you need anything. I mean it."

"I will, Joan. Thanks again," said Maggie. Tears welled up as she closed the door.

Maggie fell back onto the damp, spongey couch and put her head in her hands. How could she face anyone? How would she explain the situation? The divorce was one thing, but could she simply pretend that Lindi never existed? Was Lindi merely a week-long figment of her imagination? Her mother would be mortified that Rita's "yoga girl" had been canoodling with Andrew, as she'd say. Her father would be completely crestfallen that he'd be losing a son—who'd been sleeping with a waitress on the other side of town, as he'd put it. Irrational thoughts? Perhaps. But her ego was now bashed by betrayal all over again. Maggie felt the weight of all this craziness upon her. Fidgety, she began to pick at a hangnail as she imagined counseling her very own self.

***

Maggie, the therapist, studied the average-height, slightly toned, forty-year-old woman, who was sitting on the mildew-scented couch. The woman seemed stiff, careful not to move in a way that would wrinkle a designer suit, had she been wearing one. She crossed her legs while her grounded foot rested on its heel.

Maggie, the therapist, began the session by asking herself to reflect on any toxins or negativity that needed to come out. So, Maggie, the client, took a deep breath and disgorged a chunky batch of word vomit—the kind that requires lots of scouring afterward.

Well, she said to herself, there are my parents…not the worst parents in the world, but they need major improvement. Aren't they exhausted by their pretentious lifestyle and the way they hover over me like I'm a teenager? Do they even know how rude they are to me? It's like I was adopted or something, and they're experiencing buyers' remorse. It's been forty years, people…get over it!

Her mother's lectures flooded through her mind. *Don't speak like a teenager, dear…don't pick at your nails, dear…why would you eat at a diner, dear?*

Next, she saw her father standing in the background with a scowl forceful enough to tase her as he watched her every move. *Maggie, is that proper work attire? She's Ms. Devon to you! Run along…You're dismissed.*

Maggie took a deep breath, exhaled slowly, and opened the pizza box that lay in front of her. What kind of crazy parents talk to a grown daughter like that? Don't they realize I'm now nearing middle age? she asked herself, selecting the largest slice of pizza and taking a big bite.

Finally, she got to the pink elephant that was staring her down as she squirmed on the lake-house crazy couch. Well, she told herself, Andrew's a total douche bag. I could spend hours on that. But I'm more hurt by Lindi. How dare she be so sneaky…and distant. They made a fool out of me! And who does she think she is? She's telling *me* to get a life, when she's using Andrew for his money! What a whorelike thing to do!

After that mental tirade, Maggie collected herself. Suddenly, a realization dawned on her. Was this anxiety really over Lindi? Or was it over her very own mayhem? After all, she, too, was forty and stuck in a career she despised. She, too, had been using Andrew…collecting jewels…racking up shopping bills… scheming all along to deliver a settlement proposal. How was that any different from Lindi's behavior? The only difference was that Maggie had foolishly married the clown. And even though her suspicions of Lindi's real profession had been unfounded, she had no business judging women who worked as escorts— or Lillian's tigresses, for that matter. Perhaps, those girls were the smartest ones of all. They took advantage of drunken men who threw out wads of cash, and then they simply moved on. No ties, no turmoil. All business.

Maggie trembled at the possibility that she'd become what she'd so disrespectfully referred to as one of her *crazies*. And for the sake of preserving the lake house as her sanctuary, she didn't want this crazy to linger there any longer. She would head back to Carrington Heights that day.

***

After Maggie spoke to the Connors about the upcoming furniture delivery and gave them a spare key, Joan hugged Maggie and wished her well. In the rearview mirror, Maggie saw her lake-house neighbor blow a kiss as she drove away, heading out of Willow Circle. To keep herself from crying, Maggie focused on the trees that lined the road. How had she never noticed before that some appeared to have been damaged by storms? But they were still standing and still beautiful.

It occurred to her as she drove that she hadn't even checked her phone that morning; in reality, she had no clue where it was, but she fished around for it in her bag. *Ah, there you are…hiding out,* she thought, glancing at the blank screen. No texts, no missed calls, no voice mails. Should she have been disappointed? Not really. She wasn't up for her parents' badgering or Andrew's bogus apologies. However, there was a small part of her that hoped to hear from Lindi. After all, Lindi had been sleeping with *her* husband. A husband she deplored, but *her* husband, nonetheless. Even though Lindi allegedly knew nothing about his marital status, shouldn't *Lindi* be the one to redress the situation?

Oh…but I said so many awful things to her, Maggie remembered. *I basically called her a pathetic loser, for God's sake!*

Although there were many contributors to this mess, Maggie knew she was accountable for her life. She'd made her own bedlam. Now, she'd have to lie in it.

CHAPTER

30

It's Noisy in Hell

Maggie finally reached the Carrington Heights West exit from the highway, and thoughts of what she had to both fix and endure created a debilitating nervousness. She drove right past her street as if her car refused to make a right turn, so she decided to take a little detour toward Sal's on the other side of town. A part of her expected to see Lindi, who'd take a last-minute shift if offered. But Maggie's hands trembled, and her eyes twitched as if she were about to watch a scary movie. So, she made a U-turn and headed back to Landis Drive.

She crept into her driveway as if to burglarize the place, while mentally crossing her fingers that Andrew had taken another one of his "business trips," even though she needed to face this monstrous noisemaker she would soon call her *ex*-husband. She idled outside the garage door and then exhaled with relief as it opened far enough for her to see it was empty—no Navigator in sight! Maggie continued to sit in silence, observing her house from a Realtor's standpoint. The heavy shutters needed repair, she noticed.

"And, the list goes on," she said, thinking it would need restoration before they could put it on the market.

She lumbered into the house, dropped her bags on the floor, and fell onto the sofa she hoped would provide solace for the rest of her miserable day. But she squirmed around uncomfortably, not quite able to find a good position on the oversized eyesore of a couch that Andrew insisted on displaying in the front room. As she lay there, she scanned the room to see whether Janice had put everything back in its place. However, she was quickly disappointed in discovering that the place had not even been spot-cleaned.

Maggie got up and bumped around like a fumbling klutz, gathering magazines that were strewn about, fluffing pillows, and collecting a forgotten plate and mug from the coffee table. She was further repulsed by the bathroom mess that awaited her.

Did I really live like a disgusting pig last week? she asked herself, reflecting on her so-called days of pampering.

Maggie's stomach began to growl then, so she raided her fridge and settled on some soon-to-be expired baby carrots, Swiss cheese, and roasted-red-pepper hummus. She also discovered a nearly finished piece of chocolate-layer cake with peanut butter frosting. Where did you come from, you little rascal?

She decided to devour her guilty pleasures in the spare bedroom, while flipping through a few of her fashion magazines. But noise flooded her head again, so instead, she set the food on the nightstand and sank into bed, hoping to wake up to a clean house and a clear conscience.

***

Maggie awoke from an all-too-short respite, lying in the stillness of a noise-free house. She began to think further about all that lay ahead of her. She'd need to formulate an action plan to repair herself and heal. It was time to get down to brass tacks and write out her strategies. To hell with the iPad…she just needed a good old-fashioned legal pad. Writing had always been therapeutic for her, even if she were jotting down artless clichés or witty jabs toward her clients. It always felt good to release tension through the power of a simple pen.

Unexpectedly, she heard a clamorous melody…a ring tone had burst out of nowhere, interrupting her plan of action. Maggie stared in bewilderment at her phone, which was perfectly inactive.

Is Janice somewhere in the house? she wondered.

Maggie got to her feet and strolled through the house, following the ring tone. In the kitchen, she discovered a strange bag on one of the stools shoved under the bar. Before Maggie could even rummage through what appeared to be a cheap knock-off Michael Kors bag, the door to the basement was flung open, and a hot brunette appeared, wearing a *very* skimpy bikini bursting with *very* new boobs and holding two *very* empty wineglasses.

"Hi, you must be Janice," the young woman said. "Andy thought he heard you come in, but it really is very soundproof downstairs in his man cave."

Maggie's astonishment had resurfaced, robbing her of a voice, making her knees weak, and ridding her of any shred of dignity she'd retained. How many times would she have to suffer humiliation? Was there a certain amount of torture everyone had to endure in a lifetime? Would she soon hit her quota?

"So, yeah," the nearly naked girl continued. "I just came up for the rest of the wine. How often does a person get to drink on the job?" She giggled. "I won't be in your way at all. Did I hear my phone? I must have a missed call," she said, retrieving her knock-off. "Anyway, Andy said there's an envelope with your payment inside. It's behind the mail holder—in case his massage therapy runs past the time you're done tidying up. The place is a mess, huh?" she whispered, as if letting "Janice" in on a little hushed gossip.

"It sure is," Maggie managed to say with unexplainable restraint. "Could you please send Mr. Spencer up? Tell him *Janice* has a few questions for him."

"Oh, certainly," the girl replied. "Andy," she yelled as she descended the staircase, "your maid needs to see you."

Andy? Maid? Maggie thought. What I wouldn't do for a streak of violence so I could throat-punch that stupid bitch!

"Janice, I was hoping you'd just dig in on the cleaning…the place is a mess," said a towel-clad Andrew as he stomped up the stairs.

"Not Janice," said Maggie, standing firm with arms crossed as Andrew turned the corner.

"Mags! Hi! I'm so glad you're home, babe! I assumed you'd stay at the lake house until Sunday, as planned," Andrew said with unbelievable casualness. "I thought you were Janice up here bumping around."

"I see that," Maggie said with the same fire in her eyes from last night's eruption.

"So, does this mean you've calmed down? You're ready to talk about things… get back to our start-over plan?"

Blown away by such egotistical nonchalance, Maggie *now* wanted to throat-punch Andrew. "Start-over plan? Are you drunk? And who's the naked Chatty Cathy running around our house like she owns the place? Where's your Navigator? What the hell's going on here, Andrew? Do you enjoy making a fool of me?"

"Settle down for Christ's sake, Maggie. You know I get monthly massages. Sounds like Gemma needs to work her special touch on you as well," he said, closing the basement door.

Ohhhh, Gemma. Lillian's top dancer—or whatever. Maggie now remembered her from the Irish pub. "Gemma better not come near me! And since when do you have the Lillian's Tigress strippers, or whatever the hell they're called, come over to the house?"

"Oh, stand down, Maggie. What are you even talking about?" Andrew asked as he approached the fridge.

"Andrew, I saw you chumming it up with her at McCrery's way back in March. A cocktail server told me she was the top dancer at Lillian's. What the hell happened to her tacky-wiggish blond hair? Do you even know how cheesy you are? I can't believe I'm reliving this humiliation all over again!"

"Okay, so she's a dancer. So what? She's also a massage therapist, and I was just multitasking. Johnson's Service Center provides pickup service, so Tony came and got the Navigator. His truck's right out there along the street. Surprised you didn't see it. So, anyway, I thought I'd sneak in an appointment with Gemma. Truthfully, I was a little ashamed to have her see the house in such disorder," Andrew said, sticking his face into the fridge. "And where the hell's the rest of my dessert?" he asked, his eyes shooting daggers at his cake-thief wife.

"Oh, the house isn't that unsightly! And who gives a shit what some on-call massage therapist sees?"

"Have you looked at the place? The bathroom trash is overflowing. Your clothes are all over the bedroom. And by the way, I saw your little display of magazines on the bed. Nice touch."

"I thought so too," said a sneering Maggie.

"Geez, Janice might need an assistant to help get this place in order," Andrew snapped back.

"Oh, stop being overdramatic!" Maggie's feet remained planted on the wine-stained tiles of the kitchen floor. "Do you really think I'm some kind of idiot? Why is this massage dancer girl practically naked? And if you thought Janice was in the house, why would you send what's-her-face up to deal with her? Why would you want to put Janice in an awkward position like that?"

"We both know that Janice wouldn't judge me for my massage appointments, and if she doesn't understand Gemma's bikini gimmick, well, that's too bad. You know what, Maggie? I'm done with this conversation. I'm gonna call Tony and see if he's finished with the tune-up, so I can get Gemma back to Lil's…unless, you wouldn't mind letting me take your car?" he asked, his audacity beginning to stink up the place.

"Order an Uber, jackass! And spend the night elsewhere! Spend it with Gemma, for all I care. But you're not staying here."

"Maggie, watch your mouth. I'll go, but I think we need to talk. I think this…this wrath is more about Saff, uh, Lindi…and less about my massage therapy. And by the way, I don't buy your story that she's some middle-school friend. I think there's something else going on, and you need to come clean about your secrets, as well."

"Oh, shut up! What secrets? We weren't conspiring against you, you paranoid freak!"

"Really? You weren't taking a ride on the Spencer money train? Just like your diner buddy?"

Had Andrew hit below the belt? Maggie thought so, but she hung her head low as she envisioned herself just last week making the *choo choo* sound as she schemed to stockpile pricey assets. But she regained the upper hand once again when she heard Gemma calling for Andrew.

"Andy, we still have thirty minutes left…I wanna do your upper back!"

"Andrew, just go. Get what's-her-face out of here to do your upper back," said Maggie, giving air quotes to *upper back*. So, call Tony…tell him you need your vehicle, now. And if you aren't going to get us out of the dinner that *you* scheduled for us, then be at my parents by six o'clock tomorrow evening. You and I will get to that talk tomorrow night after dinner. But don't pull any crap like you did last weekend. Don't go over there acting like husband of the year, Andrew. I'm just pissed enough to call you out in front of my parents. So, no bullshit!"

"So, that's it? You don't even wanna get together later this evening to listen to my side of the Lindi story?"

"No, I don't. I'll see you tomorrow evening. And tell naked girl she looks much better as a brunette!" said Maggie as she marched off to the spare room, frowning in disgust at a house that was, indeed, in hellish disarray.

***

After Andrew's departure to God-knows-where, Maggie freed herself from the spare room to retrieve a legal pad from her home office. Getting on with her plan of action would serve as the diversion she needed. Instead, she lost focus, bothered by the condition of the house. So, she decided to call her mother to ask about Janice—why had she been a no-show?

"Hello."

"Hi, Mother."

"Well, hello, Maggie. Didn't think I'd hear from you until tomorrow."

"Uh, yeah. I know. I came home early. But I was curious about Janice. She never showed up for her cleaning appointment. Is everything okay with her?"

"Oh, dear, actually, she wasn't able to make it this weekend. I simply forgot to tell you, yesterday…when we spoke."

"Oh, what's wrong?" Maggie asked.

"Her mother is very ill, and she decided to visit the poor dear in her nursing home. She did call, however, to tell us that things are stable for now, and she'll soon reschedule her appointments."

"Oh, I had no idea. And I don't want her to feel that she needs to fit me into her busy schedule."

"So, tell me, dear. Why did you come home early? Did you discover that you simply felt out of place…on a weekend without Andrew?"

You are soooo clueless! "Not at all. Besides, Andrew stopped in to surprise me."

"Oh, that is so like him. Just wonderful!" her mother gushed.

Oh, you ridiculous woman!

"What wonderful plans do you have for this evening, then?" her mother asked.

"Actually, not much of anything. I'm feeling a little fatigued," said Maggie.

"Well, I certainly hope you and Andrew can make it to our Sunday family dinner. You know, it just occurred to me…we've not seen Andrew's parents for some time now. Perhaps, I should ask them to join us."

"Oh, please don't. They're such bores."

"Maggie! Please mind your manners."

"Mother…I'm really just joking." Actually, she thought, I'm dead on. With any luck, those snoozers are off traveling somewhere. "Besides, I think Andrew said they were in Maine or something," she lied.

"Maggie, I realize you're forty years old, and it would be silly to lecture you…"

Then why are you about to? Maggie wondered. Do you not hear yourself in every conversation with me? You are the lecturing queen!

"But I simply don't understand your sense of humor," her mother said. "Furthermore, the way you speak, lately, seems so very colloquial. As a professional woman who's married to a very prominent attorney in this town, you should perhaps save such…such unbecoming diner talk or whatever it is for some other occasion."

Hmmmm…unbecoming…such noise thrown my way! "So, dinner tomorrow night, then," Maggie said abruptly.

"Yes," her mother snapped.

"'K."

Click.

Wake Me When Sunday's Over

The dreaded Sunday-evening family dinner. *Ugh!* Maggie arrived at her parents' home a little flustered over everything that had gone down within the past forty-eight hours. But over all, she maintained enough stability to go through the motions. True to form, her mother was waiting at the door as the dutiful hostess.

"Hello, Maggie," her mother said. "Where's Andrew? He's coming, isn't he?"

"Hi, Mother," Maggie said, leaning in for the fake hugs and kisses. "He should be here soon."

"Oh, wonderful."

"Where's Dad?" Maggie asked.

"Well, he's in the family room…with Ms. Devon."

Ugh, kill me now! The thought of Monster Devon caused steam to blow from Maggie's ears as she swallowed a lump of undesirable gunk that had been building up in her throat.

"Hello, lovely ladies!" came from behind her as Andrew popped his head inside the door.

"Oh, Andrew! I didn't realize you were trailing Maggie," her mother said delightedly.

Me neither...sneaky bastard. Were you hiding in the bushes...having one last sexcapade before I dump your ass? Maggie thought.

"I hope you had a good trip," her mother said. "And I hear you're just full of surprises!"

Andrew's forehead glistened with a thin coat of sweat as he looked at his mother-in-law, slightly unnerved.

"Dropping in on her at the lake house. How romantic of you!" Maggie's mother said.

Oh, shut the hell up, Mother, you senseless fool, Maggie scoffed to herself.

"Yes, and I surprised her with a lovely sapphire bracelet, as well. Did she tell you that?" Andrew asked, while Maggie envisioned him placing it on Lindi's wrist...after she pole-danced...or performed some other ludicrous task.

"She did *not* tell me that," Maggie's mother said, glancing at her daughter in perplexity. "I can't believe you didn't wear it this evening, darling."

Maggie completely ignored her mother and blew right past Andrew, shooting daggers at him. Maybe this was a stupid idea. I should've bailed on this charade when I had the chance, she thought, proceeding into the family room.

Dr. Walters stood up to greet Andrew, who was following Maggie. "Andrew, hello. So glad you could make it. Maggie, you're looking well."

Is hell freezing over? A compliment!

"You know I can't say *no* to Mom's cooking," Andrew said, looking over his shoulder toward his mother-in-law, while Maggie rolled her eyes.

"Well, I'd like you to meet Eloise Devon," he said. "She was my right-hand gal from years ago when I started my practice, and we've been blessed to have her return for the transition."

We? Ugh! Kill me again, Maggie silently begged to anyone capable of hearing the tortured thoughts going around and around in her head.

"Hello, Ms. Devon," said Andrew as he leaned in to kiss her hand.

"Please, call me Eloise," she replied teasingly.

Oh, shut the hell up, Wrinkle-mug, Maggie wanted to scream.

"What a beautiful name," Andrew said.

Maggie whirled around in repugnance and headed away from the folly. She found herself standing alone in the kitchen, digging into the grilled portobello's and bleu cheese-stuffed olives intended for the canape. She caught a narrow view of the family room, where her mother stood a few steps away from the others, gazing out the window. Her distant reflection was shockingly familiar to Maggie. She looked lost, beaten down, and discontented, much like the battle-scarred face that had stared back at Maggie so frightfully in the lake-house mirror.

You can't take these fools, either, can you, Mother? Maggie thought as she continued to study her mother's wake-me-when-it's-over look.

***

The dinner table conversation had consisted mostly of Dr. Walters's retirement babble and Andrew's sickening schmoozing that everyone had fallen prey to. And when he wasn't going on with his long-winded gibberish, Eloise Devon slipped in a few boasts about her son's accomplishments. Maggie's mother appeared to be interested in what everybody was saying, while Maggie simply tuned everyone out, avoiding eye contact, and twitching in her seat.

The only place of sanity was the powder room, so Maggie had made her third visit, mostly to get away from the toxic vibes that circled the dinner table. She couldn't shake her mother's reflection in the window earlier as she looked at herself in the mirror.

Maggie's mother hadn't served much wine with dinner, which meant there was a tacit agreement that everyone would leave by nine o'clock. Just as well, since Maggie needed to have her wits about her for the dreaded conversation she had planned for later with Andrew. But she needed to get the show on the road now. She'd been hanging out in front of the powder-room mirror for way too long. She decided to push for dessert.

Maggie returned to the dining room with dessert plates and forks in hand, only to find that everyone had already moved into the family room. There was Andrew, seated in an oversized leather chair, while Ms. Devon and her father sat on opposite ends of the couch. Her mother stood near the same window as before, but this time, there was no reflection. Instead, her small frame appeared to be swallowed up by the mammoth curtains that had been drawn to block the evening sun—the same curtains she insisted looked so regal.

"Oh, Maggie, dear. We're having Eloise's fruit platter for dessert this evening," her mother announced, nodding toward the sideboard. "I've already put out the plates and forks."

"Oh, okay." Of course, you'd bring some boring fruit platter, Wrinkles!

"Maggie, come sit next to me," said Andrew, patting the leather ottoman next to his chair. "I was telling everyone what a wonderful time my parents are having, visiting old friends in Rhode Island."

Oh, I guessed right…somewhere New Englandy. Maine…Rhode Island… as long as they're not here in the family room, I don't give a shit.

"Come sit," he asked again.

Maggie looked at her soon-to-be-ex-husband, and her stomach began to churn. Eh, what the hell! Let's just get this hellish night over with, she thought, shooting daggers at Andrew.

"Maggie, we haven't heard much from you this evening," her father said.

"Yes, Maggie. Tell us all about your weekend at the lake house. I would certainly hope it was nothing less than glorious…having taken off on a Friday," Ms. Devon said cunningly.

Oh, shut the hell up, you emaciated shar-pei, Maggie wanted to blurt.

"Andrew was also telling us about his plans to make more use of the cottage. It sounds like a lovely idea," her mother said.

Hmmmm, wonder if they want to know that he's full of shit and that the lake house will soon be mine, Maggie thought.

"I told everyone that we somehow got away from going there as often as we used to," Andrew said.

Maggie turned and grimaced toward Andrew. You fools are making it so easy for me to get started with my shenanigans, she thought. So, keep it up! "Yeah, so the lake house. What can I say? It started out with the trip being just the two of us…myself and Lindi Wallace. Mother, I know you somewhat remember her. Dad, not sure if you do or not. She's a friend from middle school that I crossed paths with about a week ago," she said, looking back at Andrew and seeing him begin to squirm.

"A ladies' weekend away? At your age? I guess I'm just an old-fashioned gal," Ms. Devon said.

Yes, Crinkle-fry…old-fashioned with old wrinkles. Maggie smirked at the thought of assigning Ms. Devon a clever new name.

"She's Rita Worthington's yoga girl, Everett," Maggie's mother announced.

"Yoga girl? What exactly is a yoga girl?" Dr. Walters asked.

Maggie shot a look of contempt toward her mother for her judgy insinuation. "She actually owns her own business, Dad. She delivers personal yoga services to people's homes. She's looking to relocate, though, and buy a studio up in Laurelton; right, Andrew?"

Andrew simply gave Maggie his usual smarmy grin—this time gritting his teeth a bit.

"Oh, the lake community will appreciate that. I'm surprised there aren't several other yoga facilities in such an eclectic town," Maggie's father said, looking at Andrew as if to evoke his commentary.

"You would think," Andrew said. "But there's just the one. It's been there for several years. Can't imagine those folks selling their business. It's quite successful. Perhaps Maggie's friend has something really fantastic to offer in her studio." He smirked at Maggie.

"Well, I have to say, I admire a woman who goes for what she wants… especially when the odds are against her in such a profession. You said she's a school chum, Maggie? So, she must be age forty or so?" Ms. Devon said.

Who cares what you think, leather-face Barbie! "Well, I have to say, *for her age*, she's in remarkable shape and stunningly beautiful. She'd give any twenty-something a run for her money, don't you think, Andrew? It's like she has a perfect dancer's body, wouldn't ya say?"

An uncomfortable stillness had settled over everyone.

"Yes. Stunning, indeed," said Andrew, breaking the silence. "In fact, I'd say she's mind-blowing."

Ping…pin dropped. No one quite knew how to react to the obvious covert conversation taking place. And Maggie had been reduced to a comatose fool as inadequacy swallowed her up again. She pictured Andrew and Lindi doing *mind-blowing* things together, and she desperately needed to regain sight of the powerful, in-charge role she'd taken on over the past week.

"So, who's up for a fresh fruit plate?" Maggie's mother broke in.

"Actually, Mother, I'm going to pass. I'm completely stuffed, and I have a big day tomorrow," said Maggie.

"Yesssss, quite a bit of paperwork has piled up for your last day in the office," Ms. Devon reminded her.

Oh, go blow it out your shriveled ass, Devon!

"And, I need to be going, too," said Andrew. "I also have quite a load to take on tomorrow."

You sure do, you clueless jerk, Maggie thought, slowly returning to full control after her momentary lapse.

"But what about this fabulous fruit platter!" Ms. Devon said. "It took hours to prepare, and some of the fruit is exotic!"

Yeah, right! Take your exotic fruit and blow that out your—

"Eloise, perhaps you can take it to the office, tomorrow," Maggie's mother suggested, interrupting Maggie's thought.

"Yes, good idea, Mother. Instead of having doughnuts and bagels for the Monday morning meeting…we'll have some fabulous exotic fruit!" Maggie said.

"Very well, but I'm not sure how fresh it will be then," said Ms. Devon.

No one gives a crap about your stupid fruit platter, so get over yourself. That line was *so* ready to roll off Maggie's tongue, but Dad jumped in.

"Eloise, it was very thoughtful of you to prepare such a lovely platter, but it will be perfectly fine to serve at tomorrow's meeting," said Maggie's father as he walked toward his right-hand gal and patted her on the shoulder from behind the couch.

Way to placate that high-maintenance freak! Maggie thought.

What was left of Ms. Devon's hair stood on end, but she refrained from further scolding. Dr. Walter's stoicism went into overdrive, and Liz was completely befuddled…not knowing who to stand up for.

"Well, good night, folks," Andrew said abruptly, waving to everyone while walking toward the door—and cleverly escaping hugs and kisses.

"Good night," everyone said in sync.

"Yes, good night, all. Mother, thanks for dinner," said Maggie, not waiting for a reply. She advanced toward the door that Andrew *affectionately* held open as her mother followed.

"Maggie, could I see you in the kitchen for a second?" Liz asked.

Ohhhhh, whyyyyyy? Maggie thought. "Andrew, I'll see you at home," she said, giving him the run-along look and practically shutting the door in his face. She stood motionless for a moment, waiting to hear his Navigator start up. Ahhh, one less pink elephant in the room, she thought and then made her way into the kitchen.

"I baked a celebration cake for this evening," her mother said on the down-low.

Yes! Let's celebrate your daughter's divorce that you know nothing about!

"But I thought it would be rude to serve it, since Eloise brought the fruit platter," she said.

Maggie had had all she could take from just about everyone. "Mother, who gives a shit if you upstage her stupid dessert?"

"Maggie!"

Oh, chill, woman! I'm breaking out of my cocoon! "Sorry, but my filters have left the house. And you'd better get used to it."

Throughout Maggie's entire life, she'd never spoken to her mother in such a way...nor had she ever seen her mother's smile so genuine. She was beaming from ear to ear. What was happening, here? Was Maggie's blatant disrespect toward Eloise Devon really that amusing? By the look on her mother's face, apparently so!

"Anyway, let me send some of this cake home with you. I think you'll enjoy it. It's one of those poke cakes, infused with caramel, and topped with buttercream frosting and a few celebratory sprinkles."

And there's *so much* for me to celebrate!

"Shall I send some home for Andrew, as well?"

"If you'd like." Although he won't have much to celebrate.

"Very well. Here you go," she said, handing Maggie a to-go bag.

"Thank you, Mother. By the way, what were you going to celebrate?"

"I thought it would be nice to celebrate your father's retirement...even though he'll be working for several more months. I thought maybe some fuss might goad him along a bit. I just feel like he's dragging his feet over this retirement business."

You sneaky devil...I love it! "Yeah, I hate to say it, Mother, but I see him and Ted working out a deal that he stays on for a while longer. And who knows? Ted hasn't exactly been pushing things along. Maybe he wants to bail out."

"Oh, Maggie, don't say that. Your father's not getting any younger. He needs to retire ASAP."

Maggie chuckled at her mother's informal dialogue. "I couldn't agree more. I mean I've never seen anyone more uptight than he is." Except when he's around Eloise, Maggie thought, having turned her filter back on out of respect.

"Well, darling, you run along. Go be with Andrew," Liz said with a little hesitancy in her voice.

Maggie stepped back and tipped her mother's face upward. Her mother stiffened then relaxed as Maggie's hands slid down to her shoulders. "Mother, if you don't mind my asking...had you ever thought about leaving Dad?"

"Oh, Maggie! Such thoughts. I'm a sixty-five-year old woman. A little too mature to be out on the prowl."

Awww, you made a little joke! "No need for prowling, Mother. But serious-ly...have you ever really assessed your marriage?" Maggie asked as she looked in on her father and Ms. Devon yucking it up with silly grown-up banter.

"Maggie, this isn't a conversation I'd like to have...right now," her mother said with a twinkle in her eye. "And by the way, I didn't want to say any-thing in front of Andrew, but hadn't he gifted you a sapphire wristlet a couple months ago?"

"Yes. Yes, he did."

"Hmmm." She didn't go on about how lovely and generous he was and didn't say for the thousandth time that he was a keeper. It was just a simple *hmmm*.

"Maggie," she said, "don't underestimate yourself as a therapist. I have a feeling you do a fine job."

Maggie gave her a half smile and nodded. She then embraced her mother in a manner that wasn't at all familiar—it was heartfelt. She left with a sub-tle spring in her step, feeling that her mother was slowly waking from *her* cocoon, as well.

CHAPTER

32

Get a Life!

Other than having the *big* talk with Andrew, Maggie's only goal for Sunday night was to take a hot shower to soothe the despair that had been gnawing at her throughout the evening. Tomorrow, she'd be giving up the comfort of many luxuries. But how much had she really enjoyed those things? How could one truly relish living in the falsehood of staged opulence?

"Oh, I really don't wanna chat tonight," she said aloud to no one as she drove toward Landis Drive. "But I need to get this over with...put it behind me."

Maybe he decided to hang out at Lillian's, she hoped.

But there was no such luck. She pulled into her driveway and scowled at the Navigator as she rolled past it into the garage.

As Maggie walked into the house, she looked around to see where Andrew might be lurking. He was nowhere in sight. Is he in bed already? she wondered.

"Hey, I'm out here," came from the sun porch. "Come out here, please."

Ohhh, I hope he doesn't have some lame piece of jewelry waiting…or some other nonsense lined up to try to woo me back. "Give me a few minutes," she yelled back as she headed straight for the master bathroom.

Maggie glanced at the dancer's pole and pictured Lindi swinging around the thing, doing all sorts of tricks and moves to show off her very physically fit body. Eh, she's got nothin' on me, Maggie thought as she took one last spin on the pole. She then proceeded to the shower, desperately needing to rinse off the day's stench. She could no longer stand it.

***

After a revitalizing shower, Maggie wrapped herself in a towel, sank onto her side of the bed, and began combing out her freshly washed hair. She submerged herself in deep thought, putting the whole weekend into perspective. Although it was hard for her to swallow, Lindi was right—desperation was Maggie's worst enemy. She'd made the biggest mistake of her life in marrying Andrew. She'd bought in to the whole marriage-clock theory…gotta be married by the age of forty. And who was the fool who penned such a ridiculous rule?

Maggie also had to come to terms with her reckless determination to find a new career. Was she really doing a fine job, as her mother suggested? Was it really the career she despised, or was it the atmosphere…the one her father had created at the office? Had she frantically clung to the promise that her working days would be over once she married Andrew? Was she really any different from mystery woman Jillian, who thought she'd found a way out of her own quagmire?

She thought for a few minutes…considered making amends with Lindi and moving forward. Was it even possible to continue a friendship that had really only sprouted a few buds?

"Maggie, what the hell?" Andrew yelled from the sun porch. "It's been like half an hour or something!"

Oh, you have some nerve! Shouldn't you be kissing my ass? "Yeah, yeah, I'm coming."

She took a deep breath…braced herself…and decided she wasn't willing to wait till tomorrow to drop the divorce bomb on Andrew. There was no time like the present. She wrapped herself in a light, airy summer robe and joined him on the sun porch.

"I suppose an apology from me would mean nothing to you," Andrew said as he leaned back and propped his feet up on a foot stool.

"Ya think?" Maggie snapped.

"Can we just speak to each other in a civil manner?" he suggested.

Maggie sighed. "Yes. I can do that." But it doesn't change the fact that I can't stand the sight of you.

"So, this…this married life isn't working for you," he said.

"It's not working for either of us. This is what I've been saying," she reminded him.

"I know haven't been a good husband."

Hmmm, by his own admission. Is hell freezing over…again?

"But I wouldn't mind having a second shot," he said.

For the first time ever, Maggie had turned to stone. Rock solid…emotionless and speechless. She simply stared back at Andrew, boring deep into him as if to find that man who once rocked her world. But who was she kidding? She'd gotten caught up in her own invention of what love and marriage were supposed to be. Andrew wasn't the only one living a lie.

"Andrew, don't kid yourself," she replied, breaking the silence. "We both know you only wanted a second chance because you don't wanna look like a failure—again. You told me that months ago when I questioned staying in such a ridiculous marriage. You're more concerned about what your parents will think…what your hoity-toity social circle will think. Why is it that you care so much about all of this? Seriously!"

Andrew dropped his head. He had no words. Maggie's newly developed unfiltered dialogue had pricked him with the truth.

"So, whatta you want from me?" he asked.

Without any hesitation, Maggie came straight out with it. "I want the lake house. We can discuss the sale of *our* house and all the other things, but I want the lake house. I feel completely calm and relaxed when I'm alone there, and I absolutely love Laurelton. I have every intention to be fair with this settlement, Andrew, but that's what I want from you."

"Uh, well, I guess you misunderstood what I was asking. I suppose I meant to ask if you wanted a trial separation or a…" Andrew's voice trailed off. He was unable to say the *D*-word.

"A divorce," Maggie finished his sentence. "Yes, Andrew. What are you not getting? I want a divorce…and so do you."

He dropped his head again.

"Andrew, I'm going to give you my best dose of therapy. I think you get bored easily, and I think when it comes to relationships, you're incapable of loving someone—other than yourself. You're all about the lust and passion, and I've done things in that bedroom that I'll probably never do again," Maggie said, channeling Jess's stupid bedroom advice. "But it's never enough. You really have no business being in a committed relationship. You're not the marrying kind. And that's okay…but live that life. Don't try to fit into some kind of life that's not meant for you."

He thought for a minute, while gazing at the back yard, which needed landscaping. "You're a better therapist than you think, Maggie."

Hmmmm…second time I've heard that tonight, Maggie thought, speechless. For once, she didn't feel like she was feeding someone a textbook line of crap.

"Anyway, I'm not sure I want to get into the whole settlement thing tonight," Andrew said. "And by the way, the lake house isn't technically mine to give to you."

True. But you can make it happen. And you'd *better* make it happen! "I realize that. But your parents never use the place. Why did they buy it to begin with?" Maggie asked.

"I think they fell in love with the beauty of it all but found that it was a little too much maintenance. I'm surprised they haven't sold it by now."

"This is what I'm saying, Andrew. I don't think they'll even miss the place. How could they?"

"Yeah, I know. They haven't been there in quite some time. I feel like they just lost interest or something. I have to say, Dean Hardy does a good job looking after the place, but he's costly," Andrew said.

Yes! This could be easier than I thought—especially since old man Spencer is a tightwad! Maggie thought, rejoicing. Andrew's gonna convince those lakehouse deadbeats to give it up!

"So, as I said," he continued. "I'm not ready to get into the nitty-gritty of everything right now, Maggie. I'm going to sleep on it. I'll stay at my private suite tonight, so I can get an early start at the office tomorrow."

Yeah, yeah, office schmoffice, but this conversation *will* continue tomorrow! Maggie thought. "Apparently, I have a lot of final paperwork to deal with tomorrow, according to Monster Devon," she said. "Not looking forward to dealing with her, but I have to suck it up, I guess. Nonetheless, I'm out of there by ten."

Andrew grimaced slightly at Maggie's new unfiltered attitude but held back from criticizing. "So then, why don't you drop by my office around 10:30?" he said. "We can try to sort this thing out with clear minds."

Perfect, I can lock in a deal, then get on with my life. "Okay, see ya then."

Maggie wasn't sure if she should shake Andrew's hand or slap him in the face. She did neither. Instead, she shot up from her cushy seat and headed for bed. She was eager to get a good night's sleep and blossom into a new life the next day.

Day of Reckoning

CHAPTER

33

Monday's Back-up Plan

M aggie awoke at 7:30 on Monday morning to the sound of nothing. She didn't set an alarm, it seemed there were no birds chirping, and the construction workers apparently had finished their
thunderous task on the cul-de-sac a few days ago. She yawned and stretched
with what felt like a rested spirit and was in no hurry to get to work by eight.
But what was this uncertain buzzing in her head? Such gnawing. It wasn't
the usual vexation of everyday life she'd grown accustomed to; it was more
like a gentle reminder of something; but what? Maggie simply scratched her
bedhead and blundered her way to the bathroom, practically smacking into
that damn pole.

Ah! The pole dude is coming this morning. Nine o'clock, she remembered.
Guess I'd better call work and tell them I'll be in when I get there!

As she began to phone the office, she took pleasure in the fact that she'd be
pissing off Eloise Devon. But most likely, the answering service would pick up
at 7:30 in the morning. "Hello, Walters Psychiatric Center."

Ugh! Do you sleep there, leather head? "Ms. Devon. This is Maggie Walters calling. Can you put me through to my father's voice mail?"

"Yes, I'm able to do so, Maggie."

No time for a passive-aggressive grammar lesson, Wrinkle-dink! Maggie thought, but she remained silent.

"Well, I suppose you're wondering why I'm here so early," Ms. Devon went on.

Nope…couldn't care less. Now put me through, Wrinkle Dinkle, then go set up your spoiled fruit platter!

"Well," Ms. Devon said, "we are insanely busy and extremely backed up. There simply isn't enough time in the day to get everything done. I certainly hope you're not canceling from your duties today."

Ha ha, insanely busy…at a psychiatric center! She's too uptight to even get her own pun! Maggie chuckled to herself.

Silence.

"Maggie?" Monster Devon growled.

"Yep. Still here. And I'm calling in to give my father a message. So, if you would kindly put me through to his voice mail."

"Maggie, you know that I handle office matters, if that's what this is about. No need to burden your father with such minutia."

Yes, but I don't want to deal with you, fruit Nazi! What are you not getting?

"I will give him a message," Ms. Devon said.

"Well, here's the message then, Ms. Devon. I will be in later today when it's convenient for *me* to tie up loose ends."

Again, silence.

"So, have a nice day," Maggie said.

Click.

* * *

By 9:30, Gregory from Oasis had dismantled the monstrosity that had been a gnawing reminder of a blemished marriage for the past several months. Maggie charged the service to Andrew's Visa card and thanked Gregory on his way out.

She entered the master bedroom, feeling the absence of the steely beast. The room was now free of obstructions, revealing the true beauty of its structure. She rushed to get herself together, wanting to get the divorce-settlement show on the road with Andrew. Maggie also stepped into her big-girl pants, making a firm decision to go see Lindi. She was well aware that her visit to the diner was going to be quite different from the others. The soothing rush that once flowed like a gentle stream during those visits would most likely be something of a stormy sea, so she decided to meditate. After a few moments of reflection, her confidence gradually rose above a flat line.

Maggie took the stairs to Andrew's office, not wanting to run into any of his partners in the elevator. It had been a long time since she'd stepped foot in his office building. She wondered if she'd even recognize the staff.

"Hi," she said curtly as she charged into Andrew's office.

He motioned for her to have a seat as he began to wrap up a call in his insufferable attorney voice. Maggie took a good look around the place, feeling the ambiance of pretense and discomfort. The designer furniture that had been staged for show. The perfectly organized and untouched magazines spread across the table in front of the couch. The sideboard with a full liquor cabinet beneath it, topped with a shelf of martini glasses.

Ugh, what is this place? she wondered, dropping her head in shame that she'd once fallen for such a sham.

"Hi. How are you?" he asked, after cutting the phone call.

"I'm good, so let's just get down to business, Andrew. I haven't changed my mind about the lake house. And please don't act like you can't make this happen. You know how to wheel and deal people, so have at it on this situation, as well."

"I slept on it, Maggie. And, I'm telling you, my dad's not going to budge on this—not in this situation. He's not going to give his house to a woman I was only married to for a little more than a year. Besides, I feel like the cottage is their backup retreat…a place to go when they aren't off to somewhere more exciting."

"I call bullshit, Andrew. We both know that's not gonna happen. I don't wanna play hardball, but let's face it. I can prove you'd been having an affair. And I'm quite sure you've been hooking up with a whole lot of other women…I'm not an idiot. *And*, I know your parents adore you. The world revolves around you, in their eyes. You'd do anything to prevent them from seeing who you really are—and we both know that's why you're fighting this divorce. The annulment from your first wife was one thing, but divorce would be completely humiliating in their social circle."

"First of all, you can't prove anything. What? You're gonna bring Lindi and my parents together for a tell-all? Really, Maggie? Have you even spoken to her? How do you know she'll ever speak to you again? For God's sake, Maggie, she didn't even know you existed, and you said some nasty shit to her. She doesn't owe you anything."

Well…that's true, Maggie thought.

"And as far as my gentlemen's club visits," Andrew said, "I'm just like any other normal man who enjoys fantasy. You think my father hasn't been inside a gentlemen's club before? Think again. So, I'd think long and hard about your plan of action, Maggie."

Truth be told, Maggie hadn't thought about the downside. In her mind, she'd crafted an infallible plan, but she was no match for Andrew's sharklike attorney maneuvers. She'd become consumed by the idea of the lake house serving as her peace and serenity fix. And that was that. Nothing could stop her. But her confidence was wavering a bit, and Andrew was ready to attack as he watched his wife pick at her unpolished nails.

"So," he began again, "as I see it, perhaps you'd like to consider *my* offer."

He'd gotten her attention.

"You're right about one thing, Maggie. I love my parents dearly…they've given me the world, and it would kill me to disappoint them or embarrass them in any way. But, clearly, you and I aren't happy together." Long pause. "Tell ya what… you can *stay* at the lake house for a while, and I'll stay in our house."

Now, he really had her attention! Okay, where's this bastard going? she wondered.

"But we'll remain married—on paper. Just until the new year, and then I'll start divorce proceedings."

"I'm sorry, *what*? You're crazy," she blurted.

"Now, just hear me out."

Oh, just throw me in front of a bus or a train or from the top of this building! Maggie thought.

"My father knows you've resigned, so it will be easy for me to convince him that you'd like to spend time at the lake house, doing projects and so forth. You know, like seeing after some renovations…perhaps serving time on a few committees. The Laurelton Art Association would be a good one for you, right? Hadn't you mentioned that before? And, you'd also still have access to our money."

Maggie was stunned. There were no words! How genius of her conniving husband to dupe his stubborn father into letting her live at the lake house until they could convince him to give it up. But she'd still be married to the freak who sat before her. There was no amount of money that would keep her in the madness of a degrading marriage…*was there?*

"Andrew, I don't know what to say to you right now. As ridiculous as this idea is, even if I were pathetic enough to go along with it, how could we possibly pull it off? I mean, as much as my parents get on my nerves, they'd wanna do dinner and visit and do the country club thing. I can't deal with any further deception. And why's it so important to carry this nonsense out to the new year?"

"You just leave all that to me," Andrew said with great confidence. "Once my parents see the hard work you've put into the place over the next four months, it'll be easier to convince them that it's *our* place. They'll see how involved you are with the community and realize how established we are there."

Maggie was skeptical about his liberal use of *our* and *we*. But this *could* work.

"I'm not proud of scamming my parents, Maggie, but I know them. We can take care of the divorce after they've officially given me the deed. And yes, you will occasionally have to throw them a dinner bone or a country club bone, but there will be no more lies between us…as a couple. We'll just shake hands at the end of the night and call it a day."

"You're ridiculous, Andrew, and we both know it won't be that easy. There will be the Ted and Ritas of the world expecting us to be lovey-dovey. There will be people who notice and judge my absence."

"A few months, Mags, just a few months," he said. "I'll take care of people's questions. You know I can smooth it all over. Besides, no need to ruin the upcoming holidays."

You drive a hard bargain, that's for sure…but I don't trust you, you slime ball!

"Just till the new year," he stated again.

"I know you're afraid of disappointing your parents, but for God's sake, Andrew, marriage doesn't always work out. And I'm not even that close to them. Are you afraid they'll cut you out of their will or something?"

"No. They'd never do that. I'm just not ready to tell them. We talked about this last night…and you brought it up—I'm not ready to deal with another failure," he said, hanging his head. "Plus, my father hasn't completely turned the firm over to me. I just don't wanna rock the boat, Maggie. Can't you help me out on this? Married on paper…just for a little while."

For the first time and just for a nanosecond, Maggie felt a little sorry for Andrew. He could talk tough about her not having proof of any of his indiscretions and say he didn't want to disappoint his parents. But the bottom line was that his ego was bigger than anything else in his world. Appearances were all that mattered to him. And that would somehow eventually be the demise of his sanity.

He really needs therapy, Maggie concluded. He is one sad, sorry dude.

"Just a few months," he said. "That's it; I promise. If you'd like, I'll draw up a legal document."

Oh, yes…good thinking!

"Besides, don't you want to be somewhere peaceful so you can read and write…and do your yoga. All the things you used to love."

"Ya know, Andrew, your parents will be easy to fool…they're never around. It's *my* parents who will be difficult to explain my absence to." Well, she thought, except for my mom, who I believe has begun to take stock of her own marriage. "They're intrusive…you know this about them."

"Yeah, they'll be a challenge in all this. But honestly, I think your father's going to be pretty content around the office, especially with Eloise Devon on the scene…with all due respect, Mags."

"Yeah, Monster Devon will hang on till she kicks the bucket, I'm sure."

"As bold as you've become, Maggie, I don't see you bringing up the divorce to your father. I mean, look how long it took you to resign. For the most part, he's an old-school dude…never expected your mother to have a career, so I know deep down, he's on board with you leaving the practice. But I think he just relies on you too much to make sure everything's on the up and up. You're someone he trusts to protect what he's built into what he considers his little empire. But he'd never tell you that."

Couldn't have said it better myself, she thought.

"My point is, the unshakable Dr. Walters has high expectations for you, and the divorce will kill him," Andrew said.

Well, you are a hell of salesman...just don't quit your day job. You'll need it! she thought. "Can I think about it?" she asked, shocking herself with such lunacy.

"Absolutely."

***

As Maggie drove away from the offices of Spencer, Decklyn, and Mackenzie, she considered Andrew's offer. Crazy as it was, what was a few more months? She didn't have to sleep with him. Didn't have to check in with him. She'd hardly have to see him at all. So, she'd have to feign the happy-couple face around all the self-important people in his social circle, now and then. She'd have to put on a cheesy smile at the country club functions on rare occasions...around his parents and hers. She could always fake the flu. Andrew would be an expert at weaving that tale. And he'd be freed up to spend a quarantined Christmas with his "wife" in Laurelton—code for having an out-of-town romp with his flavor of the month. Her thoughts continued to spin over Andrew's proposal. What kind of mess would she be getting into?

I can handle this, she told herself. It's not the plan I had in mind, but I'll play my cards right. Maggie decided to call Andrew later to tell him to draw up the document, which her *own* lawyer would be scrutinizing!

CHAPTER
34

The Final Shift

Maggie pulled into Sal's parking lot riddled with anxiety but ready to be a big girl and redress the situation with Lindi. She'd most likely be winding down her duties at the lunch counter and be freed up to chat—perhaps? Maggie's thoughts went dark, wondering about Lindi's temperament. Had her anger died down from that inglorious Friday night at the lake house? Could they sit down to discuss the emotions that both had been suppressing for a few days? But as Maggie sat in her car, she realized there was so much more she wanted to know. How did Lindi and Andrew meet? How long had the affair lasted? How long had Andrew been floating her money? What about those sapphires?

Ugh…the madness has to stop! she thought, noticing that her legs had become numb, preventing her from leaving the car. She needed just a few minutes to meditate, as the courage she'd felt earlier was now taking a rest.

Finally and slightly reluctantly, Maggie opened the car door and walked slowly across the parking lot. What do I really have to lose? she asked herself.

She entered the diner, took her usual seat, and looked around for Lindi. She didn't see her anywhere, but she wasn't leaving until she knew for sure. Out of the blue, the sassy figure of a server approached her. She slapped down a healthy-choice menu and said, "I'll be right with you."

"Oh, hey, Lindi…I'm actually here to chat with you for a couple minutes. I assume you'll be getting off soon."

"Well," said Lindi, walking back toward Maggie, "it's not a good time. I'll be leaving soon. So, unless you're ordering, I have no time for you."

Rather saucy and a little unforgiving, I see. Maggie lallygagged, staring at a menu she had no intention of ordering from, while Lindi stood there impatiently, tapping her watch-free wrist.

Okay, there's no need for a timer. "I really just want a baked cinnamon roll and a cup of vanilla chai tea," Maggie said.

"Cinnamon rolls are gone for the day. Sal only put out a single batch. And we don't have special teas," Lindi said, rolling her eyes. "I can offer you plain old Lipton tea. Do you want it or not?"

"I'll just have a coffee with cream to go." Quite the salty attitude coming from the "other woman," Maggie thought.

While Lindi prepared the coffee, Maggie realized she was deflated because she'd quite obviously lost the opportunity for what could've been a good friendship. She expected there'd be friction lingering after all the hoopla that had gone down. But couldn't they simply apologize to one another and call it a day?

Lindi shoved the coffee in front of Maggie along with the check and disappeared into the back room. Maggie waited for a few minutes, but Lindi never returned to the counter. Her harsh words of Friday night resurfaced in Maggie's mind.

Maggie, I know you think you're better than people like me or Jillian…but you're not. In fact, you're quite pathetic. Why don't you get a fucking life! And get some friends, why don't you! While you're at it, lose that needy, desperate thing you have goin' on.

Maggie decided she wasn't up for the emotional spillage after all. She left two dollars on the counter to cover the coffee and scurried out the door.

As she approached her car, something tugged at her. This had been her now-or-never moment, and she'd just walked away. There was no time to plan or rehearse what needed to be said. Lindi was going to hear what Maggie had to say, even if it meant Sal would throw her out. So, she whirled around in the parking lot and marched back into the diner. Lindi sat in a nook in the back room, rolling silverware into paper napkins. Maggie headed her way.

"Lindi, I have something to say, and I'm not leaving till I say it," she said, fuming. "I'm sorry for all the nasty things I said, but you *were* in fact sleeping with my husband."

"Maggie, I—"

"Yes, yes, I know you weren't aware that he was married at first, but even though Andrew and I have been over for quite some time, it still grinds me that he's been sneaking around with other women…coming off to the rest of the world like he's some kind of…of heroic stud. I was tired of the constant humiliation, and that's what came out of me."

Lindi was bowled over by Maggie's gutsy approach. "Maggie! Keep it down," she warned in a hushed voice. "Don't wanna piss Sal off. He'll kick us both out of here."

"I'm sorry," Maggie whispered. "I'm just a little crazy right now. I can't even stand myself."

"Have a seat," Lindi suggested, seeming to want to dig into the can of worms Maggie had opened.

As Maggie sat on the cool vinyl seat of the booth in the back corner, near the waitstaff's nook, she felt the weightiness of her fears begin to lift. Had Lindi's welcoming nature returned?

"This is why I don't get close to people," Lindi said, twirling both hands toward Maggie. "What a freakin' mess, right? Now you're coming into the diner, stirring shit up?"

Hmmmm…nope, Maggie thought. Not so welcoming.

Awkward silence.

"I guess you hit home with me, calling me an aimless user," said Lindi.

"Yeah, I was nasty."

"I guess that's my Achilles heel. I know I don't have much ambition…and time just marches on. I guess I gave up trying to figure out what I wanted to do with my life. It just felt good to let someone pamper me. Not that it matters, but once I found out Andrew was married, I stopped seeing him. And then he told me he was separated. I knew he was lying, but I…well, I was so pissed that I decided to use him."

Yep, I'm well aware of the scam, Maggie thought. I've been doin' the same thing.

A heavy silence surrounded a newly formed tension. Lindi continued to roll silverware into napkins.

"Well, you hit home with me, too, Lindi. It really has very little to do with Andrew. It's about friendships. I'm just not good at them, apparently. I kept trying to hold onto my college girlfriends when our lives went in very different directions… but they couldn't care less. I should've moved on. It's like I got stuck in a time warp or something. I bet I *did* come off needy and desperate. I just poured out all my shit to you…someone who was different…someone who…well, someone who wouldn't judge me for wearing gray sweatpants, for God's sake."

"What the hell do gray sweatpants have to do with anything?" Lindi said.

"You know! You're not judgy!"

"Well, you're right about that."

"So, tell me about him," said Maggie, taking a sip of her coffee.

Lindi looked up and swallowed what seemed like a lump of coal or a golf ball—something that could make a girl choke. "Maggie, no. I'm not gonna do that."

"What I mean is, well, is he telling the truth about knowing you before me? Stuff like that."

Lindi took a deep breath and pushed the silverware aside. "I believe so... it was about three years ago. He was assigned to me by the physical therapist I've spoken of, Donnie Hayworth. So, he'd been treating Andrew for a knee injury. During that time, Donnie had been taking my yoga classes. I was a fairly new instructor and mentioned providing personal yoga for my clients. So, he brought me on board for a while. Andrew did yoga with me in Donnie's rehab center."

Oh, yes! The downward facing dog positions, Maggie recalled.

There was a long pause before Lindi began rolling silverware again.

"So, are you just saying that all this time...for three years, you've been together or what? I'm confused," said Maggie.

"Oh, no. It was off and on...mostly off. I feel like I'd run back to him when Dagger and I were having issues.

"Yes, Dagger. What does he think of all this?"

"Oh, he doesn't know everything...and I don't want him to know, either. He did meet Andrew the other night at my apartment," said Lindi.

"What?" What kind of freaks *are* you people?

"Yeah, Andrew stopped by the other night...I guess to talk, but Dagger was there. He wanted to know if we could talk over the weekend. I told him I was going to see Jillian, which he knows all about, by the way. Well, he knows Jason's side of the story."

"Oh, I bet it's Jason Charles," said Maggie. Andrew had mentioned that colleague.

Lindi simply nodded her head. "Here's the thing, Maggie...I never felt like I was good enough for Andrew. He'd never take me around his crowd...I guess for fear they'd find out I was a waitress. But I was just as bad. Dagger would always come first when he was in town, and that really bugged Andrew. It's like he couldn't handle someone 'lesser' winning the prize," Lindi said, pointing to herself. "Anyway, I'm sure you don't wanna hear any more."

You're right. I don't. But don't be surprised if I hit you up later...for collateral, Maggie thought. "I just need to know one more thing...about the sapphires. Did he give you a sapphire bracelet?"

"He tried. He got back from some trip back in June, I believe. Said my eyes remind him of sapphires."

Uh huh, his cheesy tactics were consistent.

"But I refused it," Lindi said.

Yep! The jackass regifted it to me!

"I had already broken things off with him completely, but he said he wanted me to think about things…that he wanted to start fresh…no lies between us."

"Ha! He basically said the same thing to me," Maggie said. "He was just willing to be with whichever one of us decided to give it a go!"

"No, he would've never been with me. I wasn't part of his social scene," said Lindi.

"Well, I'm just glad we dodged that bullet," said Maggie.

"Me, too. Ya know, Maggie, I'm embarrassed to admit this, but I allowed that jackass to install a dancer's pole in my loft."

"Ha ha. No worries; Gregory from Oasis can get you de-poled in a jiffy," Maggie said.

"Nuh-uh! You had a pole *too*?"

"Yep…Andrew had been badgering me about installing a dancer's pole for-like-ever, and I'm the dumb ass who thought it would be a great surprise for him on his birthday—back in January," Maggie said.

"Oh, that's hilarious! I got de-poled a few months ago. My landlord wondered why I had the thing in there to begin with. I just told him it was for yoga conditioning. Ha ha!"

"I got de-poled only a few hours ago," said Maggie.

"Are you serious?" Lindi asked, bending forward to chuckle.

"Yep! Better late than never," said Maggie, barely containing her laughter.

Maggie and Lindi roared with hilarity while *both* of them mindlessly rolled silverware.

"So, let me tell you what *I'm* embarrassed about."

Lindi stopped laughing and zeroed in on Maggie's disclosure.

"I was foolish enough to get the arrogant bastard's initials tattooed on my butt cheek."

"Oh, lots of women do that, Maggie. That's an easy fix. Dagger has an ink guy—he could probably remove that for you in no time," said Lindi.

"I'm sure it's an easy fix, but in the meantime, I have a semifaded tattoo on my ass that looks like it says AMISH!"

"Huh?" said Lindi.

"AMSIII," said Maggie, taking Lindi's pen and drawing the initials on a napkin.

"Ha ha! You're right! It does look like *AMISH* at a quick glance!" said Lindi, roaring with laughter all over again. Then, wiping the tears from her eyes, she said, "Maggie, I just thought of something. What if you, you know, hook up with someone before you get that thing removed? How funny would it be if somebody *really* thought your tattoo said *AMISH*?"

"Oh, not the least bit funny! Ha ha! And no real chance of me moving on so quickly, so that's least of my worries. I'll get with Vaughn, my tattooist, as soon as possible. I don't care if he has to scrape that thing off with a power tool—it needs to go!"

Maggie looked down at her husband's monogram on the napkin and traced over the letters, forming them into a semblance of *AMEN*. "How's this?" she said, turning the napkin so Lindi could read it. "As in, 'Andrew is history—*amen.*"

"That's more like it," Lindi said, smiling. "I don't wanna get too personal, Maggie, but seriously…Magic Mike? Please tell me *you* didn't assign that name to his—"

"Oh, hell, no! And let's table that discussion for right now," Maggie said.

"Ha ha. Truth be told, Maggie, it's gonna be a while till I can truly forgive myself. I mean, here I am, deep into yoga instruction, its health benefits, and all-around wellness. How did I fall into such a sleazy lifestyle?"

"Lindi, you're preachin' to the choir. For months, I've been stashing away cash and jewelry…and scheming to find a way to take possession of the lake house. But I told you this already. I'm such a hypocrite. I've counseled clients with the same issues and secretly judged them. Do you see how I suck at my job?" Maggie asked rhetorically.

"So, where do you think you'll go from here, Maggie?"

"Well, I've already asked to take possession of the lake house," she said.

"Oh, great! I know how much you love it."

"Yeah, so, he and I will try to work something out."

"Oh, I'm glad he's being cooperative," said Lindi.

Cooperative…puh! I'm too ashamed to let you in on the crazy deal, Maggie thought.

"So, Maggie, now that you've resigned, what will you do for work?"

Oh, no worries…I'll be milking my "husband-on-paper" for a few months. "Well, I plan to eventually take interior design classes. I've always had a flair for style and visual aesthetics. And the decorating part has always been very calming to me. But mostly, I'll be taking care of myself for a while. You wouldn't happen to know any good therapists?" Maggie said, winking at Lindi.

"Actually, I think I do. And good for you! Be sure to get a fair settlement from that jackass," Lindi said.

"Oh, I will! But it might take a while for the divorce to be finalized and everything to be settled. Ugh!" Maggie moaned as she threw her face into her cupped hands. And I have to be bogus Mrs. Andrew Spencer till this scam is over!

"Well, hang in there. Here's to fat assets," Lindi said as she raised Maggie's coffee cup.

"Yes indeed!" Maggie said, trembling with laughter.

"What's so funny?"

"Nothing. It just sounded like you gave a toast to fat *asses,*" Maggie said.

"Ha ha ha ha! That's funny!"

"I can't stop laughing!" said Maggie, wiping her eyes.

"Are you still on the fat-ass thing?"

"No! About the whole Magic Mike nonsense," Maggie replied, now deeper in hilarity. "It's just so damn ridiculous!"

"Ridiculous and…not so magic!"

They both roared with laughter like silly middle-school girls. "Ahhhh, I gotta get out of here," Lindi said, pulling herself together. "Gotta give hugs and tell everyone good-bye."

"What? As in *final* hugs and farewells?" Maggie asked as they stood up.

"Yep, I'm outta here!" Lindi announced.

"Where are you going? Have you decided on the business in Laurelton?"

"Actually, no. I'm gonna give it a go with Dagger. We'll be living just outside of Nashville…big music scene. He'll do well."

"That's fantastic!" said Maggie. "Will you start up your personal yoga business there?"

"Absolutely! Can't wait, in fact. But I'd still like to get to that dockside happy hour one day."

"That would be great," said Maggie.

"And what about you? When do you think you'll move to the lake house?"

"Very soon. Very, very soon," Maggie replied. She simply didn't have the guts to tell Lindi that Andrew had made a ludicrous proposal…and that she was going to *accept* his offer. Eh, it's only for a few months, she told herself. And she was going into the deal with her eyes wide open this time.

Lindi reached out and gave Maggie a big bear hug, and they assured each other that a dockside happy hour was next on their friendship agenda. Maggie was disappointed that Lindi was moving away, but she knew deep down that they'd always be friends. They'd both survived Andrew, and they'd survived each other's worst fury.

"Maggie, about this dockside happy hour…" Lindi said.

"Yeah? What about it?"

Lindi's eyes were laughing. "Just don't be lounging around the dock in gray sweatpants…they might make your ass look fat!"

CPSIA information can be obtained
at www.ICGtesting.com
Printed in the USA
LVHW020716250220
648116LV00005B/873